SAïD KHATIBI is a novelist, tr
journalist born in 1984 in Bou S
lives in Slovenia. He writes in Ar....
lates between both. His novel *Sarajevo Firewood* was short-
listed for the 2020 International Prize for Arabic Fiction.
His other novels are *The Book of Errors*, which was published
in 2013, and *Forty Years Waiting for Isabelle*, which won the
2017 Katara Award for Arabic Novels. He has written a travel
book about the Balkans, *The Inflamed Gardens of the East*
(2015), and has written extensively on raï music, including
the book *Wedding Fire* (2010). *The End of the Sahara* won the
Sheikh Zayed Book Award, young author category, in 2023.

THE END OF THE SAHARA

Saïd Khatibi

Translated by
Alexander E. Elinson

BITTER LEMON PRESS
LONDON

BITTER LEMON PRESS

This edition published in the United Kingdom in 2026 by Bitter
Lemon Press, 47 Wilmington Square, London WC1X 0ET

www.bitterlemonpress.com

First published in Arabic as *Nihayat Al-Sahra* by Hachette Antoine, Beirut, 2022

The publication of this translation has been made possible through the financial
support of the Sheikh Zayed Book Award at the Abu Dhabi Arabic Language
Centre, part of the Department of Culture and Tourism – Abu Dhabi.

The authorised representative in the EEA is Easy Access System Europe:
Mustamäe tee 50, 10621 Tallinn, Estonia, gpsr.requests@easproject.com

PB ISBN 978–1–916725–225
eBook USC ISBN 978–1–916725–232
eBook ROW ISBN 978–1–916725–249

Typeset by Tetragon, London
Printed and bound by the CPI Group (UK) Ltd, Croydon, CR0 4YY

جائزة الشيخ زايد للكتاب
Sheikh Zayed Book Award

CONTENTS

To the memory of Taos Amrouche

He realized that his own brief romance was over, that he was outside and beyond this desert drama of which he had only touched the fringe.

E. M. HULL, *The Sons of the Sheik*

AUTHOR'S NOTE

This novel tells the story of the end of socialism in Algeria almost one year before the fall of the Berlin Wall. The novel's events culminate on October 5, 1988, when scores of young Algerians took to the streets to protest the country's single-party system that had been in place since the country's independence from France in 1962. A state-led massacre followed, along with the violent emergence of Islamism and the beginning of the civil war that left hundreds of thousands dead.

In a country on the verge of collapse, much of the action is centered in and around the Sahara Hotel, where people from all over the country, rich and poor, come together. The hotel stands in for Algeria, and Algeria for all countries that cultivate historical amnesia and indifference to others.

The End of the Sahara is narrated by many, allowing the characters to tell their own stories in their own voices. It is a tribute to the more than five hundred people who died fighting for freedom on October 5, 1988, and to women who fought on this day and every day, resisting a violent patriarchal system that aims to control them.

This is a novel about the end of one era and the bloody beginning of another. It speaks of the silences of a country we rarely see and recounts the crime of forgetting that we all are prone to commit.

BOOK 1

A SILVER PEARL
EARRING

IBRAHIM

SEPTEMBER 9

They called me Ibrahim, or Brihoum, or Briha. Names aren't important in this place.

That's what I was thinking about when the shouts of a cookware peddler woke me that morning. "May God give you canker sores," I cursed him. He'd kept me from sleeping in after I'd spent the night previewing new movies and hadn't closed my eyes until dawn. Two Westerns, an Indian movie, and three adult films. I wrapped the videotapes in sheets of newspaper and made my way to the kitchen.

"We're out of coffee?!" I grumbled to my mother.

"Go drink some poison!" she shot back as she hung the laundry to dry in the house's interior courtyard. Whenever the pain in her molar came back, she spoke with a sharper edge.

My head felt heavier than usual, so I left the house, slamming the door behind me, indifferent to her abuse. She isn't happy with the job I've been doing for two years now after scrimping and saving to open a shop that rents out videotapes and VCRs. This was the business that yielded the most in return for the least effort, especially since the city had converted its only movie theater into an administrative building.

The more she complained, the more I reminded her that getting a government job required me to complete my compulsory military service, and I wasn't keen on spending twenty-four months in some far-flung army barracks. Once, my uncle had suggested I go with him to the Rubber & Plastic Co. and take a temporary job there, but I said no. "A young man like me? A university graduate? Working with morons?" That company hires people who, unlike me, haven't completed their education. I would rather starve to death than go work there. "You like doing business with haram things?" my mother often chided me. She had heard from our neighbors that, contrary to Islamic religious practice, all movies show women smoking or kissing men, and she avoided these movies whenever they were shown on TV. I preferred to bite my tongue rather than fight with her. Or I might press some coins into the palm of her hand, which she would then stuff into her bra. "What's forbidden is what comes out of the mouth, not what goes into it," I'd tell her. I once heard someone say this and have hurled it at her many times since.

I walked for fifteen minutes, passing the Christian cemetery, then the vegetable market, before reaching the Khayma Café. Pictures of soccer players covered its walls, just to please its customers. The café was at the edge of a traffic circle known as the Pitcher Roundabout, so named for the jug-shaped stone fountain in its center that hadn't flowed with water since its ceremonial unveiling. As the caffeine coursed through my veins and I regained my equilibrium, I muttered to the waiter who, like everyone else, called me Brihoum rather than Ibrahim: "Where do you buy your coffee?" He snapped his fingers and quipped: "We grow it." Even though it's not available in stores, you can get strong coffee in cafés which tastes as if it's been mixed with ground-up garbanzo or fava beans. "A country with no head nor foundation," I mumbled as I got up and headed downtown, nearly two miles straight down Fifth of July Street. I counted the potholes as I walked, then turned right down an empty side street, where my shop, the Desert Rose, was tucked away. On Fridays, people didn't roll out of bed until after prayer.

After lighting some incense, I arranged the new movie jackets, hiding the adult films under a wooden table at the entrance that I'd made into something resembling a welcome desk. I wiped the front window with a rag and checked on the back of the store, which was hidden behind a curtain. The space was mostly occupied by an iron bed where I sometimes laid down for a nap, practiced guitar, or enjoyed a passing fling. I was twenty-seven, and sappy love stories no longer did it for me. Instead, I contented myself with sexual adventures that had a lifespan shorter than a butterfly's. I felt pretty confident I could remake the hit song "Salma ya Salama." I'd send it to *Talents* on Radio Algiers, it would get played on-air, and if I got the most listeners' votes, I'd win a cash prize.

From under the bed, I pulled out the novel I'd bought as a gift to myself from a sidewalk vendor who also sold fabric and spices. No one else had remembered my birthday. I looked at the title, *The Sheik*, and the name of the author, Edith Maude Hull. I had seen the movie and smiled at the municipal library stamp on the first page. In the markets, I often came across items that had once been government property. Perhaps a day will come when they'll sell the employees too! A warm feeling had drawn me into *The Sheik* from the very first sentence: "Are you coming in to watch the dancing?" I enjoyed the love story of a tomboyish girl and an Arab sheik from the Sahara. I was engrossed in its last pages when a man with

17

a receding hairline walked in. He wanted to rent a VCR to watch his brother's wedding party.

"Come back tomorrow," I told him. A young woman with wavy tufts of hair peeking out from under her veil had rented it the other day. Rather than hand over her own ID card for me to hold onto as was normally done, which would have given me her name and address, she'd left her fiancé's. I went back to my reading, taking advantage of the street's calm as it approached midday on September 9, 1988, not realizing then that that book would be the cause of the worst days of my life.

ACHOUR

If I hadn't plunged the knife into my cousin's shoulder, I wouldn't have been saved from death and lived to tell my tale, which began that morning when the heat started to scorch my bald spot and I became angry at the people who had made me leave the village. I was startled by what was before me. I frowned and staggered over to a juniper tree. I banged the ground with my staff to block my sheep's path. I counted them off from one to six, then drove them home, where I saw my daughter, Louisa, who was not yet twelve. She leaned her pencil-thin body against the door as she played with her brother, who had just learned to walk. Except for a green shirt that stopped at his belly button, he was naked. I shouted at her to put the sheep in the pen. My staff landed on the ground in front of her, where I had thrown it like a javelin. She straightened up to carry out my order. When she called out to ask, "Where're you going, Papa?" I was already gone, leaving dust behind me.

I went back to where the body had been dumped on its back, legs spread, on the sloping ground among the wormwood plants. Dear Lord, I thought. I stroked my chin, which I hadn't shaved for a week, then raised my right palm to my temple, horrified at the sight of drying blood running from her nose to her left shoulder. I turned my eyes to the opening of her beige shirt, where a gold necklace peeked out. "God forgive her." I felt a sharp pain in my stomach.

Her long black hair ended in half-twisted tufts. Her eyes were brown, and she had black kohl on her eyelashes. Her round nose looked like a grape dusted with bits of dirt. As I imagined her family's anguish upon hearing the news, I noticed a scar on her lower jaw. She looked like she was in her twenties. She was thinner than my wife and had softer skin, and I guessed she was a nurse or a teacher. I was baffled. How had she got here? No woman in her right mind would venture alone into this wild meadow, full of poisonous and medicinal plants, that was attached to the city's edge like an appendix (something a municipal employee once said to me). The only people here were the poor souls who crowded into informal dwellings they built out of tin, cane, and straw, hoping that one day the world would look kindly on them and they could move into houses with running water and electricity.

I wanted to place my hand on her forehead and recite some verses from the Qur'an ("My Lord's words heal the dead"), but I couldn't bring myself to touch her. I was still shy around women, something drummed into me by my mother when I was young. When a woman I don't know crosses my path, I still lower my eyes and blush until she disappears from view. The dead woman wore a pearl earring, and I realized that my daughter had never worn jewelry. I took two steps back, scared that someone might see me and accuse me of a crime I had not committed. There was a watch sparkling on her right wrist and pink polish on her long nails. I wondered what might be in the handbag lying between her legs. Money? Gold jewelry?

There's a security barrier located on the road opposite the meadow, where they check vehicle documentation and issue speeding tickets. It's set up every day from seven in the morning to eight at night – two patrols alternate shifts. I rushed over and saluted the policemen stationed there, my jaw trembling, then added some broken sentences: "Dead... saw her... lying there..." I pointed in the direction of the body. One of the policemen craned his neck toward me and said, "You're sick!" as he scratched his right calf. "Come... look... look for yourselves." The two policemen exchanged puzzled looks. Then I got into their car with them and pointed the way.

We followed a dirt road dotted with stones and lined with dried-up streams. The sound of the Qur'an being recited came from a loudspeaker at one of the nearby mosques, calling people to Friday prayer. I was terrified they would accuse me of something I hadn't done.

One of the policemen put a glove on and felt the woman's neck for a pulse. "Oh my God!" he said, then spat on the ground to his left. Slowly, he looked up before addressing his colleague: "She's been struck on the back of the head."

He got on his wireless radio (I had learned the word "wireless" from the imam) and specified his location. We waited less than twenty minutes for the ambulance to arrive, passing the time in silence as we watched the hopping locusts that had invaded the city months ago and that no one paid any attention to anymore. A doctor came forward to examine the dead body, which took no more than a couple of minutes. Then another police car arrived. Two men got out. They marked off the area with yellow tape. One took pictures of the victim, and the other grabbed her handbag without looking at what was inside. Then they left. "These sons of bitches," the ambulance driver whispered to the doctor, and gestured with his head toward my neighbors, who had started to emerge from their dwellings to take a look, not one of them daring to come close. Louisa stood in the distance in front of our door, her arms around her brother. Then, two paramedics picked up the body after covering it with a white sheet. A policeman asked me for my name.

"Achour Hadeeri."

As he pulled the glove off his hand, the other officer barked: "Come with us!"

Fear gripped me. I remembered that I hadn't finished grazing my flock yet. I usually drive them for three hours or more so they can gobble down the wormwood that quenches their thirst, or I might give them some leafy carob branches to fatten them up. I thought about asking the two policemen for permission to give the sheep some of the dry bread my daughter collects from the neighborhoods downtown or to ask my wife to do it instead, but I was afraid of what they might say. Their frowns told me they knew who the victim was.

As soon as we got to the police station, the first policeman disappeared, while the second one spoke to a colleague standing behind the front desk: "Has The Boss arrived yet?"

"He has."

I went with the policeman to the first floor.

He sat me down on a wooden chair in a smoke-filled waiting area. He went into an office, the door creaking as he opened it. As soon as he came back out, he ordered me in. My face went pale as I thought about what I had done over the past few days. Maybe God was punishing me for a sin I'd committed. I couldn't think of anything of note. Mine is the life of the hardworking stiff. I wake up in the morning a little before or after seven. I perform my prayers, then listlessly sip my tea. I fill the metal basins with water from the well next to the mosque. I pasture my sheep, then gather up some wood for the cookfire. After negotiating the price, I might buy some simple items from a store or a sidewalk vendor, after which I return home to inspect the animals' pen before lying down on my straw mat. I gnaw on something to warm my stomach and wait for nightfall before getting into bed. Every Thursday, I head to the cattle market, where I watch the rise and fall of prices, waiting for the best time to buy a head or sell another to keep my business going. From time to time, I get a day of work on a construction site; the wages help me make ends meet.

My mind was drifting when the police inspector suggested I sit. I was embarrassed by my appearance. I wore a crimson-red shirt with only the bottom two buttons remaining, dusty black trousers, and white plastic sandals with my big toe sticking out.

"Are you married?"

"I am."

"Any children?"

"Two."

The inspector, who they called The Boss, wrote in a green-covered notebook that I was born in 1955. He guessed I was no taller than five seven. He didn't think me guilty because I spoke directly, had reported the dead woman and had agreed to come to the station; as he put it, all the evidence exonerated me. Another policeman sitting next to him typed what I said on a typewriter whose clacking sound could be heard several yards away.

The inspector, whose name was Hamid, told his colleague that the forensic police on the scene had found only a white silk handkerchief, some nail polish, a bottle of perfume, and a wad of cash in the dead woman's handbag. There were no documents that might point to her identity. "We'll await the missing persons' report to identify her."

I sat still in my chair, which had arms and was quite comfortable. I only spoke when spoken to. How did I spend my days? The names and occupations of my neighbors? An image of my son popped into my head. He's my firstborn son. I'm closer to him than I am to my daughter. Sitting in that spacious, almost empty office with its electric ceiling fan and the smell of deodorant – that's right, deodorant, not perfume; I know the difference, even though I don't use either one – made me miss him.

"Over the last few days, have you noticed any strangers wandering around the meadow?"

"No."

While I was there, I thought I should lodge a complaint against my neighbor, Sheikh Lahmar, who dyes his beard red with henna. Women line up daily in front of his door for amulets, their screams ringing in my ears as he rids them of the spirits that inhabit them. Before I could say a word about that, though, a policeman entered the office carrying just-developed photos of the victim. The Inspector gasped as he grabbed his head, his lower jaw trembling: "No… I must be dreaming!" he yelled, then ran out of the room. It made me regret ever reporting the body.

HAMID

I looked around for the Sahara Hotel owner's car, but it was nowhere to be found. "Gone when you need him the most," I grumbled. Then, after stomping out my cigarette at the hotel entrance, I hurried into the lobby, at the end of which were some red-carpeted stairs that led to the rooms on the upper three floors.

The receptionist, Kamal Belattar, was busy finishing up with some customers who had formed a short line in front of him. He looked up with his slicked-back hair and flashed me a fake smile. I shot him a frown in return. He knows I hate him as much as he hates me.

"The Hadj didn't come in today?"

"No, Maimoun's on vacation."

"Where is he?"

"In Sétif."

"Is there a number where he can be reached?"

Kamal left his customers waiting as he dialed the hotel where his boss was staying. Straightening his red tie, he listened to the voice on the other end tell him that his boss had checked out of his room. "He must be on his way back."

I didn't find it reassuring that Maimoun had been out of town the day Zakia Zaghouani was killed. Why had he let her out of his sight? In the nightclub, she'd been like a freshwater spring thirsty patrons flocked to because of her enchanting voice and suggestive dancing. I had asked him to notify me if he felt like anyone was harassing her. To keep what had happened under wraps, I opted to wait for his return. I gave the two forensic police officers who had come with me permission to leave and called the traffic policeman stationed at the northern entrance to the city to ask him to keep an eye out for a white Peugeot 505 being driven by a man in his fifties named Maimoun Belassal. Then I went to the hospital to look at the victim.

As I passed by the post office, some questions came to mind: Was her murder meant to send me a message? Did my enemies, wealthy people whose temptations I had resisted, know she was my eyes and ears on all their movements inside the nightclub? Would my turn come as well, or did they just want to frighten me? I hit the steering wheel with the palm of my hand and pursed my lips as I drove along Fifth of July Street, lined with closed shops. I reached the Pitcher Roundabout and continued straight, pressing down hard on the gas pedal until I got to the hospital, where two old men were lying down at the entrance waiting to receive dialysis. Snippets of imams' sermons came out of the loudspeakers of adjacent mosques and got all mixed up in my ears. Were they out to frighten me? Zakia had always confided in me about her concerns and submitted to my assignments. She was my messenger in reaching out to those I didn't know. And from my chats with her, I had learned all about women.

It occurred to me that the killer might have been someone I had previously prosecuted. A person certainly doesn't forget about exacting revenge just because they have served their prison sentence. I decided to investigate those released in the past few days, taking all the necessary precautions when

I went out. I bit my upper lip so hard it almost bled and remembered what Abderrahman El Mejdoub, that poet of wanderers, lovers, and mystics, had said:

Do not saddle up until all is bridled and well fastened,
Do not speak before thinking to avoid scandal once again.

My heart racing, I entered the autopsy room, which contained two metal beds. There, I met the crime scene policeman who had a face that betrayed many sleepless nights. He spoke first.

"We only found one earring. In her right ear. The other one's missing."

There was a silver earring with a pearl dangling from it. I doubted the criminal had snatched the other one. I turned to the medical examiner, seeking more from him. "She likely died between one and two in the morning after some sort of blow to the back of the head," he went on to explain.

I glanced at the victim's white-shrouded face. She looked like she was sleeping or unconscious, not dead. I avoided removing the lower covering so as not to have to see her stomach, which had been slit open to determine the cause of death. I paused at her lips; they were pursed in a way that made her look like she was expressing surprise, as if she wanted to say the name of the person who had done it. I buried the overwhelming urge to cry deep inside my chest. Crying washes away the heart's murk, but I tend to avoid it. It isn't something proper people do, as my mother always said.

"Did you find any signs of a struggle?" I asked the medical examiner.

"A bruise on her left cheek, along with traces of isopropyl alcohol."

"Women sometimes use it to clean their skin."

There were no contusions on her arms or hands, which indicated that she hadn't put up a fight before drawing her last breath. But where was the second earring?

I had to inform her relatives and arrange the funeral, but her family lived far away in Nezrama. Not to mention that she had once told me her father was dead, and that her four brothers had disowned her after learning the nature of her work. They had forbidden her from visiting her mother, too. They had threatened to kill her because she had sullied her family's good name. Was one of her brothers involved in this?

"Did you take blood samples?" I asked the medical examiner, who had gotten shorter with age. He was no more than five feet tall.

"Yes."

"And?"

"O negative."

"Do you think the samples will be of any use to us?"

"I don't know."

My throat was dry and I craved a cigarette, so I went out to the hospital garden. I examined the plastic bag that contained the dead woman's things. I took out the Japanese wristwatch with gold hands that I had given her as a gift three years ago. It had cost me half my paycheck. I slipped it into my trouser pocket. She had been carrying a large amount of money with her. Enough for an entire tribe, I said to myself. I reconsidered what I thought had happened. It hadn't been a robbery. After an examination of where the corpse had been found, the forensic report had shown no blood on the ground, which meant the body had been dragged there from another location.

I heard a commotion from some nurses and patients in the hallway. One of the patients yelled angrily: "Then close the hospital if you don't have enough medicine!" I tried to make out his face through the broken window but could only see his broad back. I put out my cigarette and hurried back inside.

I returned to the medical examiner, who was leaning back in his chair, chewing a piece of gum, his outstretched hands on his thighs. This was the tenth corpse he had seen in the last four days. He was used to bodies that were charred or had missing limbs – children run over by trucks, adults whose bodies were pierced with stab wounds – and he had come to thank God whenever a fully intact body arrived. I didn't know how he could close his eyes at night without nightmares of the dead visiting him.

"Do you need to examine her again?"

"I'm done."

I decided to issue permission to bury her the following day, then headed to the police station. As soon as I finished one cigarette, I lit another.

Calling my wife, I told her not to leave the house, and to keep our two children from leaving too. Experience has taught me that no crime is an isolated event. One is always followed by another one like it.

"Do you mean to put us in a prison?"

"No, it's for your own protection. I'll tell you everything when I get home this evening." I stopped her torrent of questions before it could start by ending the call.

I called Nezrama security, and the person in charge of answering the phones picked up. I expressed my condolences for the deceased and told the man of the need to inform the family to attend the funeral, with the understanding that I would provide an official telegram soon after. The person on the other end of the line was confused and asked me to repeat her name twice. I preferred not to get too much into it, convinced that news of her passing would put her family's minds at ease. I remembered the last time I met with Zaza, as she called herself to hide her true identity; that's what nightclub singers usually do. That was a week ago, when she had talked with me about wanting to spend some days off in a city on the coast, to breathe in the sea air that would lift all her worries away, to bury her feet in the sand, to fill her lungs with fresh air and dive into the salt water. I'd suggested she go to Tipaza, provided a friend of mine could make an apartment close to the beach available to her.

"Is he a ladies' man like you?" she laughed, flashing her bright white teeth.

"He's married and has a daughter."

"Just because a man gets married and has kids doesn't mean he doesn't love women."

But she had gone to her death, not the sea. I pictured her standing in front of me and thought about her plump breasts. Whenever I described them as "partridges," she would flirtatiously joke: "But they'll never fall into any traps!" Her skin had been a darker brown when I had first got to know her, but it had gotten lighter.

I bit my lower lip and shook my head, grabbing my right hand with my left, sorry I wouldn't see her anymore as she turned her body toward the mirror before starting to sing. I wouldn't see her taking care of her nails the way a policeman takes care of his gun. And I would no longer exchange jokes with her as we had done the past four years.

My guess was that whoever had done this hadn't been strong enough or had not sufficiently planned, so had attacked her from behind. He had caught her unaware because he had no way of overpowering her. I had investigated stabbings in the chest and the stomach, as well as stranglings, but this was the first time I was investigating a victim who had been killed by a blow to the back of the head. "There's no mercy in people's hearts anymore… look after me, O Exalted One," I sighed.

Then came a call on the radio. It was the traffic policeman telling me he had stopped a Peugeot 505 being driven by one Maimoun Belassal.

MAIMOUN

Police Inspector Hamid looked me up and down, noting my sweaty, dust-blackened collar.

"Is this some sort of circus, Boss?"

Generally, this is how I addressed him. For his part, he called me "Hadj" like others did, as I'd gone to Mecca twice, the first time by myself and the second time with my wife.

"Why didn't you tell me you'd be gone?"

I was confused. Since when did I have to tell him everything I did?

"I didn't plan on taking more than a day off, but I met up with some old friends and ended up staying longer."

I wasn't comfortable with the way I was being questioned and wondered whether he had come because of that damned woman, although I hid my suspicions. I squeezed the Camel cigarette between my index and middle fingers as I leaned back in my desk chair.

"Something terrible has happened."

I froze, but he went on.

"We found Zaza. Murdered."

I looked at his square face in disbelief. He told me what had happened since her body had been discovered in the meadow; about being informed about her death while watching a French television program, as he has done every Friday morning since buying a satellite dish that picks up foreign channels; about looking at photos of her at the police station before seeing her body in the morgue. Still, I was determined not to take what he said seriously.

"Maybe it was some other girl who looked like her."

"I wish that were the case."

I stood up, put out my cigarette, and clapped my hands together. Then I rubbed my sweaty bald spot. Hamid broke the stillness of the office.

"Anyone you might suspect?"

"She hadn't told me about anyone threatening her."

He asked me about the last time I'd been with her. I swallowed and told him all about it. We had chatted the evening before I traveled to Sétif. She announced that she wanted us to change the nightclub's decor: "Change is refreshing," she said. She also wanted me to hire a new backing musician for her. She didn't like Farhat's playing anymore.

"Do you have the key to her room?"

"It's at reception."

Two policemen joined us, arousing the tourists' suspicions as we went up to the third floor. The few rooms on that top floor were reserved for permanent residents, in contrast to guests just passing through. Among the permanent residents was Zakia, who had occupied room 301. Next to her, in room 303, was Merzaka Soualem, who had left teaching to go into politics before her body fell from the balcony, causing her soul to ascend to heaven.

We were met by a tidy room. The wallpaper tended toward yellow. There were brown flip-flops to the right of the door. The bed had a purple cover and two red pillows, and above it was a picture of Zaza standing next to the hotel swimming pool in a light blue summer shirt and white shorts, her eyes hidden behind sunglasses. Her clothes were in a wardrobe that smelled of cologne, and there was an air conditioner above that. Her beauty products were in the bathroom, and next to them was a medicine cabinet with just a bottle of aspirin and some cough syrup, along with three sanitary pads.

The two policemen felt around the furniture with their gloved hands, but nothing unusual caught their attention. One glanced underneath the bed, but all he saw was a pair of two-inch heels. The other one lifted prints off the chair's armrest and the doorknob before opening the refrigerator in the far corner. All he found was two sausages on an earthenware plate and half a bottle of soda. He then moved his hand over to a wooden table, where a television and VCR sat. Underneath the VCR was a letter written on a sheet of legal paper in rushed, shaky handwriting that slanted from right to left as if written by a child. It was folded in two. He handed it to Hamid, who read it.

Zakia,

This is the last letter I will write to you. Please understand my situation. We have no option but to part ways and put away our differences, to cast love aside with its good and bad, its tender and harsh moments. My mother said no, which means we cannot get married as we wanted to. Leaving you is difficult, but it cannot be helped. Please stop calling and chasing after me. It has become intolerable. If you try calling me again, you will pay the consequences. I will not indulge you any longer.

Bachir

The police inspector furrowed his brow and looked sharply at me in exasperation. "Who is this?"

"Her boyfriend," I responded after a silence. I'd thought she had left him.

He pursed his lips in surprise, then addressed me: "Come by the station tomorrow to sign the interrogation report."

The inspector had the two policemen gather up the victim's belongings and take pictures of the room before sealing it off. I felt as if the ground was quaking beneath me, and I had an overwhelming desire to throw up.

IBRAHIM

SEPTEMBER 10

Six came into my shop that afternoon and, as always, called me Brihoum rather than Ibrahim, my given name. Red-eyed, he waved a plastic bag in his right hand and came at me with a hug.

"You never hug me unless you need something!"

"Who needs a short guy with puffy lips?" He let out a laugh as he stuck his left index finger in his ear to clean it out.

"I may be short, but at least I don't have teeth like a mouse!"

Our friendship had begun when I'd bought a set of dishes from Six in the contraband market to show my mother how much I loved her. After that, he'd become a middleman for me and his hashish-selling friends (I'd made a habit of filling my lungs with it ever since my university days). He provided me with good-quality stuff at its actual price, and I repaid him by setting aside the latest movies before anyone else had a chance to watch them, especially adult films. He used a garage adjacent to his home, converting it nightly into a screening room where he always shows two features, the first a combat or police movie, then one that arouses the audience to the point where they ejaculate under the cover of the darkened room.

"Have you gotten the new movies in yet?" Two days ago, when we'd been out drinking, I'd told him about a new shipment of cassettes.

"I've got a real winner," I replied.

He smiled and pulled a sandwich out of the plastic bag. It was no more than half a piece of bread stuffed with olives and a chunk of hashish in the middle. We used this trick to avoid getting caught by the shop's customers. He handed me his product. "I just tried it."

"That's obvious to anyone who looks at your eyes!"

He began to rub his palms together like someone preparing to devour a feast. New movies meant more customers, which meant more money.

I handed him the new adult films I had hidden under the pinewood counter like a young woman hiding her wedding dress until the big day. "Tell me how the audience reacts," I said. Then I bent over as he busied himself looking at the movie jackets. I took out the ID card left by the woman who'd rented the VCR. I looked closely at the name and picture, along with the address. I quickly put it back where it was and asked Six about it. He's like a postman; he knows everyone, and everyone knows him.

"Do you know Bachir Labtam?"

"Do you mean my cousin?" he stammered, and his lower jaw went slack.

"He lives in the Twentieth of August neighborhood?"

"That's right."

I lied to him that the guy I was talking about had rented some movies and hadn't returned them.

"He's gone away," Six said.

"Where to?"

"Abroad."

Then he stepped back and hiked up his baggy trousers that dragged on the ground, their back pocket emblazoned with an American flag. He said he had to prepare for that night's screening.

"I looked for you Thursday night, but the garage was locked."

"I was tired and went to bed early," he said.

That woman had never returned the VCR to me. Had she ripped me off? I sat up straight on the bed and calmed my nerves with a joint. Then I pulled my guitar close to my body as if embracing a baby. I took a deep breath, legs wide apart. I moved my tongue back and forth and rubbed my upper gums with my lips to loosen up. I played a few notes to make sure I was playing them right and started to sing: "In the great big world... Across its many countries... I went around... and around... and around." I started singing as a child after learning to play an instrument at the neighborhood cultural center, where I joined an orchestra with more kids and teenagers than it could handle. That's where I learned about solfège and strings and keys. My fingers hurt at first, but then my playing improved by listening to gospel records I found at home, along with Bob Marley and Cat Stevens.

I was unsatisfied with the practice session I had recorded. Before closing up for the evening, I took some cash out of the register that my only brother, Khamisi, had asked for. He was almost twenty-six and wanted the money to travel to Constantine to compete in a boxing tournament.

"Why doesn't the local athletics division help you?" I'd asked.

"They've already spent this year's entire budget."

"No doubt they spent it filling their bloated bellies."

Khamisi had tried selling vegetables and bread on the sidewalk, then washing cars and trucks and doing oil changes and lube jobs. Then he'd settled on work as a porter in the farmers' market, a commercial center that's as big as a football field and provides people with groceries and other things. He drifts from job to job, anything that requires more brawn than brains. He's a character straight out of Mouloud Feraoun's novel *The Poor Man's Son*. Like me, Khamisi hasn't done his compulsory military service, which prevents him from considering work with a regular paycheck. He starts his mornings with strength training, jumping rope, and cardiovascular exercises, and at the end of every day he spends three hours or more at the gym.

My father was martyred in the spring of 1962, just weeks before independence, according to my mother. We have never been able to find his grave. My brother, who was no more than a fetus in her belly at the time, is now the man closest to her heart. He benefits from the kindness she shows him and doesn't eat any food unless it's full of protein, whereas I make do with whatever satisfies my hunger. She devotes the meager salary she makes as a cleaning woman at the Sahara to making sure he doesn't lack for anything. She brings him whatever the tourists leave behind in their rooms, from razor blades to perfumes to underwear. These things make him as happy as a child getting new clothes for Eid. I promised him a cash prize if he came back from Constantine with a medal.

I decided to proceed slowly and deliberately before heading to Bachir Labtam's house. When I saw him, I'd either get my VCR back or receive payment for it. Otherwise, I'd lodge a complaint with the police.

BACHIR

When the two policemen approached me in the Khayma Café, I feigned indifference, imagining they wanted to ask me about someone else. They surprised me when they said: "Come with us to the car."

I took off and ran as fast as I could, past the Pitcher Roundabout and toward the First of November neighborhood. There was practically nothing in my way. My legs moved on their own. I pictured one of the policemen firing a bullet at my leg if they couldn't catch me, but they reached me at the Gas & Electric Co. I took a blow to the back with a thick baton that knocked me to the ground. Then they cuffed me and forced me, panting, into the car with them. I could feel people watching, as if it were a rehearsal for a chase scene in a police movie.

In the police station, I stood before an inspector with a thick mustache. I wasn't wrong that he was Hamid, the one Zakia had spoken about. I had also heard about him from some hashish dealers. They were in and out of prison so much they had come to talk about him as if he were a close friend. He didn't give me a chance to catch my breath and spat loudly in my face: "Why'd you try to run away?!"

"I didn't attack that drunk. He attacked me!" I went straight into explaining what had happened to me the previous day, but he paid no attention to what I was saying. He put out his cigarette by crushing it under his shoe and yelled, saliva gathering in the corners of his mouth. I was afraid I would share the same fate as the cigarette butt. I recited some verses from the Qur'an to myself.

"Why'd you kill her?"

"Who?"

"Are you claiming you don't know, you piece of garbage?"

He said Zakia Zaghouani's name, and my vision blurred. Zakia was dead?

"I didn't kill anyone."

Hamid leaned over his desk to write something on the paper I had signed without reading. The two policemen remained standing behind me. I could hear them breathing. It was as if they were expecting me to jump out the window behind the inspector, even though the shutters were closed.

The two inspectors led me to a basement that smelled like the bus station, a combination of piss and exhaust. I was handed over to three men who had their faces covered. "You've deprived us of our Friday off!" one of them sneered, obviously annoyed. They handed me over to a gentle-faced young nurse so he could take my pulse and blood pressure before leaving without saying a word. Then they locked the door. Someone was moaning on the other side of the wall. It occurred to me that this was no more than a performance meant to scare me. The one I thought was in charge demanded I confess: "God is all-forgiving, all-merciful." But I held to my innocence. I got down on my knees. One grabbed my head from behind and pulled it back as if he wanted me to look at the ceiling. Another put a wet towel over my mouth, and the third poured water over it.

"If you want to confess, raise your index finger."

I felt as if I was drowning in a well. I could hardly breathe and my body trembled, but I didn't raise my finger, knowing that any pain that did not consume me now would erase an older pain. They couldn't bear my silence any longer, so the water stopped.

"I swear on my mother's head, I didn't kill her!" I screamed through my tears. Fear tore away at my heart. They hadn't got what they wanted from me.

"You'll be educated in prison!" the one who had reminded me of God's all-merciful nature screeched in my face.

I threw up everything I'd eaten that day. Then I was handed over to someone else. He seemed to be the most merciful of them all. He put me in a room on the station's second floor. The room was no larger than twelve square feet. A throng of men, young and old, were crowded in there. I couldn't sleep at night, and my bladder hurt the following morning. They took mug shots and fingerprinted me. Then they brought me to the courtroom. I answered some questions about my relationship to the victim but denied the charge once again, so they took me to prison, pending an investigation, where they shaved my head and provided me with a blanket and pillow. I spent my first hour in silence, watching the prisoners as they moved about, stood still, whispered, and yelled. The place was filled with a rotten stench that mingled with the smell of sweat and feet. This is ass-backward, I thought. Someone they called Slit-Nose (because the part of his nose between the nostrils had been cut) asked what I was in for. I ignored him, but he insisted, so I responded: "I've been wrongly accused."

I worried I might lose my job at the Rubber & Plastic Co., whose aim is to export its products to friendly nations. The job gave me a set salary regardless of how many hours I put in. I used to steal items and sell them to vendors in the contraband market so I could buy presents for my girlfriend. Sometimes I would be absent for days without my supervisor even asking why. One time, we schemed to break one of the machines, and all the workers got a week off while they fixed it. I'd taken advantage of that time to travel with Zakia to Béjaïa, a seaside city she loved as much as she did all coastal cities.

Slit-Nose didn't comment on what I said. But a young, cross-eyed fellow with a broad forehead and a sore on his lower lip stood in solidarity with me. "We're all innocent," he said, to which another guy missing his front teeth responded: "The one with the money plays while the poor man pays."

I recalled an image of Zakia frowning when, during my last days of military service in Nezrama, I'd suggested she come home with me to this city. I would help her find work as we prepared to get married.

"Shouldn't you ask my family for my hand in marriage first?" she asked. I told her how my mother had insisted I first find a job to keep me out of debt, which made her doubt my sincerity and grow cold toward me.

At that time, Zakia's relationship with her father had worsened. He wanted her to cover her hair with a veil, to put on a show of virtue, following the example of the neighbors' daughters. She went against his wishes, so he hit her with a screwdriver, leaving a scar on her lower jaw. She became obsessed with the idea of leaving home after she saw an announcement in the paper for a hotel resort that had just opened in a northern city and had job openings.

I was upset at her choice. "You'll work with drunks?"

"No, I'll be making pastries." She had acquired that skill at the Professional Training Center.

43

She was gone almost two years. She only made rushed calls to me on holidays, and I didn't dare go to her. I was scared she had traded me in for someone else. I started smoking regularly, crying at night, and engaging in silent conversations with her ghost. I lost my appetite. My longing for her ate away at me until she finally returned my calls when the resort had to close because it was illegally allowing unmarried couples to stay there. Terrified her family would punish her, she couldn't return to her hometown.

"I arrive tomorrow at noon."

She ended the call by blowing kisses into the receiver.

I had just twenty-four hours to get things ready for her. The only person who came to mind who might help was my friend Kamal, who worked on the Sahara's reception desk. We had gone to school and played soccer together at an amateur club. His specialty was penalty kicks. He played attacking midfielder, and people often compared him to Garrincha, the Brazilian star player. I played defense, wearing number four. We shared in certain delights, and together we accumulated stories and engaged in pranks only we knew about. I asked him to make a room available for Zakia and told him what was going on between us to put the brakes on any impulses he might have toward her. He responded coldly, as if he were the boss and not a mere worker: "She can work as a waitress."

The red uniform suited Zakia, and she would meet me when she had time off. She hid her desire to sing, which she had acquired during the nighttime shows she went to at the resort after developing her vocal cords, improving her breathing, and gaining confidence. Only after the fact did she tell me about her conversations with Maimoun Belassal, who found pleasure in her company and whom she convinced to give her a chance in front of the microphone. Without my knowledge, she moved from the restaurant to the nightclub. Kamal thought I was aware of what she was doing. But she waited two weeks before telling me about her new job, which set off a round of arguments between us. One time I asked her, "Do you want to become a prostitute?" to which she responded, "Only bastards call women prostitutes."

I learned when I was young that singing was not what women did, and I hoped it was just a passing thing, but Zakia's love for money made it necessary that she continue. Her circle of relationships widened, and she informed me that the police inspector had tasked her with watching Maimoun and observing the comings and goings of wealthy people who spent their evenings listening to her. "I agreed to provide him with a service in exchange for him doing the same for me, should I need it someday," she said. I feared one of them would find her out. She was registered as missing in her hometown and was always scared the police would return her to her family, after which she would never again see the light of day. She pressured me into getting engaged, claiming that she had other suitors. "I want to carry your name," she said.

In the summer of 1984, when Zakia came to live here, I got a job at the Rubber & Plastic Co. with the help of my aunt's husband, a former Liberation Army resistance fighter. I saved some money and told my mother last spring that I intended to get engaged. She was opposed to the idea. I tried again last month, and she responded: "I don't want ladies of the night in the house." My beloved girlfriend figured our plan to live under one roof had gone up in a puff of smoke. I could see the disappointment on her face. I promised to try again, but we got into an argument and she refused to see me. When I got home late the night before my arrest, my sister was braiding her hair and told me Zakia had called while I was out. Had she been missing me in the moments before her untimely death?

I can't believe that she's left me, that she's gone. Had the owner of the Sahara taken revenge on her because she was spying on him? Or had she discovered some secret that involved him?

HAMID

As I was thinking that Zaza's ghost would disappear from my mind as soon as her body was buried in the dirt, a woman knocked once on the door and entered without waiting for me to let her in. She wore a white *melhfa* wrap, and the lower part of her face was covered with a brown veil tied behind her neck. A short young woman in an oversize dark-blue djellaba followed her. She had covered her hair with a black veil. I thought they were members of an arrestee's family; every time a criminal or suspect is taken into custody, their family rushes to the station to try to elicit some compassion and forgiveness.

"The policeman downstairs sent me to you," the woman said. I waited for her to identify herself and tell me why she had barged in on me, interrupting my phone call with a colleague in the capital. As if she understood what I was waiting for, she added: "Halima, Zakia Zaghouani's mother."

This was the last thing I expected: that the family of the deceased would respond to my wishes not to renounce her after having kept their distance while she was alive. I apologized to my colleague on the phone, got up from my chair, and suggested they sit on the couch along the edge of the office rather than in the two chairs in the middle of the room. "May God increase your reward. I'm so sorry for your loss," I said.

It was only then that she realized her daughter had died. At first, she had not believed what the policeman who came to her home had told her, hoping against hope that a mistake had been made. The *melhfa* fell from her shoulders and the veil came off her face. I guessed she was in her mid-forties. She burst into sobs and I tapped my right foot with my left. She began to scream, hitting her chest with the palm of her hand: "My daughter, O God… my daughter!" I tried to console her, knowing full well that crying might help make her feel better, but I couldn't find my handkerchief. She cut me off, panting like someone who had just finished running a marathon: "Can we see her?"

The young woman next to her was likewise unable to comfort her, surrendering to her tears with a reddened face, knees trembling. I guessed she was the murdered woman's sister, although Zaza had only told me about her brothers. I knew they would continue feeling sad as long as they remained in the office, and one of my weaknesses is that I cannot stand to look upon others' misery, so I suggested we go to the hospital. It was close to eleven o'clock, and since I had no experience in burials, I asked two policemen to come along.

Qur'anic verses lined the walls of the morgue, which smelled of camphor and was chilled by a generator (in case of power cuts, which happened frequently). I showed Zaza's mother inside. Glancing at the younger woman's sunken eyes, I asked her who she was, and she responded, "Zakia's cousin."

I was disappointed I had guessed wrong and that she might not be of any help in the investigation. I snapped my lips shut and prevented her from entering with her aunt. "Only immediate relatives are allowed in."

As I looked at Halima, wailing as she slapped her tear-stained face, the popular saying *Only your mother cries for you* came to mind. At the same time, I kept wondering why they had disowned her.

The two policemen helped me drag the dead woman's mother out by her arms and then moved the body to the washing station. An old woman took care of shrouding her before an ambulance left for the cemetery with the coffin on board.

I brought Halima and her niece back to the station. I explained that transferring the deceased to her city of birth would require a lot of administrative paperwork and would take some time. She moaned: "A mother gives birth to her children. She doesn't attend their funerals." I reprimanded the policeman at the front desk who had let her come up to my office without consulting with me first; then I had someone get the two women some fruit and water, asking them not to leave until I returned from the burial.

Lalla Ammoura Cemetery is about half an hour from the station by car, past the Pitcher Roundabout and over a bridge that joins the two banks of a river, as the dead must sleep close to flowing water. It couldn't be easier to get to the cemetery; the city was built along a straight downward slope, which allows people to walk to visit their dead. The cemetery is divided according to clan and lineage. Strangers are only buried deep in its far corners. It is mostly bare dirt, with green plants scattered here and there. Some graves are marked with marble or stone, whereas others have no grave markers at all, and people walk all over them. Based on the many people who visit, it seems to me that death is not so grim. It's just a joke.

The imam stood up straight to pray. He was wearing a white robe and rubbed his graying beard. He wore a yellow skullcap and had a string of black prayer beads hanging from his right wrist. I hadn't told him the cause of death, because imams generally avoid funerals for murders or suicides. Several mourners were lined up behind him. I examined their faces and wrote down the names of which hotel employees were there and which were not. I saw Maimoun Belassal, Khayati the chef, Khalil the waiter, Fouzi the horse-drawn carriage driver, Hadi the cleaning supervisor, Krimo the gardener, Youssef the tourist guide, and Ajroud, who made a living taking pictures of tourists and videotaping the nightclub acts. There were a few mourners I didn't know. I figured they were curious unemployed folk who spent their time attending funerals to make themselves look good in God's eyes. Or were they customers from the nightclub? I wasn't authorized to ask them. And anyway, there are no secrets in this city. Gossip acts like a drug that loosens tongues. I was surprised to see them jostling one another to secure a spot carrying her coffin, as if she were a family member.

Over her final resting place, the blind reciter I had paid chanted Qur'anic verses. I stood alone with Maimoun, who was baffled that someone would attend a funeral for someone they didn't know. "We're mourning ourselves here. We were her family," he said. His forehead was sweaty, and he was squinting in the bright sun. I asked him not to go anywhere, as I might need another statement from him at some point. "You know where to find me," he replied.

Then I headed back to the station, meeting up with Halima and her companion, whose name, I learned, was Nassira. I felt uncomfortable with Nassira there, so I called my friend who owned the Nour motel and asked him to give the two of them a double room. I didn't want them spending the night at the Sahara, because the owner wouldn't be able to leave them alone without revealing whatever information he had, thus breaching the confidentiality of my investigation. I have learned not to trust those closest to me while working difficult cases, and not to allow anyone to interfere with what I do.

Nassira left for the motel with a policeman while Halima remained sitting in front of me. I assured her that her daughter's funeral had been well attended and that the Qur'an had been recited. She then removed her veil completely and lowered her wrap to her shoulders. When she informed me that she was about to turn forty-six, I was pleased I had guessed correctly.

She began telling me about Zaza, periodically breaking into fits of crying – her childhood, her fights with her brothers, from whom Halima had hidden news of their sister's death before coming because she didn't believe it herself. She ended with a story of her daughter's disappearance from home six years ago. "I showed her picture to the police, but they couldn't find her," she told me.

Halima had left the outside light on that night in the hope that Zaza would come back, obsessed with the idea that a gang had torn her body apart to sell her limbs. However, she never stopped praying for her, and her daughter returned the following day.

"She came back listless and weak."

"Where was she?" I asked.

Zaza said she had spent the night at a wedding, which was difficult for the family to confirm, since it had been full of both invited and uninvited guests. She had quarreled with her older brother before disappearing, and when she got back, he had given her a beating: "He tied her hands together and gagged her, then punched her repeatedly in the stomach and face."

When her father got home that evening after finishing his shift as a sharecropper on the farm of one of the rich people in the area, he forbade her from going out again. Zakia lay in bed for a whole week, complaining of fever and pain in her joints. Some months after that, she disappeared again.

According to her mother, the police had added her name to a list of missing persons, while, in order to avoid the neighbors thinking anything bad of her, Halima spread word that her daughter had gotten married in a distant town. I realized now why the policeman in Nezrama had been confused when I'd told him of Zaza's death, and surprised Halima hadn't reported that she knew where her daughter was living. Instead, she had chosen to protect her little girl by disregarding the law. No one keeps secrets better than mothers, I decided.

Zakia's father had passed away three years ago from pneumonia, coughing up blood in his final days. His daughter had not been at his funeral, and the neighbors were suspicious about what her mother had told them, but Halima dodged their questions. "We were always in touch," she told me. To avoid her brothers' wrath, Halima forbade her from visiting, so Zakia made sure to send money. "She sent an unusually large sum the last time," her mother said.

In a final phone call two weeks ago to Nassira's mother's phone (which she regularly called), Zakia had spoken of her intention to marry.

"Who did she want to marry?" I asked Halima.

"She didn't say."

Her mother's words, "May the Lord help you," were enough for me to understand that their relationship had been better than I had first been led to believe.

"Did she tell you about anyone threatening her?"

Halima wiped a thread of snot from her nose with the back of her hand. She lifted her head to look at the corner of the white ceiling, searching for an answer. "She didn't like the people she worked with."

"Who was bothering her?"

"I don't know."

"Try to remember."

"I never asked. I figured they were just passing fears."

Her answer made me uneasy. Had one of the hotel workers killed her?

Halima tried to ease her distress by telling stories about her "stubborn" daughter. She talked about her mischievousness and the solid relationship they enjoyed. She believed stories could bring the dead back to life.

"We used to call her Zerboute when she was younger because she kept changing her mind and couldn't keep still, like a spinning top."

My gaze fell on a gold tooth in the top of Halima's mouth as I continued jotting things down in my notebook. Unaware she was doing so, she answered questions floating around in my head about the victim and her brothers.

After talking herself hoarse, Halima asked me the question I was waiting for: "Who killed her?"

Although Bachir Labtam was nothing but a suspect, I didn't have any evidence pointing to others who might have been involved. Given that, I answered: "A young man who was close to her."

She arched her thick eyebrows, waiting for more.

"They were romantically involved."

She covered her mouth and round chin with her hand, like someone who had just heard an unsavory slur. "Why'd he kill her?"

The contents of the letter I had found in her room were still in my head. It was difficult for me to accept that she had loved another man, that she had in fact pursued him and that he had loved her in return, without her considering my feelings toward her.

"We'll know everything once the investigation is concluded."

I figured she needed to be alone to attend to her grief. Her skin looked dry, not at all like my wife's. I handed her a suitcase containing her daughter's belongings, clothes, and money she had left behind. I held onto the earring that had been in her earlobe. Finding the other earring will make my job easier, I told myself. Then she put her fingerprint on the receipt for her belongings, and I promised to go with her the next day to the cemetery to recite the Fatiha over the spirit of her deceased daughter.

Before I left the office at a little before five that afternoon, Hassina, a lawyer, called to ask how one of her clients, who had diabetes, was doing in prison. I assured her that I had asked the guards to be kind to him. Then, by way of conversation, I told her about the awful thing that had happened, without mentioning the victim's name. I knew she didn't like Zaza, but she was insistent, so I recited some of what was included in the forensic report:

… on Friday, September 9, 1988 at 10:30 a.m., the body of Zakia Zaghouani, born March 11, 1964, was found…

– We saw a gash, approximately 1.5 inches long, on the back of the victim's neck.

– We did not see any blood on the ground.

– We took prints.

– We did not find any items that would identify the victim.

– The identity of the victim was later confirmed.

She was silent for a moment before saying: "I can only imagine how sad you are about this."

I felt terrible when I learned the suspect was related to Hassina's friend Noura.

"What do you intend to do?"

"Make sure her killing does not go unpunished."

I hung up, thinking again of what Halima had said: that her daughter had been on her town's missing persons register. Why had the hotel owner hidden her? Why had the deceased been unhappy with the people she worked with?

There was no doubt Maimoun was hiding something.

NOURA

When I was younger, I wanted to become a veterinarian, but I just couldn't make peace with math. I imagined those professors were all dull, so I chose law. Although unconvinced at first, I reconciled myself to it after graduating. Law is a dodgy profession. The odds of winning are good, as lawyers get paid without having to ante up. The worse people's problems get, the more money I make. I spend all my time at work, with all the boredom that comes with it. The defenses I put together are basically all the same, dealing with divorce or inheritance or the like, to the extent that my mother calls me the Godmother of Divorced Women. That is, until that day when I couldn't believe my ears: A murder case! And the main suspect was my cousin.

When I picked up the receiver, my mother's voice took me by surprise. She was yelling as if I were standing on top of a mountain. At first, I thought she was calling to remind me to pick up a few things on my way home, but then she said, "Bachir... he's in jail!" I was dumbstruck, and grabbed my neck with my left hand as if afraid my head might fall off. Then, before hanging up, she hurled one last sentence at me: "Get yourself ready!"

Because I'm a lawyer, she figured I must possess the cunning to get him out of prison. And if I couldn't, I didn't deserve to consider myself one of her children. I swallowed hard, biting the nail on my index finger while trying to absorb what she had just told me.

I had never heard of Bachir misbehaving before. His record was impeccable. His family's old house was just two blocks from ours, two hundred and thirty steps away. We'd spent half our childhood building castles out of stones and mud and trading stories and myths about the War of Independence that we'd heard snippets of from the grown-ups. Then, following their grandfather's death in the same year the government nationalized the oil industry, his father had quarreled with his uncle over ownership of their grand-father's house, and, as a result, Bachir moved with his parents and brothers to another place, close to the meadow.

When I enrolled in the girls' high school at fifteen, Bachir, a year older than me, used to keep guys from harassing me, which sometimes resulted in him getting into fistfights. When I got annoyed at this, he told me: "You're like my sister."

"Look after your sister, then."

I realized later that he used to follow me not only to protect me but because he had a crush on a girl in my class. But that girl ended up getting married off to someone who had moved abroad. She was proud of the fact that he owned an apartment and a car. She called him Uncle Sassi, and I learned that he was twenty years older than her. She went to live with him in a Parisian suburb without knowing any French except for *Bonjour, Monsieur... Bonsoir, Monsieur.*

"I fell in love with her quickly and forgot all about her just as quickly," Bachir told me the day I learned about it.

I got my high school diploma and studied law after moving to the capital, where I lived with my aunt in First of May Plaza. If not for her, my father would not have been sold on my decision to move to a faraway city. I came back from that city with the requisite diploma just days before the newspapers celebrated the release of American hostages in Iran. For his part, Bachir failed to get past the third year of high school. He spent a useless year pacing around the city or leaning against walls, staring at people walking by. Then, he graduated from the Professional Training Center as an accountant. He did his military service and was persistent enough to get a position at the Rubber & Plastic Co., five miles outside the city. He'd never given up his old habit of reading love poetry, astronomy and geography books, and biographies of famous people. He also loves filling notebooks with thoughts and daily musings.

My friend Hassina, who knew everyone's secrets and what women hid from their husbands, had told me about Zakia Zaghouani.

"She isn't that beautiful, but she's younger than us. An expert at making men follow her like hungry puppies."

Hassina hated Zakia as soon as she suspected she had stolen a man from her.

"Do I know him?"

"I don't think so," Hassina answered as she chewed on a fingernail.

"But you know everything about me!"

"Ignorance is bliss."

After that, I had decided to keep my stories about men to myself.

It surprised me that Bachir had fallen in love with such a woman and was intent on getting engaged to her, as my mother had told me on the phone. But my aunt was against the idea, which frustrated him. Had Hassina been insinuating that the dead woman had stolen my cousin, Bachir, from her?

I walked the length of the contraband market, around five hundred yards. It starts at a narrow bottleneck and then widens before narrowing again at the other end. It is crowded with people selling smuggled and stolen goods, with shops and tables facing one another and displaying their wares. The owners don't have the proper permits, but the police look the other way. Used clothing merchants, customers, and porters all mix. As I walked, it occurred to me that I could take a taxi to the Sahara to ask its owner for details about what had happened, but I changed my mind. I opted instead to interview the accused before proceeding any further. I couldn't find a taxi to take me home, and I wasn't inclined to wait for a bus that stank of sweat and feet and was full of passengers who see nothing wrong with rubbing up against any woman they get close to, so I chose to walk and burn a few calories. I weighed over a hundred and fifty pounds and had stopped growing at five two. My belly was starting to sag, and my thighs were getting chubby. The diet I was following wasn't doing any good.

Before long I arrived in First of November, known as Gambetta before independence, where the houses and their gardens are lined up next to one another. Distracted, I followed my shadow, upset that my makeup was running because of the heat. I sauntered into Big Belly's shop where everything that could be sold retail, from candy to aspirin, was sold. As he looked me up and down from my hair to my waist, he informed me that there was still no coffee available and that my only option was to take tea instead.

"The wholesalers said there'll be no sugar soon."

To which I responded: "So? We have honey."

He stroked his chin with his right hand, and I could smell a mixture of spices and Savon de Marseille soap. I bought two containers of yogurt and five loaves of bread as I listened to his complaints about the state's failure to eradicate the locusts that had swept over the nearby farms.

"A year of drought and bad crop yields."

"It'll pass," I said, then paid him for a quarter qantar of semolina. My brother, Faudel, whom everyone called Six because of the six fingers he had on one of his hands, would carry the semolina home.

All my brother did was wander the streets, take care of his goldfinch, play dominoes and cards, and exchange cigarette butts with his friends, who were terrified by how quickly and easily he got into fights. Since flunking school, he now came home late every night with bloodshot eyes. We didn't know where he got the money to supply himself with new clothes for every occasion. When he was younger, his speech had been delayed and he was hyperactive. My father only saw him as an out-of-control boy and didn't extend any help to him, and my mother insisted he learn a skill or join the army, but all he dreamed of was emigrating to France. "There'll come a day when you'll want to come and stay with me there," he'd say to silence our mother's attempts at convincing him to look for a steady job. "No one would want to stay with an idiot like you," she'd answer him.

I entered the house and found my mother standing upright in front of me like a gendarme, covering her hair with a scarf. She always knows I'm coming in when she hears the key turning in the lock of the teak door. She grabbed my wrist and asked in a whisper what needed to be done to help my cousin.

"May the Lord set him free," I replied.

"Your aunt is here."

I left the groceries in the ornately painted foyer and fixed my hair and clothes so my aunt wouldn't notice how nervous

I was. When she saw me, she jumped up from where she was seated in the spacious sitting room. With a pale face and looking older than the last time I'd seen her, she moved toward me, dragging her dark-green djellaba across the floor. She kissed my cheeks and stared desperately into my eyes like a thirsty kitten.

My aunt spoke at length, as if pleading Bachir's case. She enumerated her son's commendable acts and good upbringing. She told me he had argued with her when she'd said no to his getting engaged to that girl when she found out she sang for a living. ("If I had known things would turn out this way, I would have said yes.") She spoke about her husband and his mood swings, and she cried bitterly as she talked about her other two sons and her daughter, all of whom were feeling the loss. ("Bachir's like a father to them.") Then she told me she couldn't keep any food down. Her stomach was still aching. ("I feel like a snake is wriggling through my intestines.") She imagined her son alone in solitary confinement and with tough guys constantly pummeling him.

I tried to speak clearly and succinctly to assuage her panic and confusion, telling her that her son was no more than a suspect. As I did so, I couldn't help but envy her light skin, not at all like my mother's, which was a few shades darker.

"I'll visit him tomorrow and find out what's going on."

Before I could even finish my sentence, her eyes widened, and she tried to insist on going with me.

"We'll arrange for you to get permission to visit him another day."

She rattled off a shopping list of things I would bring him: nuts, chocolate, expensive shaving gear, toothpaste, a toothbrush. I couldn't help but feel that my cousin was living a life more befitting of a wealthy man than that of a low-level employee in a national company.

"We'll give him some money and he can ask for whatever he wants from the prison administration," I assured her.

My aunt left, but before she did, she advised me to beg Bachir to remain patient and steadfast. "It's a dog-eat-dog world," I responded.

My mother asked me again what needed to be done and how we could get him released. She imagined I was a judge rather than a mere lawyer. I reminded her that his story was not entirely clear, but she paid no attention. "The important thing is that he gets out of jail," she said.

I lost my appetite after my mother told me that my father, who had split up with her and married a woman in her early twenties, had sent a relative over to try to get them back together after confirming that his new wife was infertile. "He's gone mad," she said. "And you wish to drive me crazy," I wanted to say, to shut her up.

Rouna, who shared the same letters as my name, purred as she started to rub up against the leg of the couch. The cat's head was small, and its ears stuck straight up. It had a white belly, brown patches on its back, and a black tail.

I retreated into my bedroom, which had a double bed. I took off my clothes and put on a light robe. The videotape of *The Sheik* caught my eye. It had been tossed carelessly onto my makeup table. I put the tape into the VCR to watch the movie again; I was a sucker for the love story it told. I followed the actors' silent performances in black and white, imagining what they wanted to say and inventing colors for their clothes and skin. I loved Rudolph Valentino, who played the lead, even though I didn't like how the character abused the female lead and forced her to obey him. I didn't simply love him as an actor. I loved him as a man as well. I loved a dead man whose face I had seen in a silent movie! This made me doubly sure that people understood one another through body language more than words.

Before the final scene, my head began throbbing out of anxiety about what had happened to Bachir. I needed to find a thread I could grab to get him out of his predicament, and I thought about the questions I'd need to ask him. I touched my underarms and was satisfied with how they felt, but I was annoyed that I had spotted a white hair on my head. I plucked it out like a farmer picking out a harmful weed, ignoring the voice in my head telling me that pulling out a gray hair would cause ten more to sprout up in its place. After I made sure I had locked the door so my mother couldn't barge in and recite her passionate plea for me to look for a man to "protect me" or marry me, I lit a cigarette. The smoke rose to the light-yellow ceiling. "Men don't like women who smoke," she would shame me, forgetting I was already over thirty and that men were lining up for women younger than me, just as my father had done. She knocked on the door and said: "Some woman wants to talk with you on the phone."

I figured it was one of my clients wanting to ask about her case, but I was surprised by Hassina's voice on the other end.

"Can we meet tomorrow?"

"How come?"

"It's about your cousin."

IBRAHIM

SEPTEMBER 11

It was close to midnight. I was annoyed as I approached the house and heard one of the drunks gathered at the entrance to the dusty neighborhood say, "Here's the little shitball," his tongue heavy with diluted rubbing alcohol. I'd been given the nickname due to my round head. "Say it again and I'll stuff a piece of shit up your ass," I retorted. He didn't say another word.

In the kitchen, where strainers lined the wall and dishes were piled in one of the corners, all I could find was a half loaf of bread, a piece of tomato, and a plate of rancid fava beans. With the return of water to the taps, I took the opportunity to rid myself of the sweat lingering on my body.

Standing in front of the bathroom mirror, I rubbed my chest hair and neck. I was convinced that I possessed a handsomeness that struck at the hearts of the most delectable women. I couldn't find any faults except my sunken eyes, but I told myself that fortitude, not eyes, is what makes a man handsome. My intimate adventures, few as they have been, have made me more confident in my masculinity. I examined my face and remembered Noura's sarcastic words: "The only difference between you and a beast is that you know how to kiss." Before her, I knew a girl still in high school who loved music and drawing. I thought we would be each other's destiny, like Yoko Ono and John Lennon, but she failed the baccalaureate exam and her father forbade her from leaving the house after that. Then I met a divorcée whose scent I couldn't bear after a while, so I broke up with her. The lawyer after that made me forget all about the divorcée. As Cat Stevens said, she really made me feel like a king without a crown. Whenever I embraced her, imitating scenes I had seen in movies, I felt her warmth in my arms and was confident that the blood of Casanova flowed through my veins.

I poured a bucket of water over my head, the briny taste reaching my tongue. I shaved, put on a shirt and underwear, and threw my jeans over my shoulder. Then, I tiptoed to my room to avoid waking up my mother and brother, who each slept in their own bedrooms.

My bed had a sticky smell to it. My mother, who cleans strangers' rooms and takes care of my brother's, refuses to go into mine as punishment for my choice of profession. She often scolds me: "It's as if you're living with a corpse." When I try to defend myself, she silences me: "Find a woman you can marry and have her wipe your ass!" She knows I don't have any money to get engaged, pay a dowry, put on a wedding, then take on the needs of a wife. I looked at the rolls of carpet lined up against the wall in the corner – stuffed with strong-smelling mothballs to keep the bugs and moths away – and estimated how much I could get for them. A decent amount of cash, perhaps. More than once, I'd tried to convince my mother to let me put them on display in the contraband market, but she'd always refused: "I wove those before you were born." She describes them as an inheritance that isn't allowed to be sold off, similar to the old Singer sewing machine she holds onto in her room, like a soldier holding onto his last bullet. When she was young, she used to enjoy weaving, sewing, and embroidery, but after she was widowed, she gave those things up.

I wanted to watch a new movie that might put me to sleep, but the power was out. The sound of yelling and shouted insults rose from the street, where the drunks argued with one another. They measure manliness according to how rough your voice is or how much you fight and get wasted. Their evenings would often end in bloody noses or stab wounds in the arms. The next day, though, they shake hands like boys who are quick to forget.

In my head, I went over the list of people who hadn't paid me yet for VCR rentals or videotapes. I intended on pressuring them all except for Kamal Belattar, who had paid what he owed without knowing it yet. Before closing my eyes, I heard my mother's groans from the bathroom, which has a small window above it that lets the moonlight slip in and opens into the courtyard of the house. She vomited and complained that her stomach hurt. Besides the pain in her tooth, she had a stomachache that had gone on for months. I got out of bed and rushed to her, asking, "Should I take you to the hospital?" Her hand shook, which showed how much she was suffering.

The hospital's hallway was filled with shouts from those waiting, as if they were at the weekly market, and only one nurse was working the night shift. The nurse's hair looked like a bird's nest because of the bald spot in the middle of his head. He had big ears like Mickey Mouse's, and he had a stethoscope hanging over his chest. In the absence of the doctor on call, he settled on giving my mother a shot without even examining her first, using a syringe I wasn't sure was sterile. If you don't have connections, you have to bear the pain, I said to myself. The sobs of a young woman whose baby was crying pierced my ears. My mother moaned: "O Lord… my life is devoted to Your satisfaction." She said my father's name over and over: "Ben Kaddour… you've left me like a pot without a handle." Whenever she was in pain, she longed for him, which made me even sadder. When I was young, she cried when she talked about him, hugging me and calling me by my pet name, Briha. As I'd got older, though, she'd forgotten all about that name and had become ashamed to cry in front of me. I didn't care that my father wasn't around until I started school the week Che Guevara died and ran into kids every morning who were accompanied by their parents. Once, one of them asked me: "How come your dad doesn't come in with you?" I didn't answer and felt like an orphan. I've spent half my life fruitlessly searching for my father's grave, and right then, I decided to reclaim his due. He had been martyred in the War of Independence. Still, Si Mahfoud, the secretary of the Veterans' Club, refused to issue a martyr's widow card to my mother, claiming there was no evidence that Ben Kaddour had been involved in the war. He advised me to gather testimonies from former Liberation Army soldiers, telling me they would fulfill my request if I did so. How was I supposed to convince them to testify on behalf of a father I didn't know, buried in a place unknown to me?

NOURA

Pale-faced and anemic-looking, Bachir sat in front of me in a cramped, whitewashed room furnished with nothing but an oval table and two chairs. The door was ajar, and we could hear footsteps outside the room. He stared at me for a while, then rubbed his chin with his palm and lowered his eyes. I remembered that when I'd become a lawyer, he'd read a book explaining the profession's origins, picking out words he would frequently use in conversation to show that he was just as good as those who had completed their studies. He had a complex about his failure to attend university and struggled when he saw graduates occupying higher positions than him.

"I didn't kill her... I didn't kill her," he repeated, arms waving in the air, until I was sick of hearing those words. And I guessed that the muscular guard who kept bursting in and out of the room was just as sick of them as I was. I made it clear that I hadn't come to the prison to accuse or absolve him. Rather, I'd come so I could fully understand his relationship with the dead woman and what had happened between them during her final days so I could prepare a defense for him. I waited a few moments for his dry lips to stop trembling enough for him to express himself coherently.

He'd met Zakia in 1982 in Nezrama, where he'd been stationed for military service. (The women in this city weren't to your liking, so you fell in love with someone from another town? I groaned to myself.) He helped her find work at the hotel where he began to regularly attend her nighttime shows. This reinforced my suspicions that my cousin had gotten used to a life of luxury. Entering a hotel nightclub required the customer to pay an entrance fee, as he told me, which also obligated him to buy a drink or something to eat every hour and not leave until his pockets were empty. He hadn't been blessed with a sense of responsibility. I figured that was a criminal trait.

"I first ran into her next to the Professional Training Center," Bachir told me. She'd charmed him with her pretty face and svelte body, and he was drawn to her like a moth to a flame. He's always valued the beauty of the body over that of the spirit. I once heard him say: "If the desert's beauty is in its silence, then a woman's beauty is in how she walks." She insisted he leave her alone, threatening to scream and get the attention of the people around them, but he begged her to calm down. She quickly let him know she wasn't interested in a relationship outside of marriage. "Tough broad," I muttered as I looked at his shaved head.

"She promised she would go with me wherever I wanted as long as I proposed to her," he continued.

Reluctantly, he gave in, and they spent the following weeks dating and flirting with one another, dreaming of a life of happiness: the house and children they'd have, the belief that they would live to a ripe old age... "Whenever we got close to one another, I felt like I was melting into her," he told me.

Bachir called his mother and told her he wanted to propose, but she advised him to wait a bit until he got a job that would provide for him. He completed his military service and returned home without giving his beloved what she wanted, the fire of longing consuming his heart all the while. Their connection was almost undone by the distance that separated them, but she revived their passionate love after nearly two years and finally joined him. He indulged her by saving enough money to get married, but, with time, they started to fight, so he devoted himself to writing to her – thoughts, lines of love poetry taken from romantic ghazal collections – to soften her up and renew their journey of love and devotion to one another.

He was not happy with the life Zakia led at night, and for her part, she wanted nothing more than to be done with it. Her desire was to become a homemaker, and she was convinced that loving a man teaches a woman selfishness, whereas giving birth to a child teaches her generosity. This is what he told me.

He told me that, last month, he realized his mother opposed him getting married to Zakia Zaghouani because of a plan she had in mind, not because she was opposed to what she did for a living. "She wanted to marry me to my cousin, my uncle's daughter." (Why hadn't she suggested he marry me? I thought. Because his other cousin was younger than me?)

"Did Zakia have any enemies?" I asked him.

"There was another singer in the nightclub who she couldn't stand."

"What was her name?"

"Safia… They call her Cheikha Edahabia."

At first, the two singers enjoyed a good relationship. "In fact, Safia took it upon herself to deliver my letters to her when we were fighting," Bachir said. Then they argued, and Cheikha Edahabia wanted to get Zakia out of the way so she would be the nightclub's only star. Zakia would often tell stories of how mean the other woman was to her. She told him that once Safia spread a rumor that Zakia had secretly put a spell on the hotel owner's food. I had to stifle a laugh when he repeatedly told me that Safia had accused Zakia of being a professional slanderer, describing her as a *zerzoumiya*, a gecko that's only active at night; when its tail is severed, it grows another one in its place.

Bachir could barely continue before he broke into a fit of sobbing. I covered my nose, he smelled so bad. His tears flowed, and he clenched his fists like a boxer preparing to get in the ring. His teeth chattered as if he had caught a cold.

"I'm innocent," he said. He looked at me, his lips parted.

"The criminal never admits to his crime," I muttered inaudibly. "Patience and steadfastness," I said out loud, repeating his mother's advice in an attempt to make him feel less tense. What I didn't tell him was that his case was a difficult one.

I gave him some money to buy what he needed from the prison administration. He told me he was sharing a cell with twelve men. They shared one toilet, with just a piece of oilcloth for privacy. He hadn't eaten a thing since his arrest. Nor had he slept. "They want to pin her murder on me," Bachir said, covering his face with his hands.

At this point, a guard who had not stopped rubbing his belly the whole time I was there stepped forward and returned my cousin to his cell.

Back in my office, which I keep cleaner and fresher-smelling than my room at home, I called the hotel, hoping to make an appointment with the owner.

"He's not in right now."

"I'm the lawyer for the defense in Miss Zakia's murder case."

The person on the other end of the line was silent, as if busy doing something else. Then he said: "Call back later to set up an appointment."

I felt sorry for my cousin and fought back an urge to cry *It's dog eat dog in this country.*

Memories of us as children floated around in my head – Bachir's foolishness when he was stealing worshippers' shoes at the mosque or when he was lifting my skirt without my noticing and me calling him a bastard. His crime was that he'd loved Zakia, written to her, and lived next to the meadow where her body was found. Had that woman, Safia, been involved in her killing?

I was lost in thought when the telephone rang. It was Hassina, reminding me that we had arranged to meet.

Calling me Gentle Noura, as she loved to do, she welcomed me to her family's house on the road leading to Lalla Ammoura Cemetery. The house is no different from those of other middle-class families who live as well as they can. Bars cover its two outer windows. There is no garden next to it and no greenery in its little yard. Hassina is a year older than me and nearly an inch taller. She's a more experienced lawyer and often helps me defend my clients. I don't hide the fact that I'm jealous of her legs, which are softer than mine and which she constantly moisturizes with lotion. When she speaks, she moves her hands more than her lips. Her voice is soft and sharp, well suited to singing opera. She's always telling dirty jokes and never misses an opportunity to talk about how government officials lap up what's in the pockets of the oppressed. We view life in this country very differently. I'm optimistic about where it's heading, whereas she rejects such optimism. I read the national magazine, whereas she only reads the foreign press. We've found a middle ground in our shared profession, where we forget about life's burdens by enumerating all sorts of disgusting things and poking fun at ourselves and others.

It was close to three in the afternoon. As soon as we sat down on the living room sofa, a wooden-framed Surat al-Falaq from the Qur'an on the wall behind, Hassina addressed me in exasperation.

"I feel like my face has started to lose its color. And I'm afraid I might be getting wrinkles." She massaged her chin, rubbed her right thumb with her index finger, and told me she had lost her appetite.

"But you're more beautiful than ever."

"Liar."

"We lie so as not to feel sad," I said with a laugh.

I gestured with my head at her pert, handball-sized breasts underneath her orange shirt, and she responded: "They're spoken for." Hassina covered her mouth with the palm of her hand and revealed that a man intended to propose to her, but she refused to reveal his name until the ceremony was done. She wanted my opinion on a new dress that a well-known seamstress had made. Navy blue polyester, short-sleeved and round-necked. Went with high heels or flats. I was happy for her. She had been at odds with love for years to the point where people thought she had resigned herself to remaining unmarried. I asked her what she knew of Bachir's case.

"Complicated." She gave me the impression I wouldn't be successful in proving his innocence.

"How did you hear what happened to him?"

"I have my sources." I know her ears can hear a fly buzzing ten yards away.

"Do you know him personally?"

"No, I don't." I disabused myself of the notion that she might have once dated him.

"Where was he at the time of the murder?"

"Sleeping, and he didn't leave home before nine the following morning."

Then I told her what he'd told me when I'd seen him in jail and what he'd said about his relationship with the victim.

"I'd like to offer you a solution," Hassina said.

I sensed that she knew things she was hiding from me.

"Have you met her family?"

I shrugged, then shook my head. "No."

"You need to get to them and question them. Most crimes you hear about, or that are established for the defense, are nothing more than a settling of family or clan accounts."

Although I didn't discount what she said, I didn't have any proof that the victim's family was involved, so I changed the subject and suggested she take on some of my cases.

"I'm already practically drowning in my own cases," she replied.

We proceeded to chat about the rising prices of some foods, the scarcity of others, water outages, and the increasing cost of electricity. Then she asked me: "What proof do they have against him?"

"A letter to Zakia that threatened to punish her severely if she didn't leave him alone. That's what I found out from the interrogation report."

"He was planning on breaking up with her?"

"That's what I understood."

"When did he send it to her?"

I scratched my cheek with the fingers of my left hand as if I had been slapped. How had I not thought to ask? Had the letter been written a while ago, or was it new?

IBRAHIM

SEPTEMBER 12

I still remember the last time I drank bottled water. I purchased a bottle the day they were discussing the Ethiopia famine on TV. I shared it with a university classmate I wanted to win over but failed to and haven't had bottled water since. I have become one with bacteria after having suffered so many skin infections and bouts of diarrhea when I was younger. So much so that I've gained immunity. When a bleach vendor passed by on his tricycle that morning, I bought a half gallon from him just as my mother had asked once her stomachache had subsided. Few houses lack this essential disinfectant for water that only flows intermittently. And when the water does flow, it's mixed with dirt and smells of rotten eggs.

In the shop, I pulled a French newspaper from a pile of old papers stacked underneath the counter. I use them to wrap videocassettes for customers rather than Arabic newspapers, which contain God's words. Then I became absorbed in a crossword puzzle as an announcer read the news on the radio ("Getting ready for school... The Algerian delegation's preparations for the Olympic Games in South Korea... Security forces open fire on protesters in Burma...") when a police car pulled up next to the curb across the street from my shop. I figured the two imposing officers who got out would head to the shop next door, where Boulanouar, the owner, had been making pastries for two decades, but they walked into the Desert Rose.

"Ibrahim Derras?"

I nodded blankly and folded the newspaper.

"Please come with us."

I locked the door and went with them. Wan-faced, I passed in front of the other shops, whose owners stuck their heads out, surprised at what was happening.

At the police station, they brought me to the first-floor vestibule. Its walls were plastered with WANTED posters. They didn't make me wait long before showing me into an office with a placard that said POLICE INSPECTOR. The office smelled of coffee. I thought this all might have to do with the bribes I'd been paying to get a card exempting me from military service. Or someone might have been plotting against me because I was in the illegal adult film business. I spotted the VCR I'd rented to the young woman who had never returned.

"The name of your shop is on this. Does it belong to you?"

"Yes, it does." I was baffled. Had it been stolen from the woman?

"Who did you rent it to?"

"I don't know her name."

"She didn't leave her ID card?"

"No, she left her fiancé's ID."

The police inspector adjusted himself in his chair and opened his notebook. "Do you have his ID card on you?"

"No, it's back at the shop."

"What's the name?"

"Bachir Labtam."

He looked at me, astonished, as he muttered, "Bachir."

"Do you know him?"

"No."

All that inspector needed to look just like Groucho Marx was a pair of spectacles. I wanted to ask him how the VCR had made its way to him, but I was too worried he would tell me it was none of my business. Still, I played dumb.

"The woman who rented it never paid me the balance."

"Did she discuss anything with you that might be worth mentioning?"

"I asked what she wanted it for. She simply gave me the ID card, then left."

A policeman sitting to his right stopped typing. Then the inspector let me take back the machine before dropping the bombshell: "The woman is dead. Go back to your shop and bring me the ID card she gave you."

She was dead?! My chest tightened, and the desire I had that day to sing just faded away. Heart racing, I left. I felt like the ground was giving way beneath my feet.

KAMAL

On the fourth morning after the calamity, I stood behind the counter and finished up with a middle-aged French customer. I made an effort to smile and show decorum, just as I'd learned at the Hotel Institute, where I'd graduated among a batch of other receptionists; I'd also learned there how to be courteous and well organized. As soon as the customer turned his back to leave, Noura walked toward me. She wore a white blouse and black trousers, and I felt a quivering in my belly.

She was on my mind day and night. I used to write her name in the margins of my notebooks and picture her face whenever I went to bed. The first time I saw her in front of the girls' high school, I was struck by how pretty she was and appreciated the attention she paid to her appearance. We exchanged smiles behind which we concealed our attraction to one another; then, we exchanged greetings filled with desire. I'd gone out with her twice, then disappeared without so much as a goodbye. I'd heard that she thought I didn't consider her good-looking enough and that I had hurt her feelings, but apparently she'd later learned from a classmate of hers (who I'd also dated) that I had left her so as not to anger Bachir; it's shameful for a man to go out alone with his friend's relative without a legal marriage contract. I was told that she hated her cousin for that and didn't speak to him for weeks, and that he thought she'd gone crazy. Finally, it seemed that she had reined in her emotions and convinced herself that it wasn't meant to be; that love was either a flood a boulder couldn't hold back or was destined for oblivion.

"How long have you worked here?" Noura asked me.

"Five years."

She had not changed a bit. Her hair was short, and her mouth looked like a heart when she pursed her lips. She looked at you sternly when she spoke and didn't move her hands like other people.

"And you? What do you do?" I asked her, even though I already knew the answer.

"I'm a lawyer."

I knew her younger brother, and her cousin, Bachir, had already told me that when she'd finished her studies, she'd worked as an assistant to an older lawyer. After that, she'd started her own practice with some money from her father, who received benefits as a veteran of the War of Independence. These benefits also include priority treatment in government offices and hospitals and having access to wealthy and powerful elites.

"I came to meet with the manager."

"Why?"

Before Noura even finished her response, I remembered speaking with her on the phone. I had forgotten to ask her name. I slapped my temple, and she nodded and glared at me. I took advantage of the moment to rest my gaze on her lips, imagining how hot they would be to kiss.

I'd been given my position in this hotel, the Sahara, after receiving an exemption from military service because I was the only son in my family. I'd replaced a man in his sixties who'd reached retirement age the same day they'd reported on the death of comedian Louis de Funès. I gained the trust of my boss, who authorized me to follow up on purchases of goods and supplies related to the restaurant, guest rooms, garden, nightclub, and swimming pool, which we refill once a month with water bought from vendors. I felt that luck had opened its door to me with this job; I worked less than a half hour's drive from the place I rented. But ever since Zakia's – or Zaza's – murder, I've lived by the proverb *Avoid problems, and problems will avoid you.* I feel sorry for the Hadj, I mean Maimoun; I'm sure he hasn't been able to sleep since what happened.

"May God have mercy on her." I sighed as I bit my lower lip.

"Bachir is wrongfully paying the price."

She pronounced her words gravely, and I opened my eyes wide. I didn't get what she was saying until she told me he was in prison.

"Are you kidding?" I loosened my tie, waiting for her to explain further.

"Didn't you know that?"

Bachir and I hadn't seen each other since the Thursday before Zakia's death, and I'd spent that day between work and various police offices lodging a complaint against an unknown intruder who had broken into my house.

I called Maimoun in his office and informed him that the lawyer was here to see him, but he made the excuse that he was too busy.

"But you told me to come today, didn't you?" said Noura angrily.

"It's out of my hands," I answered her with the fingers of my right hand clasped inside my left.

Noura grumbled as she walked out. A voice in my head told me that she blamed me for not cooperating in a case that had resulted in a close friend of mine being put in jail. Right then, the hotel owner called back, saying he'd changed his mind about meeting with her, but she was already gone.

I tried to extinguish the ember of love lit by Noura's sudden appearance, so I chewed on a piece of chocolate. After learning what had happened to Bachir, my head was spinning like a blender, thoughts crashing into one another. What should I do? Would I be allowed to visit him in jail? Should I go see his family? How could I help him? Then I pulled my little mirror out of my trouser pocket to make sure the face I'd met the lawyer with had no blemishes. I looked up at the ornate light fixtures ensconced in their gypsum spheres.

The Sahara Hotel is a tourist destination. In this city that sits between two mountains, it looks cube-shaped from the outside and is painted the color of desert sand, with a neo-Moorish facade. Some French people built it half a century ago, and it was renovated by Fernand Pouillon, who also built Victor Hugo's villa and the Old Port of Marseille and designed libraries and schools. Incidentally, he also published a novel entitled *The Stones of the Abbey*, which takes place in the twelfth century CE. Senior officials make their way to this place to spend hours in the pool or evenings in its nightclub, which has become renowned thanks to Zakia's singing and dancing.

When Bachir first told me about Zakia, I smiled and shook my head. "Did you go to an army barracks in Nezrama, or were you off hunting pretty gazelles?"

I met her and liked her cheerful face, which reminded me of a flight attendant's. I noticed that her loose-fitting shirt hid her beautiful figure. I introduced her to the restaurant staff, showed her the ropes, informed her of the working hours – three shifts a day – and that she should pay attention to her clothes and appearance.

"Don't you like how I look?"

"What matters is that the customers like it."

She was unsatisfied as a waitress, so after meeting with the hotel owner alone in his office, she switched to singing.

No sooner did he learn of her new activity than my friend Bachir blamed me.

"You said she'd be working as a waitress, not a prostitute!"

"I'm not her guardian."

His anger had subsided after his beloved convinced him to accept her new role. She would often sneak him into her room, where he would spend up to an hour with her, slipping out like an embarrassed child. My heart broke for him when I learned that his mother opposed their relationship. Had God created mothers only to break lovers' hearts?

"Oh shit," I mumbled, crossing my legs underneath the chair when Fouzi walked up to the reception desk. Fouzi makes his living from a horse-drawn carriage whose cabin is made of oak, with two leather seats. He takes tourists for rides or takes pictures of them sitting in it. Despite Fouzi's gentle nature, everyone makes fun of him. Except Zakia, who befriended him. She would sit or go swimming with him, although their relationship was toxic; she'd tyrannize him as if she were his mother. He'd constantly strive to win her affection, trying to avoid angering her so he wouldn't have to watch the spit fly out from between her lips as she screamed at him. Whenever he was slow in taking care of whatever she'd assigned him to do, her cheeks would puff out and her hands would explode in a flurry of slaps and punches to his face. I often saw her yelling at him or twisting his earlobe. Last Friday afternoon, he'd fallen to his knees in tears as soon as he'd learned what had happened to her.

"Can you give me back my matches?" Fouzi asked now.

I grabbed the matches I had borrowed to light a cigarette and threw them at his chest. He caught them before they fell to the floor. I was angry about what had happened between Noura and me and took it out on him even though he was trying to be nice. With drooping eyelids darkened with kohl to mourn Zaza's passing, he told me about the last time he had seen her; she'd asked him to mail a cassette tape to an address in the capital, Algiers. When he got back, he'd seen her coming out of a telephone booth adjacent to the hotel.

"She was crying," Fouzi said.

"Who had she been talking to?"

"I asked her, but she didn't answer."

IBRAHIM

SEPTEMBER 13

Grim-faced and with few words, Noura returned *The Sheik* to me.

"You didn't like it?"

"A charming movie."

She withheld her praise so as not to make me feel as if I had rendered her a service. I was used to her not thanking me for movies I recommended. She said it was to keep me from becoming too arrogant.

Noura made to leave for her office, which was just one street over from the Desert Rose. She was indifferent to my comments, faulting the director's decision not to include details that appeared in the novel it was based on, where a young English woman named Diana Mayo falls madly in love with a sheik, Ahmed ben Hassan, after initially shunning him.

She told me she hadn't slept the previous night, but I didn't pay any attention. "You're leaving without letting me savor your honey," I said flirtingly, hoping for a kiss.

I'd met Noura the day before the singer Dalida's suicide. She had come in to ask for a Mohammed Lakhdar-Hamina film she'd read about in a magazine. Because I didn't own a copy, I suggested a foreign movie instead, and she liked it.

She appreciated how generous I was to lend her videos for free. I would choose movies I liked, to prolong our discussions about them. She also enjoyed our chats about Algiers, where we both had studied, albeit at different times. Those chats usually ended with kisses. She would hide out in the back area of my shop, especially in the morning before the customers arrived, so she could smoke a cigarette or two as she swayed back and forth listening to me play guitar. Sometimes I was overcome by the urge to ask for her hand in marriage, but would quickly backtrack, using my financial situation as an excuse. She thought it unlikely my mother would accept a daughter-in-law who was older than her son anyway. "Mothers want obedient young women for themselves and for their sons," she once sighed. I didn't deny what she said, wishing that Noura would lose some weight and that her eyes were blue rather than brown. I was bored with how the women in this city all looked the same, as if they had all come out of the same womb. In the past, she had allowed me to touch her all over and let me hug her tightly to my chest. In that, she was just following my lead, not acting out of her own desire. She refused to venture any further. "When I become your lawfully wedded wife," she told me, "we can do whatever we want."

I ignored her and pinched her jiggly bum, which prompted her to admonish me.

"Pimp!"

She was even more beautiful when she was angry. But I felt that she was hiding something, or perhaps she was upset with her mother. Noura complained about how closely her mother watched her comings and goings, unlike mine, who never asked where I was going or when I was coming home.

As Noura stepped outside, she asked how my mother was doing.

"Do you want to ask her permission to get engaged to me?"

"No, I'd like to ask her to cut your hand off!"

Then she let me know that she needed to ask her about a girl who had worked at the Sahara and been found murdered.

"My mother didn't tell me a thing," I said. She had merely told me about some women she'd heard at the hammam talking about the recent discovery of some unmarked graves.

Noura told me about a woman named Zakia Zaghouani, about the discovery of her body in the meadow, and that she had been appointed to defend the man suspected of killing her.

"I'll ask my mom if she wants to talk with you."

I told Noura that two policemen had driven me to the station and returned a VCR rented by the girl, without saying a word about the cassette inside. She came back into the shop. "Did Zakia come here?!"

I described the woman, telling Noura that I hadn't known her name at the time and that she'd given me the ID card of someone she'd described as her fiancé. "His name was Bachir Labtam."

Noura looked off into space. Rubbing her neck, she left without answering my question – "When are you coming back?" It just hung in the air. Every day I see her feels like it will be our last.

I'd been surprised to learn that the dead woman was a singer. I took out my guitar. I turned on the cassette recorder to confirm that my playing was okay. I sang out loud: "*After the sun sets... We'll gather in a boat... The nights go on and on...*" Then I lay on the bed, finding it difficult to control my breathing. I remembered the victim's face. Is death not a comfort?

HAMID

On the Friday Zaza died, I returned to my apartment after work. My wife, Zinab, was leaning forward on a wooden chair in the kitchen with her hands on her knees, letting out a deep breath as if worn out from performing a difficult task. She complained about the heat and the flies, against which pesticides were useless. She was waiting for me to explain what I had said earlier on the phone about her not going out.

"You want to turn our home into a police station!"

She would lob that sentence at me whenever she was angry or things got heated between us.

"We found a young woman murdered."

"Who?"

"A nightclub singer."

"That's got nothing to do with me."

"But who can guarantee the crime won't be repeated?" I was seized by fear that a long hand was hovering above me, and if not stopped, it would grab onto the neck of one of my family members as payback for me reining in the greedy activities of wealthy bribe-takers. I wanted to explain that things were unsafe, but she dug in.

"Your job is to maintain security and safety, not to prevent me from going out."

After calling her that afternoon, during which I had smoked an entire pack of cigarettes without even tasting them, I had called the doorman of the building next to mine, where police employees like me live, and ordered him to keep her from going out. She had complied.

"I'm your wife, not your servant," my wife said as if firing the winning shot, and I took in her words without responding. I leaned on the door of the refrigerator (made in Algeria) as I thought of a line by Abderrahman El Mejdoub, whose verses I memorized like a devout person memorizes verses from the Qur'an: *"I'll put up with miserable days / until my time comes."*

Her belly had grown huge, and she was likely to give birth within weeks. This would be our last baby, even though there was a time when I wanted half a dozen children like my older brother. I always imagined myself as an old man surrounded by strong sons, me issuing orders and them obeying. However, our constant quarreling made me regret ever having children with her.

She got up and went over to the gas stove to make a cup of tea. I looked at her chignon hairstyle, thick neck, and flabby buttocks underneath the gray pajamas I had given her as a gift on our last anniversary. I closed my eyes, pained by our faded love. She seemed the opposite of the lawyer, Hassina, who had captivated me with her wide, kohl-lined eyes. I was like a teenager who responded to her every whim, violating the law to help her.

It was four years ago that Hassina had burst into my office complaining about a policeman's abuse toward her after the dispersal of a demonstration against the family law. That day, women had gathered in front of the courthouse demanding a review of that law, which did not allow women to marry without a guardian's official approval. And in the event of divorce, they needed to leave the marital home yet were obliged to continue raising their children. The law allowed men to take more than one wife, and it robbed divorced women of guardianship of their own children if the woman became involved with someone else. The police had expected the demonstrators to disperse within an hour, but the protests went on for longer than that and blocked pedestrian and vehicular traffic, so they intervened. The lawyer wanted to regain her dignity after being humiliated in front of her colleagues.

"A woman from a good family being beaten with a baton by a policeman!"

I took it upon myself to listen and absorb her anger. Hassina's pupils widened as she spoke, and I promised to refer the policeman to the Disciplinary Council.

"A month has passed since the law was issued, and you're only protesting now?"

"Just because we're proceeding slowly and deliberately doesn't mean we have forgotten."

"But it's a law that follows the Sharia."

"Sharia law does not order men to enslave women," she responded.

I kept up with her as she raged, until she finally calmed down and withdrew her complaint. I asked her if she wanted to meet the following day at the Nakhil Restaurant, next to the Gas & Electric Co., where the wealthy people went. I claimed I wanted to learn more about her work. She arrived on time, as beautiful as could be, and I teased her: "Every believer who sees you will have to rewash himself before praying!" She lowered her head and twirled a tuft of black hair around her index finger. When I became aware that my marriage would not stand in the way of strengthening our relationship, I asked my friend who owned the Nour, the motel on the road that leads to the capital, to make a room available. I justified it to myself by claiming I was prolonging my relationship with my wife, as all married men do, and fulfilling my duties as a father. I compared Hassina to one of the characters in the TV series *Dallas*, and she laughed: "It's unfair to compare Americans to people living out here in the wilderness." She breathed in the scent of my sweat and moved her hand around my firm chest, rubbing her tongue along my teeth and taking pleasure in tickling my chin hairs.

At that time, Zakia had moved to the nightclub, and at first I didn't feel a thing for her. But as the evening shows rolled on, I was struck by a light in her eyes, a purity in her face, and a fire that drew me in. I stopped meeting with the lawyer at night, making do with daytime trysts. Zinab doubted my loyalty and persisted in provoking me, hoping a slip of the tongue might give me away, but I dashed her hopes in that regard. I didn't hide that I liked the newcomer to the Sahara, and Hassina found me out. She quarreled with me and stopped returning my phone calls. One time, she even went to the hotel, hoping to catch me with Zaza, but luckily I wasn't there that evening. I sent a bunch of roses to her office, but she didn't accept them. She said I was sexually impaired, which I didn't deny. Whenever we got intimate, I would quickly be overtaken by impotence. Not even drinking ginger infusions would help. The doctor attributed my problem to anxiety and the pressures of work. Finally, we reconciled, content to keep our emotions in check and maintain a friendly relationship when I acted on her behalf to expunge a complaint that had been lodged against her by the Rubber & Plastic Co.'s manager, whom she had blackmailed and accused of prioritizing friends and relatives when hiring.

Hassina loved it when I spoke in the capital city's dialect with all its grandiloquence, where Arabic and French rub up against one another. She loved it when I told her about the Casbah, with its winding alleyways and ancient buildings, where I was born and raised.

"Don't you like your city's casbah?" I asked her.

"It looks like a zombie cave."

People here call the old city the Casbah, or the Palace, because it was constructed on the ruins of a fifteenth-century palace. Quarters branch out from it with cramped dwellings that measure no more than four hundred square feet. Packed closely together, they were first built from bricks, mud, and palm trunks, with ornate arches over their wooden doors like the capital's casbah. All of this was constantly on the verge of collapsing on its inhabitants' heads. Not a day went by without news of stabbings or robberies there. So things go in this city I came to one dusty morning in the middle of April eight years ago, when a barrel of oil was worth $35 rather than the $15 it goes for today; this city where no person makes their way through its alleyways without spitting on the ground. Its women are wrapped in white coverings and move about like ghosts. Its river is sulfuric, yet kids still swim in it, their skin covered with infections and oozing pus. I remember a stampede of people with unclipped fingernails, their breath reeking of tobacco, inviting me to eat or sip coffee, fawning and flirting with me, attempting to entice me into getting engaged to this or that person's daughter, until they turned away when I met all their requests with a hard heart. It is a city that celebrates the strange until it becomes trite.

The only thing that annoys me is how little it rains and how impatient people here are.

Hassina always wanted to get married to a man from the capital, which she likened in her imagination to European cities. She saw the women there as beautiful, the men as refined, and the buildings as laid out harmoniously, their entrances topped with stone carvings that pulse with spirit. She wanted a man to rescue her from butting heads with her mother, who burdened her with housework and constantly chided her: "When I was your age, I already had two children!"

At the university, she became enthralled with Marxism and debating the meanings of revolution. She insulted anyone who opposed her and would only swear an oath on Lenin's head. Then she started to feel she was getting on in years, and her mother's pressure began to wear her down. She failed to learn how to cook, but she never tired of looking for a man who would be happy to get engaged to her.

Would she have agreed to sleep with me if I weren't the police inspector? My job, which I came to following Anwar Sadat's acceptance of the Nobel Peace Prize, satisfied my mother's wishes for me as a martyr's son and conferred certain benefits. Sometimes I would intervene directly on Hassina's behalf. Other times, I would turn a blind eye to her clients if they were involved in minor infractions. I dreamed of becoming a pilot or a ship's captain who traveled the world, but I went off course and found my way to a police station in one of the capital's suburbs, where I spent the first part of my career until my relationship with the police chief soured. He took his revenge by requesting my transfer to this southern city, without realizing he had sent me into the arms of a beautiful woman named Zinab, who was two years younger than me. I used to run into her at the post office when I received my paycheck or drew on my savings. She seemed to be from good stock, and I saw in her the makings of a housewife, unlike other women I knew. At first, she rejected my advances, which only made me love her more. Her parents were delighted at the prospect of me becoming their son-in-law, so I married her a day before an earthquake hit the city of al-Asnam, or Chlef, and buried its people underneath the rubble, just as Zinab assured me she had buried the memory of her previous love, who had moved away to work at the oil company because he couldn't ask her to marry him. The first year, during which we listened to Joe Dassin's songs, went nicely. The way she moaned in bed was music to my ears. We had our first son, then a second child, before our love faded. After that, it got to the point where I only slept with her rarely, and it felt like I was having sex with a wooden doll. We exchanged none of the words couples or lovers do, kissing half-heartedly. I was not happy when she got pregnant again. When she became a mother, her softness turned rough. "Beauty is for unmarried women, not mothers," she told me one day when I criticized her for not caring about her appearance.

My wife plunged a sugar cube into her cup of tea and walked out. There was no cooked food to be found that might satisfy my hunger, as she never gave a thought to my needs anymore. I took a piece of bread out of a bag and searched for some apricot jam in the refrigerator, which clanked like a drum. The jar was practically empty. I had been so busy that I had forgotten to ask Maimoun to send over a basket of things that had run out at the grocer's. As goods began to disappear, I depended on him more and more to get what I could not procure myself. He would set aside a certain quantity of staples for me at wholesale prices.

I was chewing the bread to the rhythm of my sons' laughter as they entertained themselves playing with Legos in their room when the phone rang. I figured it was my mother-in-law wanting to check in on her daughter, but Zinab called me: "It's for you."

What really gets me is when someone calls on a day that's supposed to be a day off. I was about to answer coldly and reject the call when the police commissioner's screeching voice beat me to the punch.

"Is what I heard about the singer true?"

"I'm afraid so."

He swore, something I was used to hearing whenever he was in a bad mood. "Who did it?"

"We suspect someone who lives next to the meadow."

"Why did he kill her?"

"He was in a relationship with her, but they had a fight."

Even though Zaza denied any connection to him, I'm not sure if she and the commissioner were ever involved. I saw him once at the nightclub, exchanging laughs with her. He sat at a table close to mine, pulled out a wad of bills, and asked that I join him in scattering them over her head as she sang. I could only do as he did but with a smaller wad. My boss approved, and then we raised our glasses as if we were good friends. He never returned; I learned that he spent his evenings elsewhere, but I could never determine exactly where.

Turning on the television in the middle of the living room, I lowered the volume so as not to bother my wife, who was lying down in the bedroom. It was almost 8 p.m. The weather reporter appeared on the national channel, and behind her a map of the country showed temperatures for the following day. She predicted an oppressively hot day, with the heavy sky pressing down on our heads. That was followed by the news, which focused on an egg-producing farm in Tlemcen and road paving in Batna and Relizane. Then, she discussed a meeting of ministers from the nonaligned countries and the "Resistance of the Afghan Mujahideen to the Communist Soviets." I thought about taking a shower to calm my nerves and wash the sweat from my body that was making me smell like a prisoner.

Right then, there was a knock at the door and the yelling of the building's doorman, who was stooped over at sixty years old: "Boss… Boss!" He was panting after having run up three flights of stairs. "They smashed your car window and then ran away. They were wearing masks."

I turned Zaza's earring over with my fingers in my trouser pocket, then put my hands on the back of my neck. I noticed the silver-framed wall clock ticking, sure that on that particular Friday, her death would drag me into even more disasters.

IBRAHIM

SEPTEMBER 14

My mad search for my father's grave transformed into a craving for Zakia's image, which had not left my mind since I'd first seen it on the concert tape the inspector had left in the VCR he'd returned to me. I thought he had left it there on purpose, waiting to see how I would react in the coming days. Did he suspect me? I didn't care one bit about his speculations. I liked her quasi-mezzo-soprano voice, even with its slight hoarseness and lack of vocal range. It seemed that she'd never learned how to play an instrument, and I was convinced that the best singers played an instrument. She didn't have a sharp ear either, as if she'd only learned to sing in front of a microphone the way they do it nowadays. However, her self-confidence drew me in; the way she swayed her upper body and moved her legs back and forth as if she were doing the samba; her wandering eyes and her skill in exciting those there with the lyrics *Dance and prance and leave the world to its jubilance*, which garnered applause from an audience out of the camera's view. I guessed there were a few dozen people in a nightclub lit by colored lights. The camera showed a face more worn out than the one I'd seen when she had come into the shop. I would have helped her develop her performance skills had I known her.

I was only shaken out of my reveries when Nabil walked into the Desert Rose. At first, I didn't recognize him, although his long nose and narrow eyes looked familiar. He regarded my face and then approached me with a hug.

"Ibrahim... brother."

Nabil had given up the life of frugality he had lived before. He was fat now, and his face had lightened. He looked like a newscaster in his four-buttoned black suit, white shirt, and blue necktie. His left wrist was adorned with a watch that glinted whenever the sun hit it through the shop window.

"I passed by your house and your mom sent me here."

I could not hide my surprise at how different my friend looked. The Nabil I remembered had been skinny and pimply, and I used to call him Bedbug because of his body odor.

"When did you get in?"

"Day before yesterday."

Nabil related dribs and drabs of things that had happened to him during his seven years in Paris. He had received the highest average grade in the south on the baccalaureate exam and got to shake hands with the president of the Republic, who had honored him with a fellowship to study abroad. He had chosen veterinary medicine and met a nurse, whom he had married. He told me that he'd gotten French citizenship after graduation, lowering his voice to a whisper as if disclosing a secret, for changing citizenship was akin to apostasy. He had come alone to visit his parents and six siblings and to check in on how construction was going on a new house: "Large enough for the family."

"What do you think of the city after being away for so long?"

"I've hardly run into anyone I know."

Everyone I knew had gone off on their way as well. I couldn't think of anything to tell him. I kept it brief as I lowered my eyes and ran my fingers through my hair. All I had done was graduate from the Institute of Translation, but I couldn't find a job because I kept putting off doing my military service. I didn't tell him how much I paid someone every three months to get me an exemption card. I told him how I spent some of my time sitting in front of the post office typing letters for old folks looking to receive back pay from building or manufacturing companies they'd worked at in France. This job did not generate enough income, though. It was only enough to buy an old guitar – especially since I made things easy for those who couldn't pay – and I had come to spend my days in this shop. Sometimes I slept here. In fact, since acquiring the shop, there was only one day I hadn't been in, and that had been for health reasons. I didn't hesitate to tell him about the hostility I faced from my mother, who had come to hate this city and its people, the dunes that surrounded it, my brother's dreams of becoming a professional boxer, and my desire to train my musical ear (I wish I had perfect pitch, something the greatest musicians strive to achieve). Sometimes I don't shower because there's no water, and I count the passing days in boredom, satisfied with making a living by renting out videocassettes and VCRs. I still refuse to eat eggs because they make my belly hurt, and I snatch momentary pleasures with brown-eyed women. If it weren't for the women, I'd surely realize the futility of my life.

"You sly fox!" Nabil said with a laugh as he looked around the shop, one wall covered with movie jackets and another with posters and pictures of actors under the watchful eyes of Charlton Heston. Given how much care I took with the place, he undoubtedly imagined it brought in a good amount of money.

I declared frankly that the most beautiful girl I had ever encountered had been murdered. She was rare among women, who generally don't take pride in their good looks out of fear that they will draw crude comments. "She had a smile like Catherine Deneuve's."

My friend didn't seem moved by that, not having much of a connection to the cinema. "Come visit me in France to meet some actresses!" he scoffed, which piqued my curiosity.

"Why not? My life here doesn't hold much promise." I asked him about the different ways one could settle on the other shore. Then I remembered I didn't have a passport because I hadn't done my military service. May the Lord provide relief, I said to myself.

Nabil put his hand in his suit pocket and pulled out a wristwatch and a purple box containing a small perfume bottle. "I bought them for you," he said.

It had been a long time since I'd cared how my body smelled, and I thought the fragrance might attract Noura and bring her lips closer to mine. I noticed that the watch was no different than the one on his wrist. I felt bad that I had nothing to give him, until I caught sight of *The Sheik* under the counter. "You're really going to enjoy reading it," I told him.

Nabil took his leave, and I didn't insist he stay, understanding full well that he had limited time to see his family and check in on the construction work. I put off asking him to help me emigrate and rested my chin in the palm of my hand, daydreaming about what my life would look like if I managed to get to Paris. The women of that city are "*gorgeous and gentle, good-natured and kind*," as I had read in some book. But before that, I needed to get some answers from my mother about the hotel singer!

NOURA

I wrote to my clients, apologizing for not being able to continue working on their cases; Bachir's situation was taking
up all of my time. "A means of making a living comes to me,
and I push it away," I mumbled. I deposited the letters in the
yellow metal mailbox, hoping they would get to where they
needed to go; I had gotten used to letters getting lost and
the post office denying any responsibility. Then I headed to
the hotel on foot, carefully choosing the words I would throw
in Kamal's face if he told me I couldn't meet with Maimoun
Belassal, like he had the last time.

I passed in front of the contraband market and looked
across the intersection at the Foreigners' Villa, which a
wealthy French colonist had left behind. No one knew what
went on behind the front gate of the villa. At one time, a sign
had hung at its entrance, saying FOREST PRESERVATION,
and people thought the government wanted to plant a line
of trees at the city entrance to prevent the sand from creeping northward. But then the sign was removed. After that, a
rumor circulated that an important official was under house
arrest at the villa. The only thing for sure was that German
cars made their way there every night. Anyone who saw them
would think the people of this city enjoyed a life of luxury
rather than poverty.

Dog eat dog, I said to myself as I cut straight across an alley crowded with pedestrians, herbal remedy shops, and a spare parts shop in front of which a group of buyers shrieked frantically. I came to a wide boulevard with scrap dealers on one side and antique furniture sellers on the other. Turning right, I passed the former Dunyazad movie theater, built sixty years prior. Its facade had been painted white and it had been transformed into a government building, although no one had fixed the broken glass in the upper windows. It teemed with workers and those who never tired of requesting personal documents. On the upper part of the front wall, there was a sign that read FROM THE PEOPLE TO THE PEOPLE. Then I passed by a synagogue that was now a War of Independence museum, the six-pointed star that once adorned its entrance having been removed. It had arched wooden windows and a bamboo door. Despite the periodic power outages in people's homes, its exterior lamp was always lit.

I finally reached my destination after walking for close to forty minutes. My trousers were stuck to my buttocks, I was sweating so much. There were some tourists standing in the hotel entrance and a bus waiting for them. Why do tourists insist on visiting this city? I asked myself. To hike among the dunes and take pictures under the palm trees? To visit the ancient quarters and enjoy the ever-present sun? To eat traditional dishes such as couscous and zviti and chakhchoukha? Or is it because of the women and ripe young boys here to enjoy? If I could travel, I'd choose someplace where it rains and is green and lush. Does it bring the tourists joy to steal glances at people's miserable lives?

Wading through the bodies, I spotted Kamal sitting behind his desk. He paid no attention to me as he finished dealing with his customers. I waited patiently for a moment until he lifted his eyes. He cracked a smile that deepened his dimples, and my heart shook. "Just a minute, please!" he said. I know that, customarily, a minute is an undefined period of time, so I sat on a sofa waiting for a sign from him, knowing full well he knew why I had come.

I waited fifteen minutes without the crowd of tourists thinning. Then, I got up to remind the receptionist that I hadn't come to waste time. I asked him if my wait would be much longer. He shot me a look and suggested I order a juice at the bar while he finished taking care of some routine matters, as he described them. I thanked him graciously for his offer, while it occurred to me not to give in to him, for sluggishness is a male trait; their sluggishness hastens the end of their sappy love stories. Ignoring men is the best response. I followed the arrow pointing to ADMINISTRATION and made my way down a corridor with a mirror on the wall. I looked at myself, smiling as I do whenever faced with a mirror, until I reached the manager's office. I gently knocked twice, then entered.

"*Bonjour.*"

As soon as I introduced myself to the hotel owner, he put down the papers in his hands and invited me to sit.

"My heart has been aching ever since I heard about her murder," he said.

He addressed me solemnly, like the tone the neighborhood imam uses when appealing to young people to pray. I wondered if the puffiness under his eyes was due to a lack of sleep. Or perhaps, given the blue veins on his forearms, it was a consequence of his advanced age.

"Do you suspect Bachir Labtam?" I asked him.

The hotel owner neither accused Bachir nor defended him.

I went right into asking questions about Bachir's relationship with Zakia Zaghouani, her life at the hotel, and the people she interacted with. My eyes moved around the office, which looked like a royal salon. It was furnished with two broad leather couches, there was not a speck of dust on the floor, and pictures of Maimoun were arranged in a triangle on the wall, along with Rabah Driassa, Mustapha Dahleb, Yahia Benmabrouk, and other high-profile artists and athletes I only see on TV or in the magazine I read regularly. The Throne Verse was embroidered in gold thread on black silk and hung on the opposite wall. He responded calmly to my questions, emphasizing that Zakia was like a daughter to him. Happy with her life. All the hotel employees were her family. News of her death had come as a shock to everyone.

"Bachir maintains his innocence," I said.

"Justice will be served."

Deep down, I sensed that the man I was speaking with did not intend to cooperate or that he had nothing useful to add to the case. His broad, sun-kissed face didn't suggest he was a violent person. I thanked him and left, apologizing for the interruption.

"I hope to see you again under better circumstances," he replied.

He accompanied me to the door, and, without turning around, I felt him stealing a glance at me from behind.

When I passed in front of him, Kamal was finished dealing with the customers, who had left for the bus. I hope the court summons him and he provides good testimony for his friend, I thought. I said goodbye, staring at him with a smile that, he later told me, got him into trouble with his boss, who was very upset when he called him on the phone.

I couldn't stand the idea of waiting for a taxi. Nearby was a carriage. In front of it stood a man rubbing down a black Berber horse's neck. I offered him a reasonable sum to take me to my aunt's house in Twentieth of August, a neighborhood next to the meadow on the other side of the city.

We passed the stone frontage of St Philip's Church, built in 1931, and I gazed up at the two brass bells in its bell tower. It was a shame that it had been closed since independence in 1962; the story went that municipal officials couldn't agree on whether to turn it into a mosque or a craft workshop. Then we drove past the Martyrs' Cemetery and the Peace of Mind Café. Before we got as far as the post office, I asked the coachman, whose face was smoother than mine, what his name was.

"Fouzi."

I plunged right into asking him about what he knew about the victim.

"She treated me like a brother."

"Do you have sisters?"

He told me about his four older sisters whom he hadn't seen for two months, even though they live in the same house. He gets home late at night after everyone has gone to sleep and leaves early in the morning to avoid fighting with them and his parents, who don't accept him for who he is.

After passing the police station and the security workers' building a few hundred yards beyond it, I tried to find out what he knew about Bachir.

"He loved her. I don't believe he killed her."

He spat twice to his left as he urged along his horse, whose tail was so long it practically touched the ground.

"But since he's in prison, he must have something to do with her death."

I understood that his words were distilled from what was generally being said, and that every rumor contained a grain of truth. We passed by the hospital and continued straight until we reached our destination. I thanked him as I got out of the carriage.

As I entered Twentieth of August, which was lined with garbage bags and echoed with the squawking of boys throwing mud left behind by a burst pipe that supplied drinking water to the houses, a question dogged me: When will I have children to play with or chase off? All the Lord has provided for me is Rouna the cat, who I play with and pour my anger out on.

My aunt was looking forward to my arrival. Yesterday, after I'd told her I was going to come take a look at her son's room in the hope that I might find something to help me in my defense, she hadn't been able to sit still. She'd asked her husband to take the day off from his ambulance-driving job so they could speak with me face-to-face. He was the one who had transported Zakia's body from the meadow to the hospital, not knowing his son would be implicated in what happened. As soon as I looked down the long street of redbrick houses, I saw them waiting for me in the doorway. I used to be so scared of her when I was younger – she'd always grabbed my ear or slapped my bum as she said over and over: "When someone hits you, they only want what's best for you" – but now she made me feel like someone special, not just her niece.

"Noura's come with some good news!"

My anguish was compounded, as there was no good news on the horizon.

The three of us sat in the living room around a small wooden table with a vase on it that contained a bunch of plastic tulips.

106

"What's up with Bachir?" my aunt's husband asked with a puzzled look. His mustache covered his upper lip, and his gray hair was combed back.

I could not forget the image of their son's pale face and the tears he was unable to hold back, but I avoided bringing that up. "He's fine," I said.

Silence shrouded the room without further comment from me. It was eleven o'clock. They had expected me to bring them some cheerful news that might lessen their gloom, such as telling them a mistake had been made in putting my cousin in jail or that the case was pointing toward his exoneration. To break the silence, I asked my aunt whether Bachir was in the habit of going to the meadow, but she said no.

"That place has changed," my aunt grumbled, telling me that families used to stroll there on weekends. "People we don't know go there now." According to her, these people have built huts for themselves, and fights break out between neighbors and the new residents, sometimes with words and other times with punches or rocks being thrown. Sometimes, they crowd in front of the mosque's well and prevent others from filling their buckets. Their kids piss on the walls and steal shoes from the worshippers on Fridays. Apparently they cut open stray dogs and throw their corpses onto piles of garbage, resulting in a disgusting smell.

My aunt offered me some pastries, but I declined. "I'm on a diet."

She didn't like my response; she agrees with my mother, who thinks men like full-bodied women with some fat on them. I looked up at the ceiling fan. It was buzzing and vibrating so much, I worried it might fall on my head at any moment.

I asked if I could look around my cousin's room, and she showed me the way. As soon as I was alone with my aunt, I seized the opportunity to ask: "You intended to marry Bachir to his other cousin?"

"Yep, but he wouldn't listen to me."

"You only remember me when there's something wrong," I said into my chest. Am I not suitable for marriage? I asked myself. I let her know that I wanted to go into the room alone, and she asked me if she and her husband could pay the dead woman's family some blood money to secure their son's release. "That's not how things work," I replied.

There was a poster of Umm Kulthum hanging on the wall, and one of the national soccer team facing it. Two clean, folded shirts lay on a table, and next to them were some cassette tapes of Arab singers from the Middle East, a bottle of perfume, two collections of love poetry, and a book on the history of ancient civilizations. There was also a Waterman pen and, under the bed, three pairs of shoes. I pulled out some clothes from the bottom of the closet and found myself looking at a wad of bills. If not for the shit Bachir had stepped into, I would never have known about the luxurious life he enjoyed.

I didn't find anything of note, so I left the room. My aunt was standing right there in front of me, as if she had been spying. She was the one who had tidied up after the two policemen had left after conducting the search the day Bachir was arrested. She handed me a light-green short-sleeved shirt with a Lacoste insignia on it.

"I found it with the dirty clothes in the courtyard before the police arrested him."

My arms went limp and my head started to ache. The shirt was smeared with blood. Could the blood be Zakia's?

She whispered nervously to me: "Are they going to put him away for life?"

I stuffed the shirt into my briefcase without responding and headed back to my office.

IBRAHIM

SEPTEMBER 15

I was possessed by a feeling that love had led to Zakia Zaghouani's death. "She probably left her lover, so he killed her." (I, too, had almost strangled a previous girlfriend.) But my mother refuted that theory and told me about an argument the victim had had with another singer in the hotel. "She was jealous of her."

There were two light knocks on the door. I found Noura standing there before me, head buried in her shoulders, eyes lowered. She was smiling. "I came to meet with your mother," she said.

Noura had hurried over without giving me time to ask my mother whether she wanted to speak to her or not. Her audacity offended me and I hoped she would leave immediately, but my mother called from the kitchen: "Who's at the door?" I understood that the lawyer was intent on doing what she had come to do, so I let her into the low-ceilinged, cramped living room, as cramped as my worried heart. With a visitor there, I became conscious of the chipped paint on the walls and handwoven rug in the middle of the floor. Along the side, there was a couch that could fit three people, next to it a low-set table facing a black and white television. The window was closed, as always, to keep out the foul language from the street. A picture of my father with his wide eyes, light-brown skin, and thin mustache faced another one on the opposite wall promoting the agricultural revolution. In it there was a boy raising his finger to the sky, with the following words written underneath the image: THE LAND BELONGS TO HE WHO CULTIVATES IT.

"A woman's come to see you!"

My mother thought one of her relatives had come to see her after getting her sore tooth pulled, even though they never came to our house and forced her to make the rounds to see them on special occasions and weddings. She put down the earthenware plate into which she was shelling fava beans, wiped her hands with a towel, and headed barefoot (as she usually was in the house) toward her visitor. Noura kissed her on both cheeks and spoke as if she knew her.

"How are you, Mama Wannasa?"

Noura told her what she did for a living, making it the first time my mother had met a lawyer. I withdrew to the hallway, listening in from behind the wall. Noura did not hesitate to say why she had come.

"May the Lord have mercy on her."

My mother had started working at the Sahara after years of cleaning the floors at City Hall. At first, she'd washed dishes in the restaurant. Then she'd become a cleaner, responsible for the reception area and the rooms on the first floor. Another woman named Fatiha cleaned the second and third floors. My mother feared Fatiha's scheming and tried to curry favor with her so she wouldn't publicly accuse her of stealing things from the tourists.

"Can you tell me about the deceased?"

My mother was afraid what she was doing might get her boss, Maimoun Belassal, in trouble, so she tried avoiding the question and offered to make her a cup of tea.

"I just came to talk," Noura said.

The room fell silent, and it occurred to me that Noura, as anxious as she was, might light a cigarette, which would make my mother realize that women smoked in real life, not only in the movies. But the lawyer kept her composure.

"What's said here will remain between us and won't be heard by another soul."

"I'm scared I'll lose my job."

"God will not provide for the one who is silent to the truth."

My mother could only describe Zakia by saying: "She was on a path pleasing neither to Our Lord nor the angels." She added that the victim used to sing and that women singing was haram, according to the imam. And there were rumors she spent time alone with men.

"Did you ever see her with a man?"

"No."

"Your suspicions are wrong, then!"

"That's just what I heard."

"From who?"

"From people who work at the hotel."

"But I know she was a good girl."

"Only God knows what's in people's hearts."

"Did you ever go into her room?"

"Never."

"Who do you think killed her?"

"Lord knows."

Noura felt that the statement of this woman whose hair smelled of henna and who had dark circles under her eyes would not do her any good. Despite that, she left her office number, knowing full well that we didn't have a telephone and made do with the booths in the street on the rare occasions we did make calls. She begged her to get in touch if she had anything else to say.

The lawyer made her way to the front door, and I shut myself in my small room. I sat on my bed and looked around. On the other side of the room, there was a small table with books and newspapers piled on top. My eyes passed over a small radio and an alarm clock, and a metal wardrobe where I kept my clothes. To its right were rolled, woven rugs piled on top of one another. I pretended to fix the small television set that sat below my framed university diploma. I kicked a beetle, causing sticky liquid to fly out from its midsection, and wondered: Why was my mother hiding her suspicions that another singer had been involved in Zakia's death?

BACHIR

TUESDAY

The prisoners make up stories about me.

One of them says I killed my neighbor. Another one thinks I killed my mother for the inheritance. Yet another claims I killed my wife, though no one has even asked whether I am married. I avoid arguing with them. They've already passed judgment on me and adjourned the court session. "Whoever kills once might kill again," one of them whispered to his friend.

I record my thoughts in this notebook I bought from the administration with money Noura gave me, along with a Bic pen that doesn't write as smoothly as the Waterman I'm used to.

The only one who bothers me is The Pharmacien. He is fat and looks like a lizard. He tried to rip my pillow from me to provoke me into fighting him, but Rahhal ended the argument from the get-go: "Avoid friction with the other prisoners to avoid solitary confinement." I followed his advice, and his intervention allowed me to get closer to him. He's the only one who believes I'm not a killer. He was sentenced to five years, two of which he has already done. The day before yesterday, he was kind enough to wash my shirt with his. Or, more to the point, he plunged them both into water and laid them out on the ground to dry. "We're brothers," he said when I protested, looking at me with two eyes gleaming like cups of coffee. What I like the most about him is that he doesn't cut me off when I talk. He compares his condition to Job's: "I proceeded righteously and patiently." I compare my situation to Jesus': "My suffering is a sacrifice for the sins of others."

WEDNESDAY

I find myself crammed into a life that moves slowly. Guards slowly walking through the corridors, opening the dormitory door every morning to slowly conduct the roll call and count the number of prisoners, slowly searching every corner. Prisoners slowly amusing themselves or fighting, walking slowly around the yard during rest time. A heavy time, slower than slow. They say slowness is wisdom, but here it's madness. I am beset by nightmares when I close my eyes. Was Zakia slowly tortured before she took her last breaths, or did she die a merciful death? She favored me over others and remained faithful, preferring me over wealthier men and those who proposed marriage. Did one of her lovers take revenge on her? Love blinds and makes disappointed lovers commit the worst deeds.

It's one in the afternoon now. I should be in the accounting office at the company, taking care of the workers' pay and preparing memos and work schedules, but I'm in prison. Rahhal told me the story of a British singer who embraced Islam. As I listen to him, I long for the taste of nicotine. A feeling of jealousy that he has quit smoking takes hold of me.

THURSDAY

Rahhal, standing at over five five, consoled three prisoners who had abandoned themselves to silent weeping: "Men are not afraid." I have lived as a son, a brother, someone without a job, a drifter, a soldier, a lover, an optimist, and a pessimist, but I am also afraid of what will happen to me. I am not a man, and as long as I remain in prison, I won't be one. I'm nothing but a piece of shit people step in.

FRIDAY

The newspaper is more expensive than a piece of meat. I pay a guard a handful of dinars to read it; then I let my colleagues know what's happening on the outside, even though the news is basically unchanging from the beginning to the end of the week: settlement of illegal construction cases, combating waterborne diseases, the government urging women to space out births to protect maternal health... Nothing interesting. But The Pharmacien, who had made peace with me to get into Rahhal's good graces – because Rahhal is the eldest here and everyone reveres him – grew curious when I read out news of a drug bust in a nearby city. He began to list names of people he imagined might have been arrested. I think he's an infiltrator who informs on us to the administration. The only article that caught my eye was THIRD HORSE EXHIBITION IN NEZRAMA, an exhibition in which 1,300 horses would participate; among them were 840 for the Fantasia, 100 for a horse training competition, and the rest for long- and short-distance races. Nezrama, a town of women more than one of horses, still lingers in my imagination; whoever wrote that article was not interested in saying much about that side of things. I would have told him enough to fill an entire newspaper if he had asked me.

I turned the page and began reading the Culture section, where I found news of seminars and new books, along with verses by two poets from the capital and a translated short story by a Russian author. The Culture page is of no interest to anyone except me. I quote lines from it that I supplement with Umm Kulthum lyrics I have memorized or romantic ghazal collections to incorporate them into letters I write for Slit-Nose, who intends to send them to his fiancée.

SUNDAY

Neither my father nor my mother has visited me. I don't want to see them here anyway, especially my mother, who I've had a falling-out with in a fit of anger after she objected to my relationship with my girlfriend. I imagine that what happened to me might facilitate my father's reconciliation with my uncle. They had a dispute over their inheritance from my grandfather and haven't spoken for almost seventeen years. My mother sought to bring them closer together when she suggested I get engaged to my uncle's daughter, but I squelched that idea, reiterating that I thought of no woman other than Zakia.

MONDAY

Since high school, I have applied myself to writing in my diary. I have blackened pages upon pages and filled notebooks with words. My hope was to become a writer, but I failed in my studies. Is it right to presume to write without holding a single higher education degree?

From all the reading I'd done, I'd thought I possessed the secrets of language, but I spent days mastering the language of the prisoners around me. They call guards "locusts." A "visit" means a rest period in the courtyard. As for family visits, they refer to them as "baskets" because their families bring baskets of food. They refer to soap as "rocks" even though they only use it rarely, given how scarce water is here.

They have lost their freedom, but they have freed up their language.

BOOK 2

GHOSTS

HAMID

A week has passed since Zaza's death, and I have only gathered a single piece of information. It was reported to me by Fouzi, who, they say, was born with feminine tendencies. A little before her time came, he saw her coming out of a telephone booth next to the hotel. I asked for a list of numbers dialed from there that day, and I learned from a Grand Taxi driver who works the Nezrama line that she had lied to him, pretending she was a nurse.

"She would give me money, which I would place in her mother's hand and then leave."

I returned to the nightclub, which had regained its previous rhythm, but I could not erase Zaza's image from my mind. I found it difficult to comprehend that she could have loved the man I'd begun describing as The Camel because of his broad nose. Along with his ID card and the earring she'd worn, I forwarded his love letters to the court. I conducted another search of her room for the second earring, but to no avail.

Sitting at a table in a dark corner scarcely lit by the colored light that filled the center of the lounge, I rubbed a cigarette between my fingers before putting it down, taking a sip from a small glass and undoing my top shirt button. Maimoun approached me, his shirtsleeves rolled up to reveal two thin arms. He was twenty-one years older than me and eight inches shorter. He hadn't been able to believe it when he heard that the deceased had been on the list of missing persons in her hometown. He regretted having trusted her and neglecting to look closely into her past: "I believed her when she told me she was the only daughter of divorced parents who had disowned her." He recommended that his employees show some discretion and tell the customers she had gone on vacation, even though I doubted we could keep secret what had happened.

My relationship with Maimoun dates to when I first arrived in this city. A fire had broken out in his warehouse next to the meadow, where he stored foodstuffs earmarked for retail sale. Quintals of wheat and dried seeds were lost, and the perpetrator was never identified. Even though Maimoun accused Si Miloud, his competitor, I never found any evidence to corroborate that. I did arrange for the police to take shifts guarding the place, pretending it was to maintain security on the nearby road, and there were never any problems again. In return, he flung the hotel doors wide open for me, allowing my family to spend time in the pool on vacation days for free. He even gave them anything they wanted to eat or drink.

The nightclub was not as crowded as usual, with some tables empty. And Maimoun had not changed the decor, as he had promised the dead woman. It was still the same as before, with its double doors, wooden carvings in the corners, and impressionistic paintings on the walls that appealed to customers who included white-collar workers and the self-employed. Ceiling fans turned without bringing in any fresh air, and jazz came out of the speakers, which drowned out the conversations of people sitting there, most of whom were clean-shaven. The waiter, Khalil – broad-shouldered, blond, with clear eyes and a freckled face – made his rounds.

I drew on my cigarette as I imagined Zaza coming toward me, her eyes sparkling, her curves accentuated by her short black dress as she leaned in toward me with her lips painted bright red, transmitting into my ear Maimoun's and his visitors' movements, all without hiding how dissatisfied she was with her job and how much she wanted to make a change in her life. "All women envy you for how far you've gotten," I would assure her.

Although I had invited her to spend a weekend with me more than once, she had always declined. Now, the only way I could smell her scent was on the wristwatch I had given her as a gift three years ago. After her death, I had found it in a bag of her things, and I hold onto it like a pagan holds onto an idol. "She was a light that filled my heart," I whispered in French as I moved the small glass around on the table. Then I fixed my gaze on Maimoun, who had not quit smoking despite his last heart attack, against his doctor's advice.

"How's business?"

"Fine."

I told him about the crowds that formed every morning in front of the farmers' market, but he refused to believe food was scarce. "The good stuff is there, but people act as if they've gone crazy. They buy more than they need, believing rumors and ignoring what the government tells them," he said. Nonetheless, he resented the fact that pharmacies did not have essential medicines, and he told me of his intention to purchase antibiotics, pills, and vaccines.

"Are you planning on opening a pharmacy yourself?"

"Just helping out the pharmaceutical field."

I winked to indicate that I understood what he meant. *Oil comes from the olive / and the one who easily grasps things can understand the language of birds*, as Abderrahman El Mejdoub said. I knew full well that the man I was sitting with would only be satisfied reaching his hand into everything that could be bought and sold. "Maimoun will throw you in the water and pull you out dry," Zakia used to say. No one was as shrewd as he was. Although she had devoted herself to watching him, she had never learned a thing about his secrets. "His own welfare is more important to him than his health," she once laughed softly under her breath.

As Maimoun dove into the topic of the scarcity of medicines, a tall young man I had never seen before walked in. He had long black hair and wore a short-sleeved shirt and sneakers. He sat down at a table next to ours. He ordered a drink and a plate of nuts from the waiter as I stared at him silently. Then I remembered it was Zinab's birthday. I slapped my forehead, which startled my friend.

"Are you alright?"

"Yes… yes."

The jazz music faded, and it was almost 10 p.m. when Cheikha Edahabia appeared. She was wearing trousers that were loose around the buttocks and tight lower down, with a shirt that revealed her belly. She had put a summer hat over her dyed blonde hair and concealed her hands in fashionable lace gloves. She got up behind the microphone, gave a friendly smile, and then leaned toward the few people there as they clapped for her. I adjusted myself and leaned back in my chair to listen to her first song as Maimoun scanned what was going on around him, like a radar that detected even the slightest movements on the ground.

*"O, Lalla Turkiya... I just heard the beats of the bendir drum...
I came to ask for your blessing... for I am fragile and barren..."*

I kept touching the edge of my mustache with my tongue, enjoying how the lights shone on Cheikha's chest as it rose and fell. The more she turned around, the more I focused on her. She had never aroused me before, but my desires had ripened since Zakia's burial. She took off her black hat, and it appeared that her hair was actually a wig.

"She's lucky to have taken the dead woman's place."

"They were rivals."

"What do you mean?"

"Cheikha Edahabia was hard on her."

Could Zakia's murder have been the result of jealousy between the two women? I wondered.

I had just decided to give my wife the watch I had retrieved from Zaza's belongings when the tall young man sitting next to us stood up, burped like a lazy frog, and spoke with the waiter before leaving. The scene piqued my curiosity, so I called over Khalil, whose neck smelled of French perfume.

"Do you know him?"

"No."

"What did he want?"

"He traveled fifty miles to see Zaza tonight."

The place is nothing without her, I thought as I looked at Maimoun.

Cheikha Edahabia's voice got louder and mixed with the melodies of a synthesizer played by a new arrival who was bald and had a long nose.

"Who's that?"

"A new musician. I suggested we try him out."

"What was Zakia's issue with Farhat's playing?"

"She complained that he kept playing wrong notes."

I wasn't convinced by that explanation. He had accompanied her for years, and she could have requested his replacement before now.

"Do you think she was hiding something else?"

"I don't think so."

"Did you get rid of Farhat?"

"No, he asked for a leave of absence. He got into an accident on his moped near the meadow Thursday night," said Maimoun.

"The night Zakia was killed!"

IBRAHIM

My mother told me that the hotel's owner knows the names of the city's martyrs, few as they are, but he denied ever knowing Ben Kaddour. Who would've known my father? I asked myself, without finding an answer.

Six walked into the Desert Rose humming the Ahmed Wahby song "What's Passed Has Passed." He was carrying a wrapped sandwich in a plastic bag as usual, thinking my eyes would light up with happiness when I saw him, but I met him with a gloomy face. I indicated that he should leave, then pushed him toward the door. He stood on the sidewalk, waiting, searching for an explanation… "What's up, Brihoum?" he asked me.

I told him that I'd heard rumors that the gas station owner's car was set on fire by some young guys from First of November, and I'd immediately thought of Six, or Faudel, which is his real name. He lives near there, enjoying the devotion of his peers just as Jesus did the apostles. I didn't think something like that could have happened without him knowing about it. The gas station's owner is the father of my friend, Saâdi, who lent me some money to cover the shop's rent. Now he's sitting in some prison after being

127

arrested for assaulting a tax collector who came into his shop.

"How dare you accuse me of that!"

It was said that an argument had broken out when someone tried to make off on their moped with a can of gasoline. Two workers at the station had beaten him up, after which he'd come back for revenge. Six is the only one in his neighborhood who owns a moped.

He maintained his innocence, but I didn't listen as I swept the floor, ready to tear into him with the broomstick if he dared to come in again. He begged me to let him show me the high-quality hashish he had.

"Smoke it yourself," I said to him.

Six obviously couldn't bear the insult as he stood on the sidewalk like someone infected with scabies. He told me he regretted returning the adult videotapes to me and wished he had destroyed them instead. "Tomorrow I'll burn your shop down, shithead!"

Before he could finish this sentence, I took off after him, brandishing the broom and yelling as loudly as I could: "I'll tear your balls off, I swear!"

I couldn't catch Six, so I returned to the shop and whispered to myself, "Scared of that flyweight?!" In any case, I needed his father, a War of Independence veteran, to help me by providing testimony so I could get a martyr's widow card for my mother. I had explained that to Noura, but she hadn't shown any willingness to cooperate.

"My father split up with my mother, and I don't see him anymore."

I asked for his address, but she denied even knowing it. It seemed that she was harboring feelings of rejection, but I was determined not to lose faith and stop trying, hoping that

that card would deliver me from eternal hellfire to a paradise without walls; that it would help me obtain exemption from military service and save me from the extortion of that middleman who robs me of my earnings; that it would help me get a job I actually want, or facilitate a better business venture.

"Noura, my life is in your hands." I tried appealing to her sense of compassion, bringing up her visit to my mother: "She asked me about you."

"What did you say?"

"That you're my friend's sister."

"If he knew about our relationship, he'd strangle you," she said, laughing.

I held my tongue concerning what I had learned about the hostility between Zakia Zaghouani and the other singer at the Sahara, even though I found it unlikely that a woman would kill another woman. Women are ten times less violent than men. Someone must have been working with her. I wanted to tell her to start looking into her family, but I held my tongue. There was still a suspicion bearing down on me that Six had something to do with it. I'd looked for him the night it happened, but to no avail. I'd remained skeptical when I asked him where he'd been and he responded, "I was tired and went to bed early." Perhaps he had gone to bed early, but only after having killed someone.

I decided to prod my friend Tijani, a news reporter for *Echaâb*, to refer to her death in an article. Her story might stimulate a writer's imagination to look into her life despite the lack of information.

CHEIKHA EDAHABIA

I glanced at her as she stood on the corner waiting for me to leave home, like a thief waiting for his mark. Her shy smile lingered as she alternated between lowering her gaze and fixing it on me. I didn't know her name and had never seen her face. I thought she was waiting for someone else, but as soon as I got to where she was, she approached me politely. I thought she was one of those women who tend to block my path to ask about their husbands who frequent the nightclub, and I prepared myself to respond as I always do, by saying that I don't know the customers there, but she introduced herself and told me what she did for work.

"Noura Arkoub. Lawyer."

She told me the reason for wanting to meet with me, so I responded: "May God have mercy on all the dead."

Zakia had died, and it didn't matter anymore if I said anything good or bad about her, but I still held onto a thread of reverence toward her for how well she'd treated me and how close we'd become when she first came to the hotel. That's what made me give in to the lawyer's insistence that I accept her invitation to sit with her at the Saâda Café. However, I made her solemnly swear that no one would find out I'd spoken with her.

We sat across from one another in a far corner of the café. I noticed she was a little heavier than I was.

"I answered all the questions at the police station."

"I came to listen, not to interrogate you."

As I regarded her short brown hair and sparkling eyes, I guessed she was either married or engaged, sure a man would have noticed her beauty. However, I didn't see a ring on her finger and couldn't justify asking her about it. I was scared she would say *Everything is written.* Or she would slap me down with an *It's none of your business!* Or she might bemoan the fact that she was divorced, which would make me feel awkward.

The waiter circled our table. His face was sharp and his combed-back hair thick. He reminded me of Kamal, who works on the reception desk at the Sahara. I can't stand how smug he is and how harshly he treats me and the hotel employees. Whenever he sees two people whispering to one another, he gives them an angry look, thinking they're talking about him. He flaunts his arrogance and reaps the benefits of being from the same clan as Hadj Maimoun. Whenever I run into him, I make it a point to say hi, never expecting him to reciprocate. And if he deigns to respond, he does so from the side of his mouth, as if it makes him miserable to utter so much as a word. He treats me as if I've committed a crime, while he turns on the charm with the foreign tourists, receiving tips in hard currency from them.

"What's your real name?"

"Safia Bechiche."

"Your age?"

"Twenty-seven."

Noura ordered juice and a croissant while I made do with a cup of tea, wanting to avoid looking like a ravenous young woman in front of her. I was used to deprivation, unlike the victim, who'd been lucky enough to live in the hotel, all expenses paid, eating in the restaurant and enjoying the pool. I wasn't even allowed to sleep there. I had to make do with a small room on the ground floor next to the men's changing room to change my clothes when I needed to. And I had to pay for food if I wanted it. I tore my stomach up with french fry sandwiches I bought in the shops on the edges of working-class neighborhoods, and I often cursed Maimoun under my breath for the favoritism he showed to Zakia. All because my mother was a lowly cleaning woman. Her mother didn't have such a disgraceful job!

"How long have you worked there?"

"Five years."

Solemnly the lawyer asked me to tell her about my life. I reiterated my request that she not tell anyone that I'd spoken to her. I cast a penetrating look into her questioning eyes and detected a glimpse of warmth there. Then I lowered my head and noticed her nails were painted with rose-colored polish. "My life is no different than any other woman's," I told her.

She insisted gently as she cast a curious look at my lace-gloved hands, broad shoulders, pink-colored lips, rouged cheeks, and darkly painted eyelashes. Her voice sounded like that of my cousin, the seamstress, who enjoyed a good reputation among brides. She had taught me how to keep my skin soft with a mixture of herbs, while never growing bored of stealing kisses from my lips. I straightened my bra strap, which showed through my gray summer shirt. I brushed away a strand of hair that had fallen over my right eye and pushed my leg underneath the chair, happy to have met someone who would listen to me. I took a deep breath and started with the day I was born.

I opened my eyes to a father who only spoke when angry. He would slap and punch my mother or drag her by the hair and hit her in the face with a plate or a spoon. At night, in their room, their grunts would mingle. She was as obedient to him as a child is to her father. Then my younger brother, Lotfi, was born before I turned six, and my father continued to behave the same way toward my mother. He started to abuse my older brother, Muqdad, too, who wasn't shy about digging his nails into my father's face. I went to school and made friends, but they went their separate ways and disappeared as the years passed. I volunteered collecting used clothes for kids in Vietnam; then I joined the Islamic Scouts, where I learned to play the *darbouka* drum and trained my voice by singing patriotic anthems and religious praise songs. One evening, my father came home as usual from the Rubber & Plastic Co., which some Yugoslavs had built. He didn't bathe or change his clothes and went straight to bed. He closed his eyes and never woke up again. My mother heard him snoring before he was struck by a heart attack. I left school because I didn't like the teachers and they didn't like me. They showered me with zeroes and whacked my fingers with a wooden stick. I worked as a women's hairdresser for a while but didn't stay at it for long. Then, when I got older, I learned that my father's anger at home was caused by his drinking. "He used to drink to forget his problems," I was informed by my mother, who, after he was gone, became his defender. "A good woman is obedient to her husband during his life, and afterward too," she told me.

"Do you love your mother?" Noura asked me.

In truth, I see her only as a ghost floating around the house. She cooks. She cleans. She retreats into herself in prayer and grief. She makes me feel as if I'm a mere guest, with no blood linking us to each other. I don't remember the last time she kissed or hugged me. I'm not even sure what color her eyes are, and she doesn't deserve to be called Sit el Habayeb or Lady of Beloveds, as the singer Fayza Ahmed described her mother. In fact, she was nowhere to be found the day I turned fourteen and my life was turned upside down. She'd nursed me with discontent, and I'd taken on loneliness as my mother.

I was surprised by a tear I couldn't hold back. After all these years, I still long for a mother to show me some tenderness. Whenever I meet a woman the same age as my mother, I want her to hug me and make me forget the misery of my youth.

"Whether I love her or hate her, it won't change a thing in my life or hers."

Then I bit my lower lip. I bowed my head and shook it from side to side. I closed my eyes for a moment and felt as if I were drowning in a well. The story of what happened to me that afternoon I turned fourteen got stuck in my throat.

That day, Muqdad, now eighteen and far taller than me, took me by surprise as I swept the living room floor. He put his arms around me from behind like a snake winding itself around a frog. I turned to him with a goofy smile and asked him to move away from me, hoping the door would creak open and in would come my mother, who was next door with my younger brother, blowing off some steam. I thought he was fooling around and didn't know how to hold him back. I had been raised to obey him. Then I resisted and shouted. I kicked him but he paid no attention. His eyes looked like my father's when he got angry. The door didn't creak open, and my mother didn't come back in. My brother became my enemy, and I rushed to the bathroom to throw up. I poured a bucket of water over my body while my mother's absence grew longer still. The radio announcer mourned Umm Kulthum while I mourned my loss of confidence and trust in my family. I felt as if I had aged ten years. My body gave off an acrid odor that I can still smell whenever I take off my clothes to wash. I thought I'd be stricken by cancer or some other horrible disease. Muqdad begged for forgiveness, but I couldn't look at his face as I bled intermittently over the days that followed. Whenever I conjure up the name or image of my older brother, I'm stricken by a terror that turns me into a raging bull. Since that day, I have never once forgotten to hide a knife in my pocket or handbag whenever I go out to meet a man alone.

"There isn't a mother who doesn't love her daughter," the lawyer said.

"Not all mothers are the same."

My mother, Fatiha, spends her days cleaning rooms at the hotel, praying with wandering eyes, and pouring out her resentment toward another cleaning woman named Wannasa, who she accuses of slander, polytheism, and having sex with tourists in exchange for a few dinars. She's fifty years old, and I'd like to tell her who deflowered me, but I'm afraid she won't believe me. All she's graciously bestowed on me are these nice-looking breasts. I don't have to enlarge them with cups like other women do. Oh, and one other good thing: she guided me to the Sahara after I failed the national ballet exam. During my first days there, I worked in the laundry, then moved to the nightclub when it opened. After changing my name to Cheikha Edahabia, I dyed my hair blonde because blonde hair is associated more with femininity than black, which is associated more with sadness, as was the case with Zaza. That American wasn't wrong to title his movie

Gentlemen Prefer Blondes. Hadn't Dalida dyed her hair blonde and doubled her fan base? My cousin, who changes her hair color every season, taught me that. I won Maimoun over with my voice and my experience in the Scouts band without any opposition from my mother, who figured that my being there would allow me to find a husband after I had refused to marry Hadi, the toothless head of cleaning, because of our age difference.

When my older brother turned twenty-three, his engagement to the post office's female paymaster fell through because our clan was lower status than hers, and he joined the oil company in the far south. At first, he continued to visit us occasionally; then his visits became less frequent and then stopped altogether after he married and had three children.

"And your younger brother?"

I remember calling Lotfi *bébé* until he was seven years old. I used to hug him and play with him as if he were a doll.

"He's in jail."

My mother preferred he remain there than be released and fill the house with screaming and threaten her with a knife for refusing to hand over a portion of her pay. Sometimes he would say she wasn't his mother, or even that she wasn't related to him. But he didn't deny that he was related to me.

"Does he torment you as well?"

"No."

Before he went to prison, Lotfi tried to assert his control, keeping a close eye on me when I left the house and when I came back. He would ask where I was going and then berate me if I came home too late in the evening. He disapproved of me removing the veil, but I responded to his insults in kind. I drew boundaries for him that he never crossed. Once, I screamed in his face, "I'm your sister in name only!"

"Why is he in prison?" the lawyer asked.

"Because of his work."

"What does he do?"

"He's a pharmacist."

Noura wondered out loud if he might be a colleague of her half brother, Djelloul, who owned a pharmacy next to the Grand Mosque.

"I mean he's a sidewalk pharmacist." I realized she didn't understand what I meant, so I explained that he uses forged prescriptions to buy boxes of medication intended for mentally ill people and then sells them by the pill to addicts. And sometimes he gets foreign cigarettes from people living abroad, which he doesn't sell to his regular customers. Instead, he sets those aside for important people.

After I was called to the police station, Hamid learned that The Pharmacien was my brother and cut his questions short. He asked me to describe my last encounter with the murder victim. I had run into her in the entranceway to the hotel, I'd told him. We'd exchanged cold looks, and then she'd turned away and spat on the ground. "She didn't say anything to you?" he asked. "No," I told him. I signed an interrogation report, and he let me leave.

Noura seemed like a sensible woman to me. I was happy to tell her what I knew because she was a stranger, neither from my house nor one of my colleagues. It also seemed that she didn't intend to do me any harm. But why didn't she wear a ring on her finger? Had another woman become jealous of her and mustered up some sort of charm that kept suitors away? Or did she detest men as much as I had come to detest them? I only come across single men worn out from masturbating who whistle or toss rude words at me in the street or make farting sounds with their mouths behind my back. Trash, I say to myself and walk on. Farhat the musician was the only one I liked, despite his strong body odor. Farhat, no surname, who was raised in an orphanage before being brought up by a childless cobbler, had left me when he discovered I wasn't a virgin, because he's a son of a whore who thinks other women are just like his mother! He even denies the accusation about his mother, saying that an angel visited her in her sleep and he became an embryo in her belly. However, out of pity for my broken heart, Fouzi had told me that Zakia was the one who'd encouraged him to leave me: "He always does what she tells him to."

"When did you first meet the deceased?"

"When she came to the hotel."

The first time I saw Zakia, she was wearing a blue jumper. She had a kind face. It was after her shift in the restaurant. I liked her. We exchanged our little secrets. She complained about how harsh her father had been toward her, about his ghost that slipped into her nightmares, about his words she heard in her head over and over that told her she was a failure. I would comfort her, taking it upon myself to deliver Bachir's letters to her when they were apart, sneaking a peek at them as my heart burned with jealousy. I hoped for a man like him, enamored with the one he loved, faithful to the woman, and sympathetic through her ups and downs. But being so close did not prevent her from treating me harshly at times. She acted as if she were my guardian. She thought she was right about everything and would flare up in anger if someone disagreed with her or spread rumors about her. When I happened upon her standing next to Maimoun in the hotel garden, brushing her tongue over her upper lip and letting out little laughs, I figured she had become one of his mistresses. At first, I helped her with her singing; then she stole my spot as the top act in the nightclub. She even criticized my performances. Sometimes I likened her to a gecko and other times to a viper that spits its venom at whoever vies with it for rank or honor. I was convinced Bachir would regret choosing her.

"How did you take the news of her death?"

"I'm still sad."

When I heard the news, I burst into tears, but I didn't tell the lawyer the whole truth, which is that I never forgave the deceased for coming between Farhat and me. And when my mother, who cleaned Zakia's room, told me she had seen a white dress hanging in her closet, I thought the time of her wedding with Bachir had arrived, so I dashed off a letter to her, imitating his style and signing his name. I slipped it under the door to her room, hoping to stir up a new fight between them. I didn't imagine he'd get so angry as to kill her. Afterward, Fatiha told me she found that same dress in the dumpster behind the hotel. No one ever found out what I had done, but the feeling of guilt has been with me ever since. The day after Zaza's death, Farhat followed me as I left the Casbah neighborhood. He was hoping to reconcile and addressed me in an obsequious voice. "Starting tomorrow, you'll return to your spot at the hotel nightclub," he told me. "I certainly won't go back to you," I responded and walked away, wanting to get as far away from the nightclub as possible. Ever since I started work there, I've learned how to lie. I lie to the customers by putting on a fake smile and appearing in front of them as a charming girl with a verve for life. Whenever I set out to sing, I assume a role that is not my own. Still, I pity the people who come, staring at me and drooling over my breasts, showering me with bills, turning into children when they fill their heads with drink so they might forget everything they are deprived of or how much they've failed with their lovers or wives.

I removed my gloves because of the heat, revealing the inflammation that had crept from my fingers to my wrist and which I had been hiding for the last two weeks. I grumbled that I had not recovered from it and was furious at myself that I'd been responsible for Zakia's death. "She was jealous of me," I said.

As I scratched my right eyebrow, making sure not to catch the mole in its center with my nail, I listed my virtues, things that made me better than her: I'm from this city. My father and my father's fathers were buried here. She was a stranger here. I'm better at singing scales than she is. The victim was solidly a mezzo-soprano, whereas I could jump from soprano to mezzo-soprano as I learned how to do in the Scouts and from listening to the most famous singers. The dead woman's voice was husky and came only from her throat, whereas my voice could change from soft to husky, rising from deep inside me. I've memorized Warda the Algerian's songs and dreamed of meeting her, just as I dream of singing on the radio or television, whereas she only knew a few singers. Her father wasn't wrong when he described her as a failure, whereas my father wasn't interested in me at all. He didn't know whether I was a success or a failure.

Noura continued to watch my movements, especially my fingers. "The only one who feels jealousy is the one whose heart has died."

"She had no heart."

"What do you mean?"

Merzaka Soualem – may God have mercy on her – who the lawyer said she didn't know, liked my voice. She said she'd act on my behalf and get me a gig singing in a nightclub downtown that was popular with senior officials, and that she'd split the pay with me. But Zaza objected, applying pressure and going there instead of me, knowing she would make a lot of money there.

"Where is it?"

"Only Merzaka and Zakia knew." I played with a silver chain that hung from my neck and added: "After she started singing there, she began to regularly argue with Merzaka."

"Did she ever complain to Maimoun Belassal about her?"

"All I know is that Zakia killed Merzaka. It's not true that she killed herself by jumping from the balcony of her room."

NEWS FROM THE SOUTH

YOUNG WOMAN'S BODY FOUND

Ten days ago, security forces discovered the body of a twenty-four-year-old woman dumped in the meadow on the edge of the city, and the relevant authorities have not yet issued a statement. Nevertheless, an informed source who refused to be identified reported that the victim, known as Z.Z., was working at the Sahara Hotel and that she was from the town of Nezrama. She was killed by blunt force trauma to the back of her head. While the authorities have initiated investigations with the workers in the hotel itself, we cannot rule out foul play in that meadow where faith-healers known for their rough behavior operate. Men and women of all ages flock to them. It is worth mentioning that this is the fifth body found by city security this year, after the discovery of the body of a man in his sixties who committed suicide in his house, the body of a baby in the garbage dump, the body of a man in his twenties who was the victim of a hit and run, and the body of a child who had drowned in one of the pools in the valley. — TIJANI K.

BACHIR

A guard shouted my name, and those around me looked in my direction.

I slumped forward. I felt like I had lost weight, and my short-cropped hair had grown back. I slapped my cheeks to get the blood flowing to them and rubbed my eyes I only seldom closed these days. I get a few hours of sleep at the most, waking drenched in sweat, terrified from nightmares, woken by prisoners' banter or searches by the guards. I want to swallow some pills that will plunge me into a sleep as deep as that of the People of the Cave in the Qur'an. Being in prison feels like being inside my grave.

As soon as I set foot outside, Slit-Nose's mocking voice reached me: "There are people who have family, and people who are cut off from the tree." I paid no attention to what he said; the branch of passion that had connected me to Zakia was severed, and she'd been my only family. I wasn't interested in asking him his name, but I did learn that he was accused of setting his divorced neighbor's house on fire, thinking she was engaging in prostitution. The fire had left her infant child severely wounded.

I walked down the long corridor behind the guard, whose full lips were like the guy who, when I was six, circumcised me with scissors that looked like sheep shears. Instead of turning right into the room where I had met with my cousin, he continued straight, then turned left. I entered a vestibule that led to a glass divider. Prisoners removed from two other cells stood in a straight row, their backs to me. At the end of the row was an empty corner where I found an intercom. As soon as I looked up, I saw my mother on the other side of the divider, pressing the receiver to her ear. "Mom!" I yelled, but she couldn't hear me. I could hardly contain myself; I wanted to leap toward her and embrace her. I was delighted that she had forgotten how upset she was with me. Anxiously, I picked up the receiver and asked her how she was doing, and about my father and siblings. She assured me they were fine.

She spoke in a lowered voice. My cousin had gone to the courthouse with her to get a visitor's permit.

"I'm innocent."

"God decrees and does what He wills," she responded in a defeated tone.

This was the first time she had ever visited a prison. She looked uneasy, perhaps because she didn't know how many times she would be coming to see me here. My relatives don't believe I'm just a suspect, except for Noura's mother. The court of public opinion says that everyone in jail is a criminal.

She asked me how I was doing and how I spent my days. I didn't tell her about the overcrowding in the seven-person room I now shared with sixteen men (there had been twelve when I got here), those charged with minor crimes and more serious ones all mixed together. I didn't tell her how the water has been cut off and only runs for half an hour every two days. I didn't tell her how the heat makes me hate my own body. Or about the fights that break out among the prisoners and end in bloodshed or broken bones. Ass-backward! Or the food that is nothing more than salty dough, as if it has been baked with Zakia Zaghouani's tears. I didn't tell her about the snoring that fills the place with noise, or the persistent farting. Or about The Pharmacien, his quest to impose his leadership on us, and his wild ravings as he sleeps. Or about Rahhal, who eases my isolation, sharing a plastic bucket with me to piss in to avoid the crowded bathroom, who always has a *miswak* stick dangling from his lips like a cigarette, who spends his days fasting and leading prayers by symbolically washing on the floor without performing the *wudu*. ("The guards don't let us have a *tayammum* stone to use in place of water, they're scared we'll use it as a weapon.") Out of kindness, I've started to accompany him in prayer. I didn't tell her about the light that's never turned off. I didn't tell her about that prisoner who stabbed his sister and won't stop hitting his head against the wall until he bleeds and loses consciousness, or the guards who barge in whenever they want, claiming to be conducting a search. Or about the twenty minutes of free time we get to walk in the yard, or about my giving into sobbing, or about a fear that washes over me, the fear that my cousin will give up my case and I won't find another lawyer to represent me. As I scratched my neck, I buried all that deep down inside me and summarized the answer for her: "In patience and steadfastness."

I pressed my hand on the glass divider. I wanted to touch her cheek to comfort myself, calling to mind how when I was young she used to sing in my ear while she picked the lice out of my hair: "*Such a handsome boy, Bachir, O Bachir... He's brought nothing but good cheer.*" Or she would tell me stories of the ghoul with the head of a bull, the body of an old man, and the legs of a goat. I paid no attention to the prisoners next to me and ignored the guards lined up behind us. I wanted to say so many things to her, but I didn't know where to start.

Before I could ask her to tell Noura to come back and visit me, the fire-engine-like siren blasted. A guard walked up to me and grabbed the receiver from my hand, announcing the end of the visit that had lasted no more than a few minutes, most of which we had spent in silence. "You'll finish what you were saying next time," he screamed in my face. I kept yelling along with the other prisoners, but my mother couldn't make out what I was saying. She sat glued to her chair on the other side, looking at me as if I were being driven like a sheep back to where I had come from. "We'll search the basket and then bring it to you," the guard told me. I wasn't even thinking of the basket she had brought. I wanted nothing other than for my cousin to come so I could give her the details that had come to mind about the murder victim.

I found Slit-Nose sitting on my bed. "Any sweets?" he asked me with sleepy eyes.

"The basket still hasn't come."

As if I had asked him about his future, he began to ramble absentmindedly about what he was going to do when he got out, about how he wanted to learn how to cook and open a small restaurant close to the bus station.

A guard came in carrying a basket for me. I picked out what clothes and chocolate I needed while putting aside the other food and the rest of the sweets and bread for Slit-Nose and some prisoners next to him who had flocked to me like sheep walking across a desert wasteland.

Now that I knew who had put an end to Zakia's life, why was the lawyer taking so long to come back and see me?

IBRAHIM

The municipality published the names of the people in the graves my mother had heard about in the hammam, and after performing forensic tests on the remains, it was determined that they were martyrs. My father's name was not among them. She would be subject to yet another disappointment, I predicted. I sat on the bed in the shop's back room, clutching the guitar by its neck the way a hunter clutches a gun barrel. I listened to the notes I played, moving my tongue around in my mouth to warm up before singing out: "*Love is still pure... The air is still warm...*" Then I listened to the recording of myself, reassured that my playing was getting better. I resolved to spend an hour every day going over the song. Just then, an old man with a wrinkled brown complexion, dry lips, graying hair, and a neck rumpled like an unironed dress rushed in to shake my hand and introduce himself.

"Daoud, Nabil's father."

I couldn't see any resemblance between him and his son, and figured my friend had inherited his mother's genes.

"I hope Nabil is enjoying his vacation," I said, putting on a smile and trying to present myself as a polite young man.

"He's engaged in a fight with Azrael right now."

His eyes darted around as he said this, breaking the upsetting news that his son was in a serious condition after a fall from high up at a construction site.

"He landed on his head, and blood went everywhere."

"He came to build his house, and I'm afraid he's built his tomb," I replied.

Nabil had told me about building a house large enough for his entire family, not just for himself. Had he been afraid I would be jealous?

"Every disaster that doesn't end in death is a blessing."

"He had me come to you."

Did he think I had acquaintances who might provide him with decent medical care?

Daoud returned *The Sheik* to me. On the first page, after regaining consciousness but unable to speak, his son had written that he needed money to buy medications that weren't available at the hospital. He had spent all the hard currency he had brought with him on the contractor, his workers, and construction materials.

"That disaster preceded him before he even left."

I had assumed my friend would help me with my plans to emigrate, but our roles had been reversed. I had to stand beside him now, but I only had a few dinars in the cash register. I asked the old man, a traditional traveling dentist, to come back at sunset. I headed to the contraband market with nothing to give Nabil except for what I might get for selling the watch he had given me as a gift.

It was almost two in the afternoon, and people were walking back and forth in the market like chickens in a coop. Voices and vendors' shouts blended together. I looked around before settling down next to a snack shop that smelled of fried potatoes and had neither sign nor name. Customers stood inside, eating. I took off the watch and offered it to people walking by. Not two minutes passed before a young man stopped in front of me. He had the pimply face of someone who was addicted to masturbating, and he had bad breath.

"How much?"

"Make me an offer!"

In the contraband market, nothing has a fixed price; everything is subject to negotiation. He offered me three bills.

"That isn't enough for the band."

He threw me an angry look and suggested I trade it for a hair dryer, but I rejected that idea. Four other people came one after the other, each naming a price, which caused the figure to rise. I told them the watch was Swiss-made, since people generally preferred anything from Europe. Then, a smallpox-scarred man who looked to be in his fifties came along. He offered me a price that was almost what I'd paid for my second-hand guitar. He wanted the watch to give as a gift to his son, who was going to get married. "May the bliss last forever," I said to him, before deciding to give it up to whoever paid just a little bit more, which happened to be a woman wrapped in a white sheet that covered her entire body except for her two brown eyes. She paid me what I wanted and told me in a husky voice about her jewelry business. "It might fetch me a better price from another buyer," she told me.

I returned to the Desert Rose, fried potato sandwich tucked under my arm, pleased with the money I had pocketed. Why not move my shop to this market? I asked myself. It would get more foot traffic. But that would make it difficult for me to meet with Noura, because people in this city fix their eyes on women from elsewhere more than they do their own. In the distance, I could see Nabil's ghost lying in a hospital bed.

NOURA

Hassina told me the story of Merzaka Soualem, who had worked in education and volunteered with the Women's Union for Raising Awareness of Expectant Mothers until two years ago, when she had thrown herself off the balcony of the hotel room where she lived after her divorce. In their report, the police wrote that the victim had suffered various injuries, including a fractured skull, and had broken her left upper arm.

She told me that Soualem had been a municipal representative. My father had also been a municipal representative but had left his post following a scandal. He'd probably known her better than I had. I picked up a newspaper from Hassina's desk to fan myself with and, on the bottom of the front page, I glimpsed a picture of a frowning Margaret Thatcher. I asked Hassina: "Why'd she commit suicide?"

"God only knows."

I didn't want to stay too long. I was surprised Hassina had parted her hair in the front and left it unbrushed in the back. Her breasts looked like two air bags. There was a cold sore on her lower lip, and I learned she'd had a fever all night before it had finally broken. No doubt she's getting more anxious as the engagement date approaches, I thought. I had to think of an appropriate gift to get her.

At this point I was leaning toward Cheikha Edahabia's theory: Zaza had paid the price for her involvement in Merzaka's death. Then there was the fact that the singer's honor had not been violated before she died, which made it more likely the perpetrator was a woman. Cheikha Edahabia was probably holding something back. I was lost and unable to grab onto a single thread that might help me in Bachir's defense. Fatiha, who cleaned the victim's room, had been of no use at all to me. I figured that Maimoun Belassal had advised his employees to remain silent.

I went back to my office, and the telephone immediately rang. I let out a deep sigh as my mother informed me of news that sent shivers down my legs: "The police have arrested your aunt's husband."

Bachir in jail, and now his father too. I couldn't imagine why he had been arrested.

My mother, who prolonged her silence mixed with sobs, echoed her words from before: "Get yourself ready."

I called Hassina, whom I had left in peace due to the number of cases she was now responsible for. I was sure no secret would slip by her unheard. "Could you call Hamid and ask why he arrested Bachir's father?" I pleaded with her like a drowning person praying desperately for divine intervention; she knows every official in the city, and they know her. She told me she'd call back in a bit.

After what seemed like hours, the telephone rang again, and I answered it excitedly without asking who it was.

"Put my mind at ease."

"He didn't pick up."

I wanted to let loose an insult that humans and jinn alike would hear, or smash my head against the wall. I broke a pot with a cactus in it which I had acquired two months ago to brighten things up. I stepped on it and knocked the smooth, serrated leaves on my desk to the ground. In this country, it's dog eat dog! I thought. My only option at this point was to walk down to the station myself and meet with that inspector I always made a concerted effort to avoid.

As I walked to the city center, I saw the usual bunches of unemployed people gathering in front of the wall surrounding the Foreigners' Villa; they had no park or public plaza to go to. They were dealing in foreign coins and counting the women passing by as a shepherd would count heads of sheep. They would imagine them stripped of their clothing. I thanked God when I found a taxi, since taxi licenses are hard to come by – in fact, they are monopolized by people with connections – and headed straight to my destination. I paid the driver without waiting for change, and he was pleased with what I had lavished upon him, sending me off with good wishes.

At the station entrance, I stood in front of a cheerful-looking policeman. He took a close look at my ID card and wrote down on a separate piece of paper why I had come. He called Hamid's office, but no one answered. It was almost ten in the morning. "You can either wait or come back another time," the policeman said.

I withdrew to the narrow waiting room, whose bare walls were the same light-green color as those in hospitals. It was quiet save for the sound of feet moving back and forth in the hallway. Four other people were there with me. A look of irritation rose on their faces, like water boiling, as they sat there stiff and motionless. They had come in compliance with summonses they had received and were all feeling the same anxiety.

After waiting twenty minutes, I returned to the policeman sitting at the front desk. He was flipping through a sports magazine. I asked him if the inspector had come back. Lazily, he redialed the phone, then allowed me to go up to the first floor.

Hamid's office seemed dreary to me. On one wall was a picture of smiling children raising the national flag, but no other decor that might make one feel at ease. There were papers on his table and files all strewn about. The hustle and bustle of the street came through the open window.

"I'm a lawyer. Noura Arkoub. I've come about Makhlouf Labtam."

The inspector lit a cigarette and offered me one, but I declined. He met me with a smile, but I kept my lips closed. He busied himself by shuffling through his papers, repeating the name "Makhlouf Labtam." He went on like that for a few seconds, then lifted his head like a student struck by the solution to a math problem.

"Ah, they brought him in today."

"And they left his wife in tears."

He grinned as if mocking me. "The important thing is that he's safe."

"Might I know why you took him into custody?"

He treated my question coldly and handed me a bottle of water from under his wooden desk.

"No, thank you," I said.

Then Hamid suggested we sit down on the sofa. Keeping my anger in check, I cradled my handbag in my arms like someone rocking an infant to sleep. With his legs apart, he started to speak to me in an accent from the capital. His voice was hoarse, like someone who smokes too many cigarettes.

"A doctor heard him describing the residents of the meadow as 'sons of bitches' the day a young woman's body was discovered there."

"Is that sufficient cause?"

"Perhaps he knows something we don't."

"Is he a suspect?"

"We're interested in hearing what he has to say."

Hamid placed one leg over the other and assured me that my aunt's husband would be released as soon as he signed an interrogation report. I thought about asking him if I could call my mother from his phone, but the request seemed unthinkable in the presence of a man whose cunning and shrewdness I had heard so much about.

He put out his cigarette and proceeded to fiddle with his wedding ring, taking it off and putting it back on his finger, like someone wanting to get rid of it. Then he started a monologue about the weather.

"Heat and locusts. Does God want to punish us?" True, the sky hadn't coughed up any water for six months.

I looked at him in silence before he abruptly moved on to something else.

"How's the lawyering going?"

"Fine."

I know full well that he realizes all the hardships we endure, from the government's calcification to the anxieties of clients who want quick settlements for their cases at the lowest cost. People in this city would rather have a man than a woman for a lawyer. I would have to rip my breasts off for them to trust me completely.

The inspector's telephone rang, and he said to the person on the other end, "A routine measure, and then he'll return home." He turned back to me, rubbing his hands together.

"The lawyer, Hassina Eidache. Just checking up on Makhlouf Labtam."

Certain my makeup would not hide my discomfort and that he was aware I had asked her to call him, I regretted asking Hassina for help. I was also sorry I had left the house that morning without putting on a girdle to keep my tummy from sagging and that I hadn't thoroughly checked my face for pimples, as I usually do.

"She's your friend, as far as I understand?"

"More than a friend."

I regarded his thick eyebrows. His face wasn't as handsome as I usually like. His gray hair made him look more dignified, but his mustache was as thick and black as an ant colony; it made him look years older than he was. I prefer men without mustaches.

He assumed a servile role and projected a gentlemanly air: "We're at your service whenever you need us."

I didn't need him to provide any service for me. I hated him to the core.

Hamid obviously felt the silence stretch out between us and tried to break it by asking, "Where do you live?"

"In First of November."

He proceeded to go into great detail about the patrols that roamed that neighborhood and the neighborhoods adjacent to it, sweeping up drug dealers and arresting young men who show off by carrying knives. His investigations into the Zaghouani case kept him from continuing those patrols, he said. Then he told me about the case of the faith-healer Sidi Zerzour, whom they had put in jail: "Imagine, he knows French, Spanish, and German. He's amassed a fortune from what he does."

After tying her hands and feet, stripping her of her clothes, and writing talismans on her breasts, the inspector told me,

Sidi Zerzour had used a solid brass hammer to beat a woman to death after she had entered his house. At first the police thought she had come looking for amulets, until it became clear she was his sister. Their relationship had soured due to inheritance issues.

I'd heard of the faith-healer who moved to a house next to ours the evening a mourning period was declared following Marshal Tito's death. I didn't care about Zerzour going to prison, but I resented police abuse, and it occurred to me that the opportunity was ripe to express my dissatisfaction to Hamid.

"Sometimes you wrongfully jail people."

He could tell from my tone that I was annoyed. I clasped my hands to show him the strength of my words. He could have responded with the stock phrase *Error brings us closer to the truth*, but he preferred not to allow me to doubt his work: "Anyone in particular?"

I did not mention a specific name, but I continued to challenge him sternly until my tongue unexpectedly got away from me. "And Bachir Labtam? Was he not wrongfully imprisoned?"

He looked me straight in the eyes. "We have evidence against him."

"Such as?"

"A threatening letter to the victim."

"That's not sufficient evidence."

The sly smile Hamid had met me with did not leave his face as he informed me that Bachir had been under the influence of alcohol before the tragedy. I figured they'd analyzed his urine the day he was jailed. I remained silent as I rubbed my cheeks and avoided cracking my knuckles as I usually did. I didn't want him to see how agitated I was.

"We have another piece of evidence."

"What's that?"

"The victim telephoned Bachir's family home hours before her death." Hamid informed me that he had looked at the numbers dialed from the phone booth next to the hotel, and the Labtams' number had been one of them. He also said that my cousin had written in his letter to her: "*If you try calling me again, you will pay the consequences.*" Still, I wasn't entirely convinced. He added defensively: "He stole her innocence, then doubted her loyalty to him, so he killed her."

The medical examiner who examined her body had confirmed that she had lost her virginity.

I began to suspect that Bachir's case was getting more complicated. I kept my lips closed, not believing what he said. He then came back more forcefully, saying, "I'll give you a phone number so you can speak with her mother and check."

At this point I realized that he and the dead woman's mother had exchanged words, and that this was where he had heard that the suspect had deflowered Zakia. I was in so much of a hurry to call Zakia's mother that I didn't get a chance to ask the inspector about Merzaka Soualem.

I remembered what Hassina had said: "Most crimes you hear about, or that are established for the defense, are nothing more than a settling of family or clan accounts."

IBRAHIM

I decided to publish an announcement in the newspaper about our search for my father's grave, but my mother resisted: "We ask for the intercession of Our Lord and the angels."

Khamisi returned from the boxing championship, having earned a certificate of participation. He accused the referee of bias: "Anyone who wants to win in this country has to live in the north!"

This is an opinion shared by many young people in the south. They feel that they are no more than fingernails that need to be clipped, and that their peers in the coastal cities get more than their fair share of success. Still, he couldn't hide how happy he was to have reached the quarterfinals in the lightweight division before being defeated by an opponent from the capital.

"I know how to become a professional boxer."

"On the streets?" I asked him sarcastically.

I don't doubt his ability. I've seen him beat his opponent in more than one fight. He knows when to go on the offensive and when to fall back in the ring. He protects his face with light movements and blocks direct punches with his long arms, following Muhammad Ali's advice to "float like a butterfly, sting like a bee."

"No. In an international championship."

"As a spectator?"

My response annoyed my mother, who was sitting cross-legged in the kitchen listening to our chat coming from the house's interior. "He's my son, and I know him better than anyone. He'll become a champion," she said.

She defends him more than she defends me. The angrier she gets, the more she unloads profanities on me. Same old song about how tired she is of raising me and that I don't acknowledge how much she provides. "You're the best mom," I tell her, and her anger transforms into a silent smile. Sometimes, I imagine that if I'd been given the opportunity to raise my younger brother, he would have become a musician or a singer. But she singled him out. She had hopes of him becoming a doctor, but instead he became a porter during the day and a boxer in his free time.

Unusually for me, I locked up the Desert Rose that after-noon and decided to go buy a cake to celebrate Khamisi and motivate him.

"Well, if it isn't Comrade Ibrahim."

Boulanouar, the broad-faced pastry chef, set upon me. He didn't have a mustache, and his thick eyebrows reminded me of Brezhnev. It was the end of his workday and he was busy cleaning the shop, whose air was freshened by four fans in each corner. He had a young assistant with him who'd been born deaf and mute and only spoke using sign language. We called him John Travolta because of the way he combed his hair like that actor in *Saturday Night Fever*. Sometimes Boulanouar would give me an unsold cookie and insist I bring him films on pastry-making, to which I would courteously respond: "They need to make a movie about you."

"I'd like a pistachio cake," I said.

"Are you planning to propose to a young woman?"

Laughing, I told him about my intention to honor my brother. "And I won't give up my bachelorhood," I added.

I envy Boulanouar for the spoils he enjoys even though he didn't participate in the War of Independence. He occupies a shop previously owned by a Jewish man who taught him how to make pastries before he emigrated following independence; an unknown person had attacked the man's wife and two sons with a knife and drawn a swastika on the wall of his house. Boulanouar also inherited a farm outside the city without paying a single dinar for it. Some say he plants tobacco there with the help of some sharecroppers. Others say he grows hashish. Whenever I think of how blessed he is, I get angrier at my father. "Clever people managed to appropriate stores, houses, and land. The wool business was enough for my father," I once complained to my mother. "Your father was a virtuous man, martyred before independence," she responded, her angry face as red as a ripe tomato. "He lived virtuously, and we got nothing but filth for it," I answered, for which she showered me with insults.

Boulanouar tied a decorative blue ribbon around the cake box, refusing to take money for it. Then he said to me inquisitively, "Last time I saw you, you were getting out of a police car."

I was irritated by his observation, having thought the matter was over and done with, so I lied to him. "They got the names all mixed up. They were looking for someone else."

He was silent for a bit, then went on: "Have you heard the rumors?"

"No, I haven't."

"The merchants are going on strike."

"When?"

"Next month."

"Why?"

"Scarcity of staple foods."

Nothing more than rumors. But in any case, I didn't intend to close my shop. If I stopped working, I wouldn't have the money to pay the remainder of what I owed in bribes to get my military service exemption. I had started toward the door when he stopped me.

"They're saying they're going to change the weekend day off from Friday to Sunday."

"Didn't that use to be the case?"

"But we're Muslims."

Muslims don't deal in tobacco and hashish either, I wanted to say to shut him up, but I made do with waving my hand and saying, "Our Lord will bring goodness."

As I walked through downtown, teenagers were running from Fifth of July Street – or Georges Clemenceau Street, as it used to be called – toward the post office, throwing rocks at some policemen. They looked like they were in high school. The march they'd been on, which had quickly turned violent, had been calling for the use of Arabic in schools and the removal of French. My studies, too, had been in French, but my friends and I weren't going out into the streets to protest. My teacher at the time, Merzaka Soualem, had instilled in me a love for learning languages, and I'd put her advice to good use. I hurried away from the teenagers, a touch of sadness swirling inside my head: Why hadn't Fate allowed my father to live after independence so he could enjoy the good life like Boulanouar?

KAMAL

That morning, I woke up having seen my dead mother walking next to me on a crowded sidewalk wearing a flower-print dress. She was looking at me and laughing. Suddenly she broke into a run, indifferent to my muffled screaming for her to stop, or to the vehicles in the street. After just a few moments, she was hit by a car. I couldn't make out what kind it was. Then she got up and continued running, letting out a piercing laugh. It was as if she wanted another car to hit her.

I went over the dream in my head for some sort of interpretation, but it was no use. There was a kink in my neck and the taste of beer in my mouth, which I got rid of by drinking some bitter tea and eating half a box of cookies. I decided to ask Maimoun about it. I knew him as a pious man who understood what was concealed in dreams. He prays regularly at the Grand Mosque and never tires of talking to the imam about the need for people to return to the Creator's door and perform prayers for rain.

It was 8:30. I pressed play on the tape player I'd recently bought at the contraband market. Umm Kulthum's voice filled me with delight. It reminded me of Bachir, with whom I would spend evenings listening to her songs. My heart still ached over his arrest.

My darling, everything is fated / It is not by our hands that
as unfortunates we were created.
Perhaps, one day, our fates will bring us together / after such
a long time apart.

A voice inside convinced me that Noura was involved with
a lawyer like herself or a man in a high position and that I
had to forget all about her. My shortness of breath returned,
which I attributed to the dust that filled the air after every
gust of wind. I put off going back to the doctor for a checkup
because I'd have to wait a long time for an appointment. I
told my boss I might be late and put the waiter, Khalil, in
charge of filling in for me while I was gone. I needed to go
to the police station to give my statement concerning Zaza.

I stood in front of the mirror, the upper corner of which
was cracked. I was determined to soften how I spoke to
Hamid – or, as I called him, The Scorpion. He hadn't been
nice to me since I'd refused to give him a room key without
Maimoun's permission so he could be alone with one of his
mistresses. "I'm the master of this hotel!" he'd yelled, the
smell of wine on his breath. "I am not so honored as to work
under a boss such as you," I'd replied sarcastically.

After checking to make sure my hair was combed back the
way I liked it, I turned off the tape player and left. I knocked
on the door of my neighbor, Zayyan, who has a square face
that reminds me of a cartoon character. I rent my place from
him and play with his kids whenever I see them. I buy them
presents and candy, which endears me to them.

I asked when the bricklayer would come to build a higher
wall for my house.

"Remember that cement is unavailable!" Zayyan told me.
I wasn't surprised that cement was as scarce as fresh, pure

water, as the buildings of the nouveau riche and people returning from living abroad were sprouting up everywhere. All building materials were scarce in this city, which was otherwise jam-packed with iron and locusts.

"You need to be patient."

I waved goodbye to him and went on my way, lamenting the state of the municipal library, whose sign had lost a letter so it read LIB ARY. The door was ajar. No one went there anymore, except for teenagers who occupied its half-darkened corners, stealing kisses or copping feels, pretending to read books.

When I got to the police station, I presented my summons to the policeman at the front desk, and he asked me to wait for him to finish his phone call. Then he ordered me to go up to the first floor, where I found Hamid rubbing his cleanly shaved chin.

Hamid sat with one leg over the other, arms crossed. I made it clear that I had to get to work before midday, and he said it wouldn't take long. Then he started asking questions, fixing his eyes on mine, which prompted me to respond quickly.

"I didn't see you at Zakia Zaghouani's funeral!" he said.

"I was busy submitting a complaint." That day, I had spent an exhaustingly long time waiting to complete a transaction that should have taken no more than half an hour.

On the night Zaza died, I'd been on duty until seven in the morning because some tourists arriving from the capital were late. After a short break in the hotel, I'd continued my work until the afternoon. When I returned home, someone had snuck inside, taken advantage of the low exterior wall, and smashed some appliances. It had been a Friday, a day off, so the policeman on duty said he couldn't register my complaint, claiming that the one in charge of conducting investigations wasn't in. He asked me to return the following day, when I had to wait again to complete the paperwork.

The Scorpion searched through his drawer for a copy of the complaint and replied: "We receive complaints every day, and some slip under my radar."

He made sure it matched what I had provided.

"Who do you think did it?"

"I suspect a neighbor of mine."

I told him what had happened the day before the incident, when I'd invited Bachir over.

"Bachir Labtam?"

The inspector raised his eyebrows when he learned that we were friends. He threw his cigarette butt into the marble ashtray without putting it out. I continued with my account of what had happened that day: After my friend had finished his third glass, he let out a bitter wail expressing how much he missed his beloved. This angered my neighbor, Derraji, who's a similar age to me and of similar height and appearance, so much so that one of the neighbors suspected we had come out of the same womb. He banged on my door and, in a voice thickened with beer, demanded I respect the propriety of the neighborhood. Bachir got angry, convinced he hadn't knocked on the door to complain but to threaten us. "If you don't like how we're acting, move somewhere else," he told Derraji. They then proceeded to exchange insults.

I implored my friend to stop, but he went too far, and the exchange of words turned into a fistfight. Derraji walked out and was gone for a few moments before coming back holding a knife. With the experience of a butcher, he brought it down on Bachir's left shoulder, causing him to fall howling to the ground. I tried to staunch the bleeding with a rag and some toothpaste, but the flow wouldn't stop, so I took him to the hospital at a little after four in the afternoon. I didn't see him after that. When I returned home, Derraji berated me: "You're a wretch, and you bring nothing but wretches to the neighborhood!" "When you've calmed down, we'll talk," I responded and made my way to the Desert Rose to return some rented movies. After that, I settled in at the hotel, only to learn the following day what happened to Zakia and find that some person had snuck into my house.

Right then, Hamid brought up what Bachir had yelled when he took his statement: "I didn't attack that drunk. He attacked me!"

When I'd got home, I'd discovered some smashed electronic equipment. Someone had also broken the window of my car, which was parked next to the house.

Hamid alerted me to the fact that both of our cars are Fiats, although they're different colors. "Is there a gang specializing in vandalizing these cars?" he whispered. Then he wrote down the full name of my neighbor who I suspected: Derraji Aouina. He cleared his throat and moved on to asking me about Bachir's relationship with Zakia.

"I know that he loved her."

"What else?"

"I didn't stick my nose into their business."

I stuck to answering questions without implicating myself so much that I might be required to stand as a witness in court. Thus, I didn't get into the story of the wedding dress I'd received from a delivery worker in the victim's name and paid for from the hotel's cash register, as Maimoun told me to. I knew her plan to marry Bachir had hit a snag, so who had she intended to marry then? No doubt Maimoun knew, but it wouldn't have been polite to ask and have him think I was meddling in things that didn't concern me. I was one of the reasons she had settled in this city, but she hadn't trusted me for a single day. I'd behaved too imperiously toward her, as I did with the rest of the staff, and she'd died hating me. I'd kept the story of the white wedding dress from Labtam as well.

The police inspector fidgeted in his chair and ended the session. He thanked me, and when I headed toward the door to leave, he stopped me.

"Do you think your friend killed her?"

"I think we lost an irreplaceable woman."

I went back to the hotel and met Maimoun in his office.

"That idiot, Hamid, let you go?"

"He's the same as always."

"He won't summon you again?"

"I hope not."

I told Maimoun about my dream without mentioning my mother's name, sufficing to say "a woman dear to me." He told me that dreams purify hearts and that God sends our loved ones into our dreams to remind us of the impermanence of earthly desires. Then he asked me if I had gotten my car back from the repair shop.

"Not yet."

"Use my car if you need it."

He was only making this offer so I would help him with something that would not be easy.

"I had a fight with my wife."

He said it in a lowered voice, legs crossed in front of him. He wanted me to go see her at his brother-in-law's house to convince her to come home. He made me a middleman whenever they fought, not wanting his cousins to get involved lest the story get out.

"I'll see what I can do." Then I added: "There's something I want to tell you."

"What, that you want a bonus this month?" He thought I wanted money as usual.

I never miss an opportunity to chase a bonus for the extra work I do, and my employer complies, just as he looks the other way when I rent out room 302 for double its regular price to lovers who spend a half or full day there, contrary to the law that prohibits unmarried couples from staying alone in hotel rooms.

"That's not what I mean."

"What then?"

"Someone is digging into Merzaka's case."

IBRAHIM

SEPTEMBER 22

In Art Stars next to the Nakhil, I came across some cassette tapes of singers with curious names – Cheikha Pepper, Chebba Longneck, Cheikh Ostrich, the Indian Cheb – but I didn't find anything under the name of Zakia or her alias. All singers fade into oblivion unless we have recordings of them. The only trace she'd left behind was a videotaped concert. Her voice, even with its minor flaws, was likely better than other female singers' voices that fill the country with noise. I wished I could have got to know her better while she was alive so we could rerecord "Salma ya Salama" together. Duets are in vogue right now, although listeners are more interested in what people say about them than the actual music. Had she learned music when she was young, like me? I don't even remember when I started, but no one remembers when they started to eat or walk. I've been listening to the music around me – vocal and instrumental – ever since I was a boy. A teacher at the neighborhood cultural center taught me the basics of the guitar and some simple instrumentals. After that, I learned by listening to well-known artists and by imitating a university student I knew who loved the Beatles. He used to share joints and Valium pills with me. Because we spent so much time together with our musical instruments, our classmates thought we were intimately involved. We hung out with others to convince them otherwise. My mother's words about the victim came back to me: "The Lord blessed her with beauty and people to envy her."

Kamal walked in, and his gaze fell on the movie jackets. The shop filled with the smell of perfume and cigarettes.

He doesn't hide his admiration for how much I know about what intellectuals and scholars have said, things I've gotten from leafing through books. He gains a certain amount of wisdom in discussing them with me, so asks me for advice whenever doubt overwhelms him. We often compare French and English; I help him understand the differences between Shakespeare and Jean Racine. Like me, he's had a predilection for learning languages since he was young. Before turning twenty, he mastered French and whatever he could of English too – this language that so captivated his girlfriends, as he told me. We also loved to chat about movies, fully agreeing that cinema was created to correct the mistakes humans made. Still, I was not thrilled that he rented cassettes without paying what he owed.

"Anything new?"

"There's a Western and an Indian one."

"I mean 'special' movies."

Everyone calls adult movies "special." Kamal persists in watching them because, according to him, they relax him and relieve his fatigue.

"I rented the most recent one to another customer."

"But I'm your most loyal customer."

You're a loyal fucker, I wanted to respond, but instead I said, "You haven't paid what you owe me yet." He always took his time paying, claiming his financial burdens were piling up. He was testing my patience.

"I'll pay you next month." He told me someone had smashed his car window and that fixing it would cost him a lot. *If only your head had been smashed,* I almost said, but before I could, he said: "I'll come back when your customer returns the movies."

I couldn't let him leave without first satisfying my curiosity.

"I heard that a young woman who works at the hotel was killed."

"Death is the fate of us all."

Kamal turned toward the door to leave, slicking his hair back and dragging his Italian-made moccasins on the ground. He cares for his clothes like a fashion model, even more. I stopped him: "Who killed her?"

"Azrael," he scoffed.

I waited until he was out of sight, then called him a pimp under my breath.

I'd first met Kamal the day the Albanian leader, Enver Hoxha, died; I remembered his name because it was the same as my mother's family name. I had gone to the hotel looking for a gig there, handing him a cassette on which I had recorded some pieces. Hadj Maimoun Belassal had invited me into his office. He praised my playing, but then paused when he heard my name. Although he'd promised to let me know if a job opened up, he never did.

There was a commotion coming from the street corner. It was seven in the evening. Anxiously, I hurried over and saw a crowd gathered around the zalabieh shop. I refuse to eat the fritters there because the owner only changes the cooking oil once a week, making some of his customers sick. I made sure no one was coming close to the Desert Rose and headed to the corner, where people were gathering to see what was happening. I grabbed my head in alarm when I spotted a butane gas tank on fire. A short young man was pouring a bucket of water on the flames, but it wasn't doing any good. The yelling grew louder, and someone shouted: "Call Civil Defense!" I felt an explosion was imminent, so I backed up. Right then, an old man in a white cap and with deep wrinkles on his forehead smothered the top of the tank with a wet towel, and the fire went out. The zalabieh vendor kissed his hand, and when I looked at his face, I recognized him as a newcomer to the neighborhood, although we hadn't met yet.

I let out a deep breath and returned to my shop, muttering, "Kamal is a bad omen."

HAMID

I got to my office with a pain in my lower back from a lack
of sleep after Zinab and I had argued. "You spend your days
at work and your evenings out while I sit pregnant at home
taking care of two children on my own. When will you learn
to be a father?" Whenever she gets upset, her chest swells,
and she pours all her anger out on me, so I take refuge in
silence and pity for the fetus sleeping in her belly. I forgot
to buy bottled water the day before, and she laid into me:
"No other woman would put up with you." She told me I
couldn't sleep next to her, so I was forced to sleep on the
living room sofa.

A file was waiting for me on my desk with *Illustrated
Technical Report* written across the top. I skimmed through
the report without finishing it. I turned the page over to see
if there were any attachments, realizing I had never seen
the victim's face before; pictures had been taken of him as
he lay at the base of an electrical pole. I thought of my own
smashed car window. The informants had been of no help,
and I had no time to investigate, preoccupied by Zaza's case.
I had changed the lock on my apartment door and sent
Derraji Aouina – accused by Kamal of violating his property
and insulting him, and of assaulting Bachir – on his way. I
had asked him to come back when summoned, informing

him of the charges leveled against him. I just wanted to be done with this Zaghouani story, which was forcing me to take precautions when I went out and intensify security around my family. I looked out the wide-open window and saw the movement of cars and passersby. How calm life appears when we look at it from above! I thought. I had barely finished my first cigarette when the policeman at the front desk called to inform me that Farhat, no surname, had arrived.

The musician stood before me, his left hand raised in greeting. He had a barrel chest and was tall, like a goalie. He had golden-brown skin, curly hair, small, hollow eyes, and his right forearm was in a cast. I regarded him with a frown, moving my head forward and then quickly side to side. He understood what I wanted to say. He spoke to me in a chastened tone about a traffic accident he had got into on his moped and that had resulted in the doctor putting his arm in a cast for two weeks.

"I was hit by a car close to the meadow," he said. I guessed he had been drunk at the time, because it was his first accident on his blue Peugeot 103 moped. He had been on his way home from the Rubber & Plastic Co., where he spent nights laughing and playing cards with his friends who guarded the place. But I wondered why he'd told me the precise location of the accident. Was he trying to convince me of his innocence?

"Is this why you requested a leave of absence from the nightclub, then?"

"Better than having Maimoun Belassal fire me like Zakia wanted."

Cigarette smoke streaming out of my nostrils, I begged God to show Zakia mercy as I fixed my gaze on the musician's yellowed teeth. Then I asked him to tell me what he could about the rift that had opened up between him and the dead woman who had taken issue with his playing in her final days.

Farhat had spent years playing in an amateur band, performing at weddings and family events for which he received a few dinars and lots of praise. It was his hope to open a recording studio attached to a shop that sold audio cassettes. Then Kamal, who lived next to him in the neighborhood, had introduced him to Maimoun, who immediately hired him after some of his acquaintances vouched for him and his adoptive father. Over time, he became Zaza's right-hand man. Not to overstate things, he said, but once she had canceled a show when he was stricken with a bout of diarrhea. Suddenly, though, she had turned on him. And she had died without revealing why.

"There wasn't any problem between us. It was because of Kamal."

Then he closed the fingers of his left hand. His unclipped nails were black. My eyes flashed. I had wanted to link the receptionist to the crime from the get-go. Despite what the receptionist had revealed in his statement, I wanted to punish him so he would learn to kiss my hand. Unlike the other hotel workers, I found him difficult to tame, which reflected poorly on my own abilities.

"What do you mean?" I asked Farhat.

"She used to describe him as a bastard, a scoundrel, and other nasty things."

Farhat sympathized with his friend without delving into why there was so much hostility between Kamal and Zakia. He begged her to stop insulting him, telling her that he owed the receptionist. She never mentioned him again. He thought their hostility toward one another had cooled down until Kamal had asked him to meet at the Peace of

Mind Café, next to the contraband market, where they serve the best teas to intellectuals and unemployed poets, even though some finish their drinks and then run off without paying. He'd said he wanted to speak about something important.

As Farhat narrated his testimony, I thought I might be getting closer to untangling the hidden threads of the case.

"What did he say when you two met?"

"That Zakia was blackmailing him. He wanted me to stop her from doing that."

Had she needed money? I remembered the considerable sum I'd found in her handbag the day she was killed. Had she taken it from Kamal?

"Why was she blackmailing him?" I wondered as I opened my eyes as wide as I could and stuck out my lips like a hunter approaching his prey.

"He said she wanted to leave singing and build a new life for herself."

I wasn't convinced, even though I couldn't deny that she had hated the receptionist because of his arrogance and the way he took advantage of his relationship with Maimoun, just as she had hated Cheikha Edahabia because she was a better singer than her.

"What did you do to help her?"

"I chided her again, but she couldn't stand how blunt I was with her."

Farhat had not been able to forgive Zakia for assailing his friend, and she had criticized his playing to the hotel owner.

"I knew her when she was a good person, before she became hateful."

I recited the words of Abderrahman El Mejdoub to myself:

*O heart, I will strike you with fire, and if you heal, I'll do it
again.*

*O heart, you left me in a shameful state. You want someone
who doesn't want you.*

By the end of her life, Zakia's nature had changed entirely,
just as the devilish Iblis had turned on his creator. I scratched
the back of my head and wandered around the office, looking around, puzzled, and muttering as if talking to a jinni.
No doubt Farhat realized I was mulling over something
serious, the consequences of which might fall on Kamal's
head. However, he had no way of escaping suspicion other
than by confessing everything he knew. He had come to the
station knowing I was aware of the rift that had opened up
between him and Zakia prior to her death. He was also sure
that Maimoun was angry with him for having given in to the
singer's desires, and that he would never go back to work at
the hotel.

I calmed myself and sat back down in my chair, giving
Farhat a sideways look. "It seems that you know things I don't."

He did not understand what I meant, which irritated him
like a pebble in a shoe. In a weak, cajoling voice, head bowed,
he asked for clarification, but I raised my hand and looked
sternly in his direction, indicating that I was done listening.

Before Farhat left, I addressed him: "We'll call you in
again when we need you."

I finished writing down the questions I intended to ask
Maimoun and Kamal separately to arrive at the answers I
sought. Suspicions about Farhat also swirled around in my
head. And I was unaware, right then, that my enemies were
preparing a trap for me that would change my life.

IBRAHIM

SEPTEMBER 23

On the radio I always had on to keep me company, I heard some of the president's speech: "General mobilization to face the economic crisis... Directing imports... Reforming the educational system... Encouraging youthful energies..."

"I'm a young man too, and my energy is being squandered," I muttered. I left the house, hair slicked back with Vaseline. There was a police car in front of the Christian cemetery, where people were milling about. Every day, I pass by that place, where French people who were born and died here are buried, and never has it occurred to me to go inside. In my view, it's nothing more than forsaken land, visited only by teenagers hooking up with children in exchange for money or by drunks sneaking in to smash the marble headstones. The complete opposite of the Lalla Ammoura Cemetery, founded by a pure saint who gifted her land to the dead. That cemetery bustles with pilgrims and the devout and stories of people finding talismans among the graves.

I noticed a suntanned teenager who used to come into my shop to rent Bruce Lee movies. His name was Mellah. "Have they gone mad?" I asked him.

He turned his head to me. Plugging his nose with his thumb and forefinger, he expelled some mucus, which he then wiped on his faded orange T-shirt.

"They pilfered a set of gold dentures from the skeleton."

"It's not enough for them to steal from the living, so they steal from the dead too?!"

I got on a bus next to the Pitcher Roundabout and found an empty seat, something which rarely happens. Those standing usually outnumber those sitting down. I didn't get off until the last stop, close to the hospital built four years ago. Before then, people had sought medical treatment at a clinic run by the missionaries of the Pères Blancs. I continued on foot, passing through the Bellevue neighborhood, where a Soviet company had built gray buildings with apartments that were like matchboxes. These were occupied by nurses, white-collar employees, and a few doctors. I reached Twentieth of August, which has a mosque at its far end. Beyond that, there's a meadow where trees and wild plants proliferate and piles of garbage are scattered about. A roadway along its edge leads to the Rubber & Plastic Co. I was curious about the place where they'd found the hotel singer's body, but I could not find the precise location; my mother had been of no use to me when I'd asked her before leaving the house. Some kids were yelling and playing on top of a pile of sand, tin dwellings scattered behind them. Would it make sense for one of the meadow's residents to also be involved?

My curiosity unsatisfied, I decided to head back.

I walked back through Twentieth of August, my eyes pausing on a house numbered 3/18, the address of Bachir Labtam, who was a suspect. It was attached to a row of other mid-rise houses and topped with a rubber tire to protect it from the evil eye, with three exterior windows enclosed by ornamented metal frames. THROWING GARBAGE HERE IS PROHIBITED was written on the wall. Its architecture indicated that it belonged to a well-to-do family. I hurried to catch a bus next to the hospital, which took me to the post office. Then, I made my way to the Desert Rose and arrived by noon.

There I found a baffling scene. Someone had tried to break the padlock to the shop. "O God!" I said out loud. I turned the lock over in my hands and saw scratches made by a sharp tool that had not managed to break it. I had never heard of attempted burglaries when I rented a shop on Aurès Street, or Anatole France Street as the old-timers used to call it. What had the attacker wanted from a poor shop? Even though the lock was still in place, my heart was racing. I understood that I was the target and needed to take action.

Then I noticed something scrawled on the wall in white paint: IBRAHIM IS THE SON OF A SELLOUT. My face went pale, and the blood rose to my head because of the insult to my father, calling him a traitor. I looked around at the closed shops adjacent to mine, then went in, examining the window and cash register, videocassettes, and VCRs, as well as some other items in the back room, to make sure no harm had come to them. It had been no more than a failed robbery attempt. An image of Six flashed through my mind. He'd regret the day he ever met me.

I walked around the shop for fifteen minutes like a fly buzzing around a pile of shit, then headed to the locksmith who lives in the next neighborhood over. Because he's so fat, people call him The Barrel. I got him to leave his house on his day off to secure my door with a second padlock.

"There are lots of thieves," he stuttered, chewing on a piece of gum.

"Have you been robbed too?" I asked him.

"They robbed a pharmacy across from the Grand Mosque last week."

I hurried him to do what I had asked him to. He also gave me some green paint, which cost me a pretty penny. Money comes and money goes, I said to myself.

With trembling fingers, I painted over the writing on the wall. Then I played a cassette tape of Qur'an recitation and leaned on the entrance table, staring out at the street. I live by the saying *Eat what pleases you, but wear what pleases others.* I engage in my pleasures in private and strive to display my piety publicly; my mind is always filled with anxiety.

It was me against him. I needed to punish Six myself. However, I was not entirely comfortable with that, because he never did anything alone. He was always with a group of friends and would likely incite them against me, which would make things worse.

I settled on filing a complaint against him. But his sister's a lawyer who will exonerate him! I imagined striking a deal with Noura where she would obtain a written testimony from her father to help my mother get her martyr's widow card in exchange for me not implicating her brother in something that would not end well. I pulled a local Hoggar cigarette from my breast pocket and waited till the end of Friday prayer for the customers to arrive.

FAUDEL

Ever since my friends and I smashed the police inspector's car window, the watch patrols haven't come back to the neighborhood. It was all I could think of to exact revenge on the security forces who showed up all of a sudden in the middle of the day or at sunset, ordering us to stop playing dominoes or cards and line up with our faces to the wall. They'd search our pockets and arrest anyone they found in possession of a piece of hashish, or a knife, or a blade. Obviously invigorated by the scene, Hamid would gaze at us, our heads bowed in humiliation. We've often insisted that we're nothing more than the weakest link in the illegal market because we have no gainful employment, but they've made us their number one priority.

I threw two rocks, one the size of an eggplant, at his car window. The first was out of sheer hatred for him. The second was to avenge my friend Lotfi Bechiche, The Pharmacien, who'd been arrested on assault charges even though he'd just been defending himself against the son of the director of the Rubber & Plastic Co., who had bought a box of Cuban cigars from him and refused to pay. Their dispute had escalated and ended in blood flowing from his victim's thigh after Lotfi stabbed him with a shard of glass. I spent the night hiding under a date palm by the river, which flows with distant mountain water mixed with sewage, listening to the rhythmic croaking of frogs and raucous mewing cats as they divided up bags of garbage among themselves. My thinking was that my friend had been discovered dealing in contraband and might betray me. After learning the following morning why he'd been arrested, I returned home. When my mother asked where I'd been, I claimed I'd slept at a friend's place, and when Ibrahim Derras kept asking, I told him, "I was tired and went to bed early," just to shut him up.

The Pharmacien is in jail while his sister is out free. May the Lord provide relief. Her situation keeps me up at night, and I take it upon myself to protect her reputation when he isn't around. He knows she sings in a nightclub, which goes against religious practice, but there's nothing he can do about it. He says that whoever goes out with her outside the confines of marriage or dares to violate what's between her thighs is violating his honor. She doesn't know me, but I know her secret of secrets and the color of her underwear. I've entrusted a young man to ward off anyone who comes knocking at her door or wants to seduce her. I pay him baksheesh in exchange for him standing up against anyone who dares to think she's adrift, cut off from her family. May God guide her.

I feel as if I owe The Pharmacien. I first met him in the contraband market. We exchanged jokes and hung out together on hot evenings. I used to bathe with him in the swimming hole, which claimed the life of a child or two every year. We would smoke and drink under a dateless palm. Everyone bows down to Lotfi, including me. One time, while we were sitting and passing the end of a joint back and forth, he saw a stray light-brown Berber puppy, so he called to it, then he whistled, but it didn't respond. He got right up and stabbed it, and the puppy howled. It died a few minutes later. Then he cut its tail off. I dug a grave for it, the blood practically freezing in my veins! "Why'd you kill it?!" I asked him. "He was hardheaded," he replied.

Lotfi sees nothing wrong with getting into fights with anyone, young or old. One time in the market, he almost strangled a man much bigger than him with a bicycle chain on the pretext that the other man had bumped him with his shoulder and hadn't apologized. People just watched, no one daring to intervene. He taught me the hashish business, and I'm constantly surprised at how voraciously he eats, as if his stomach were a sewer. I've broken into some houses with him, the most recent one being that of an old woman. We snuck in one afternoon while the lady was taking a nap. We thought she had hidden some money and gold in her closet, but we didn't find anything of note, so The Pharmacien took it out on her by stripping off her clothes and tying her hands and feet together. He pulled out one of her thumbnails with a pair of pliers, and we left her there unconscious.

Once he loaned me some money so I could rent a garage and turn it into a screening room at night, charging every one of the viewers a fair price, which I spend on new clothes and birdseed for my pet goldfinch. I save some of it with the hope that I'll have the opportunity to pay for an overseas visa or board a cargo ship for a fee I'd pay one of the marina workers. God will open the door of good fortune for me. The Lord created me to emigrate. Whenever my mother scolds me ("In France, all you'll find is naked women and wine-drinking men"), my tongue jumps into action to express disapproval of my father, who left her and refused to deal with me as a mature young man: "Sure, they drink wine, but they don't leave their children."

I sat on a rock in the corner of the neighborhood where the houses face one another, their fronts the same green color as the plants and bushes. I was cutting my fingernails with a razor blade – except for the sixth finger, which I keep long for when I need it – and nodding my head in greeting to people passing by. Everyone here knows me. Some of them address me by my given name, others by my primary nickname, Six, and others still by my other nickname, Mouse, because of my prominent front teeth. At first, I took issue with anyone who uttered either of the two nicknames, but with time I got used to them. I thought again about the police summons I had received. No doubt Ibrahim Derras had filed a complaint against me. I tried punishing him by attempting to break the lock to his shop, although I had no intention of robbing him, and I scrawled some words on the wall to rile him up. I heard his father had cooperated with the colonial authorities. But everything backfired on me. Things got all screwed up. I know that an unfriendly fate follows the arrival of a summons. Hamid knows me, and he knows my associates. He wouldn't hesitate to put me in jail. I begged my sister, Noura, to deal with it without our parents finding out: "Do me a solid." I sought to evoke her sympathy as she busied herself with the cat, talking to it as a sensible person might speak to an infant and pointing to where it should relieve itself rather than on the rug. I saw her end a call with a twitching hand, then rush out. She promised me she wouldn't return home until the problem was solved. I used to be friends with Ibrahim, and that Thursday, when The Pharmacien had been arrested, we'd loaded our heads up with beer. We'd laughed like fools. It didn't take long for things to fall apart, though. I'd like to get out of this summons situation, then settle the score with him face-to-face… We'll see who's the stallion and who's the coward, you son of a sellout!

Ibrahim accused me of setting the gas station owner's car on fire, but I had nothing to do with that. I did argue with the owner, Si Miloud, because he'd refused to sell me a tank of butane after I'd stood in line for a full hour under a sun that plunged me into a sweat bath, telling me that the remaining tanks were reserved for other customers. This made me angry, so I pretended to buy a can of gasoline. I got on my moped and went to take off without paying but found myself knuckled and punched like a piece of meat by two workers. I was saved by a bloody nose. My foul-smelling friend, high from sniffing glue, got involved by setting fire to the car that night, but I hadn't asked him to do that. "D'you want to go to jail?" I'd yelled at him. "He deserves more," he said in defense of what he'd done, his breath smelling like a corpse.

Grumpy Big Belly – in his fifties, medium height with a crooked back – was sprinkling water in front of his store.

"Water's been cut off for five days. You must have a well!" I quipped.

"This is Zamzam water," he replied. A relative who'd returned from the Umrah pilgrimage had given it to him as a gift from Mecca. He hoped the water would bring in customers and ward off the evil eye, but it doesn't ward off thieves, and I'm one of them. I remember when, unbeknownst to him, I used to fill my mouth with candy, or I would pull out an extra loaf of bread on top of the loaves I'd paid for, or a cigarette, or a piece of soap. God forgive me.

A locust jumped in front of me and I swatted it with the

palm of my hand, recalling what my mother had told me about how they'd eaten locusts when she was young: "We would fry them with salt, then chew on them." I'd rather go hungry than crunch down on those insects. The mere sight of them makes me sick, even though I once overheard the imam speak well of locusts in a sermon. He mentioned that there are thousands of types of them – brown, red, yellow – and that they are mentioned in the Qur'an. Will God punish me because I crush them wherever I find them?

I decided to walk to the contraband market to satisfy my curiosity about how much things cost there and to meet some friends when I spotted Kamal in the distance. "Movie Star Kamal!" I called out to him, because he looks like an actor from the sixties. I thought he'd come to buy a joint. Then I remembered he'd quit smoking hash. Perhaps he'd come to ask for my help procuring spare car parts from the unlicensed vendors who sold things out of bags. Our relationship had been firmly established two years ago. He would bring me items he stole from the Sahara, such as cookware, pillows, or blankets, and I would sell them at the contraband market. Then we'd divvy up the profits, with him taking seventy percent and me taking thirty.

"Still guarding the neighborhood?" he chided me.

"Who else will do it?"

He used his time off from the hotel to visit Sidi Zerzour, who was more famous than an Algerian soccer star. People from every city in the country, even from abroad, sought him out: women who wanted to get engaged or who wanted a cure for infertility; men who wanted women or sought to get rid of spirits that inhabited them, so they said; students looking to pass their exams; merchants seeking profit; teenage girls who came crying to him for help aborting that which violated God's law; farmers hoping for a good harvest; pregnant women wanting to give birth to a boy. No one knew where Zerzour had come from, but everyone agreed he possessed blessed baraka. Once, he wrote a talisman for Kamal's niece, and she ended up getting married. This time, the receptionist had come looking for something similar so he could enjoy some prosperity in his future, but he had found the door padlocked. He thought the faith-healer had moved, but had missed the news that he was in jail.

"How come?"

"He killed a woman."

"May God forgive him."

Then he asked me about Bachir.

"I've been too embarrassed to go to their house and ask his father about him."

I told him what I'd heard from my mother about the miserable time his parents were going through.

"May the Lord bring relief."

Then our conversation moved to more general things, until he told me about his need for "special" movies to take his mind off his worries. He used to get them from the Desert Rose, something we had in common.

"I went to Brihoum's, but there was nothing new there." He pointed his chin at me.

I was surprised to hear that. "You still go to his place?"

I told Kamal how I'd gone out drinking with Ibrahim Derras the day before my cousin's arrest. I'd had to listen to Ibrahim heap insults on him just because he hadn't paid what he owed. He'd threatened to wreck Kamal's car and trash his house.

"He's the one who broke into my house?!"

Kamal raised his head to a light blue sky, crisscrossing electrical wires ruining the view. He pinched the skin on his neck and frothed at the mouth, he was so angry.

"That's how you pay me back, you son of a sellout?!"

IBRAHIM

I was thinking about the fact that the soldiers in the War of Independence had operated under assumed names, and that neither my mother nor I knew my father's alias, when a municipal truck rumbled by like a helicopter, spraying insecticide. Its strong, burnt-oil smell irritated me. Did they kill the locusts so they could then busy themselves with cockroaches and bedbugs? Under my breath, I cursed the driver and whoever was with him: "May God punish them." There were always rumors circulating about misappropriation in the municipal budget, and I never let an opportunity slip by to curse city employees.

Standing in front of my shop, I lit a cigarette. As I watched the people walking by, I spotted a thin, brown-faced girl wearing a dusty green dress and rubber sandals and carrying a burlap sack on her shoulder. Her head was lowered, as if she were counting the spit-spotted sidewalk tiles. This was the third beggar I had seen today. There were so many beggars. People would go to sleep and wake up the next morning to find a battalion of new beggars working the public plazas or gathering in front of the mosques. Sometimes, entire families clamorously reached out their hands to people who might

190

give them something. This city has become the capital of beggars. The only time they disappear is when an official from the capital comes to visit.

As soon as that little girl reached me, I ran my hand over her head, which was wrapped in a vinegar-soaked cloth to protect it from the sun. She looked uncomfortable; perhaps she was unsettled by my behavior and thought I had something dirty in mind. I was surprised by her apprehension, so to reassure her I gave her a coin I had taken out of my trouser pocket. "Keep it," she told me, and kept walking when I tried to stop her.

"What's in the sack?"

"Dried bread."

"Why?"

"For the sheep."

I apologized for taking her for one of those kids sent by their parents looking for handouts. "Take the money."

I suggested she buy some ice cream as the heat was still lingering and people hadn't stopped craving frozen treats, or barbe à papa, or candy floss, or cotton candy – everyone calls it what they want. Its price had gone up after rumors had spread about the scarcity of sugar. She accepted my offer and changed her mind about me. Then she asked in a nasal voice: "Do you know any houses where they have dried bread?"

"People here throw it in the trash."

She made a plan to come early in the morning next time and collect what she needed from the trash cans before the garbage trucks came. That way, she wouldn't have to knock on doors.

I asked what her name was. "Louisa Hadeeri," she replied.

I found her innocent face pleasant, and her name reminded me of my aunt, who like so many others had donated her jewelry following independence to help the country get up on its feet. Her hope had been that she'd be blessed in return once the country's situation stabilized, but she'd never received a thing – neither she nor her children – and she regretted what she had done. She'd been so nice to me when I visited her as a child. She would fill my pockets with nuts, and I would hear her singing traditional songs over and over again. But, like my other relatives, she now refused to come to our house, claiming we lived in a neighborhood teeming with degenerates.

"Where do you live?"

She told me her address in the meadow and turned away absentmindedly as she watched a blue Peugeot 103 moped go by.

I waited a moment before asking: "Bachir Labtam. Do you know him?"

"He's in jail."

"How come?" I pretended to be surprised, as if he was a friend of mine.

"He killed a woman." Then she covered her mouth with her hand as if she had said something wrong. She squeezed the coins more tightly and continued walking so I wouldn't ask her anything else.

As I scratched the back of my neck, I said to myself: Do you think I'm an idiot, Six? To believe that your cousin was traveling?! I'll have you join him in jail.

MAIMOUN

I can't stand the sight of Hamid anymore, or his detectives who are walking around all over the place now. They keep tabs on when I come and go and closely watch the movements of the tourists whose numbers have dwindled and won't rise again until the new year. "He thinks I'm scared of him," I muttered under my breath as I grabbed the skin of my neck between my thumb and forefinger as if to try to extract it the way Zakia's death had extracted my peace of mind. I wouldn't be surprised if he were listening in on my telephone conversations, too. I trusted him when he first came to the city eight years ago a broken man, fired from his previous job in one of the capital's suburbs. I solidified my friendship with him and entrusted him with protecting my food warehouse. I put in a good word about him to the police chief and rewarded his cooperation by opening the doors of the hotel to him and his family. But ever since Zaza's murder, he's gotten too big for his britches.

He had taken statements from all the employees, which he'd had them sign, and hadn't given me any idea of where his investigation was heading. I could not get over how shockingly rude he'd been when I returned from Sétif. A policeman had stopped me, taken one look at my documents, and ordered me not to move until he called his direct superior.

They'd dealt with me as a wanted man. Then, the policeman had sternly ordered me to wait for Hamid in my office. All of that had happened in front of Mehdi. My son's legs had shaken like the young branches of a tree. I thought my wife, Yacout, had fabricated a charge against me after I'd expressed my intention to take a second wife, or that she had revealed the piles of cash I had accumulated in our safe because of how much I mistrusted banks. I thought the damn woman had laid a trap for me! When I learned the details afterward, I regretted ever betting on that harebrained police inspector. How dare he suspect me or one of the hotel workers, all of whom I've screened through meticulous background checks as much as a sultan screens his closest advisers? There's no way one of them would commit such a heinous act. My heart ached. The only way I could cool myself down was by returning him to the humble state he'd been in when I first met him.

In a moment of disloyal weakness, I resolved to leave the aging mother of my children; then I sent Kamal to beg her to come home again. This had been after I'd placed my confidence in Zaza, who, after Merzaka had succeeded in getting her a gig there, performed regularly in the downtown nightclub that catered to VIPs. I thought a common-law marriage to her would secure her place by my side so no other man would snatch her from me. This would allow me to send her in to act on my behalf with the decision-makers so I could join them in running the city, where I had been unsuccessful in running for office. May God forgive her, in any case. I never got over my anxiety about the white dress's disappearance from her room. She was going to wear it on our wedding night. It cost me as much as one of my workers makes in a month. She was the only one I'd hired without looking into her past, not knowing that she had run away from her family home and that the police from her town were looking for her. I was drawn to her fresh and youthful face and enjoyed talking with her. Whenever I wanted to tease her, I pointed to the scar on her lower jaw, telling her: "It makes you more beautiful." I thought she was fond of me, and she gave the impression that our age difference didn't bother her.

"I'm as old as your father."

"I hope you make me forget him."

"You don't love him?"

"He doesn't love me."

I won't forget how depressed she was the day she learned of his death. She didn't sing for two whole weeks. At that time, I still thought she had two parents who had divorced and abandoned her.

When I told Yacout of my intention to marry another woman, without revealing her name or profession, she opened fire with some choice words: "You're despicable! A collaborator who didn't fire a single shot during the War of Independence!"

After all these years together, we haven't been able to love one another. I don't share my secrets with her, and I don't trust her with my affairs. I married her in the second year of the war; when the French discovered the oil well at Hassi Messaoud, I discovered the well of her femininity. She was not yet fifteen years old. I had complied with my mother's desire for a daughter-in-law from our clan. At first, my wife and I had shared a room with a leaky roof that let the water in when it rained. We would eat barley bread when we were hungry. Later, I'd met her cousin, Si Mahfoud, who was known as Papillon because he insisted on wearing a bow tie that looked like a butterfly. He always had a Bastos cigarette between his lips, and he enlisted me in the Liberation Army the morning Charles de Gaulle shouted, "*Je vous ai compris...* I understand you!" in the capital, the shout that made us understand that colonialism would continue. Papillon introduced me to Belkacem Belattar, who worked as a gardener at the Sahara during the colonial era, delivering letters and news to the fighters and closely watching enemy activities. I was responsible for collecting donations of francs from those who had money. Then, after independence, we moved to this spacious house where colonists had lived before us. We came to eat vegetables, fruits, and croissants. I had two daughters with Yacout, both of whom got married and live with their husbands now, and an older son who works as a teacher and lives with his wife and son. Our youngest, Mehdi, is nineteen.

Once, Mehdi came to me to talk about getting into business. "Finish your studies, then I'll help you," I offered.

He did poorly in high school and repeated his attempts to convince me to help him open a shop that sold music cassettes. He promised to make a go of it and not to burden me anymore. He grew taller than five nine, and I'm convinced that the taller a man grows, the more stupid he gets. I test him from time to time to see whether he can remain patient. He accompanied me on my trip to Sétif – that city spread over hills and covered with snow every winter like washed wool – and he passed the test with his savvy and quick wit. On our way there, I told him of my desire to take a second wife, and he responded with slow deliberateness: "You know what's best for yourself."

Although I'd thought Mehdi would instinctively side with his mother, he settled in next to me, next to the stronger one. This is the most important lesson I ever learned, and I taught it to my children. I became conscious of it in the summer of 1965. At that time, I stood with Belkacem in the face of the new country's president. Belkacem helped me buy the hotel with donations I had acquired for the War of Independence from charitable people and wealthy folk. The police arrested us, and I had the chance to review my position while in prison. I found myself in the orbit of those who were strongest, and was released. I reclaimed the hotel – "my Sahara," as I liked to call it. After that, I could only rest soundly once I ascended the staircase and became one of those pulling the strings from behind the curtain.

I didn't expect to stay in Sétif for more than two days. I spoke openly with Yacout about what I was thinking and hung back to give Zaza time to prepare herself for the wedding. She gathered a considerable sum of money to buy the jewelry and accessories she needed. The receptionist did not stop calling me while I was gone, reporting on everything, and the smuggler I went to see was late delivering a large quantity of medicines that were behind schedule due to a surprise guard patrol on the Tunisian border. I didn't meet up with him until three days after my arrival. I sent the first shipment the following day with my son, to show him that I only had the best intentions. He delivered it to Kamal, who transferred it to a warehouse I kept hidden from my family. We moved the second shipment together the day after that. The police were waiting at the city's edge for my return, so I was late as I hastily got it to its hiding place earlier that night, thanking God they did not search my trunk when they stopped me. The news of Zaza's murder had shocked me; I was also upset that Kamal had not rushed to tell me, although he'd been busier than usual that day. I always covered up his shortcomings but applauded the sincerity he put into his work. I'm the one who steered him towards the Hotel Institute, and after he graduated, I hired him. I taught him how to tie a necktie and showed him preference over his colleagues, even though I never forgot what a fool he'd made of himself one day when he'd got drunk and harassed an Italian lady at the hotel... "I won't do it again," he said, chastened when I scolded him.

I made up my mind to write up a complaint against Hamid right away. What goes up must come down, and there are fat years and thin, I thought. I pursed my lips and turned my nose up. He denied leaking the news to the *Echaâb* journalist, but I don't believe him. He got me into trouble with the head of the Tourism Bureau, who called from the capital asking for details, and all I could do was persuade him that her death had come as the result of a familial settling of accounts. "Be careful, or you'll lose your customers," he warned me, knowing full well that the hotel's success and failure hinged not on the services it provided but rather on its reputation.

Whoever killed Zaza was out to ruin me. And no one wanted my ruin more than Si Miloud, because I refused to sell the hotel to him. But who could say for sure that that inspector hadn't had a hand in her murder? I repeated the Lord's name and breathed in the smell of tobacco that filled my office. The dead woman had once told me how much she resented Hamid for his insistence on being alone with her. I swallowed a pill my heart doctor had prescribed, and it occurred to me that she had wounded the inspector's self-esteem by rejecting him. No doubt he was involved in her death.

IBRAHIM

It wasn't difficult for me to understand what had brought Noura here; her cheeks were free of makeup, and her slightly puffy lips looked as if a mosquito had bitten them.

"Are you nuts?!" she said to me. Her face seemed thinner without makeup. I predicted she would resort to the usual dictionary she drew from when she was angry, like when she called me a "fucker," or said, "I'll tear your dick off and shove it up your nose!" Her foul mouth made me love her even more. I was forced to remain behind the counter as I waited for her to unload on me and stop waving her right hand in the air, which she didn't normally do. "You filed a complaint against my brother with the police?!"

She couldn't stand my silence, so I began to speak calmly. "You didn't ask me what he did!"

Noura didn't believe my accusation that Six had tried to break into my shop, and she suspected I held some sort of grudge against him. "Did he find out about our relationship?" She asked it with a gentle, wan look on her face as if she were a sick child, so I reassured her.

"Only God knows about it."

She insisted I was committing a crime against her brother,

199

who was six years younger than me. She was surprised when I told her he was one of my customers and that he made a living by showing movies in a garage. All she could say was: "He's free to do what he wants." She was dumbstruck when I told her he'd been involved in setting the gas station owner, Si Miloud's, car on fire; that old man who insisted on wearing a Borsalino hat and spectacles, who was always walking around with a newspaper in his hand and who, in just a few years, had gone from smoking rolled *arar* leaves to Cuban cigars. She struck the top of her chest with her palm, and her face turned red.

Seeing my opening, I rushed to reiterate my proposal to her. "If you convince your father to swear that my father was martyred in the War of Independence, I'll withdraw the complaint."

I didn't know the police would release her brother as soon as he appeared for the summons because I lacked a witness. She wanted me to withdraw the complaint myself, afraid that her father, who had a hand in every government agency, would find out and exploit the incident to rub in her mother's face and smear her good name by accusing her of raising her son badly.

"Don't you understand that my father split up with my mom?"

Her brother had never told me about their parents splitting up. Had he been too embarrassed? It's considered shameful for someone to state openly that their parents are arguing or have divorced, because people will conclude that the mother has done something disgraceful.

"Let's let the police do their work then."

"What goes around comes around," she sneered as she stopped at the door, her teeth clenched. "Whoever described you as a piece of shit wasn't wrong."

I could see her through the store window. She wasn't happy with me.

"I'll teach you who I am," she said as she walked away.

I spat loudly from the doorstep: "You come from a family of criminals!"

She couldn't hear me anymore. I realized a gulf had grown between us, which saddened and depressed me. I didn't beg like Jacques Brel did with his lover in the song "Ne me quitte pas." It's my fate that every woman I fall for leaves me. Love also means leaving the ones we love. I didn't get to ask when her cousin's trial date was. I wanted to hear her arguments for the defense to better understand what I was missing about the hotel singer's murder.

I locked up and headed to Nabil's house in the Moudjahid neighborhood to check in on him. His father hadn't come back to see me as promised; the last time he was here, he'd taken the money I had given him and disappeared. When I got there, I was met by a crowd of people standing in front of the door, the sound of Qur'an recitation coming from a loudspeaker hung from a window. My friend had died without finishing reading *The Sheik*, without telling me how to get out of this country.

A day that begins with a breakup and ends with a funeral is a day that doesn't count. Any ideas I had about emigrating and following in Nabil's footsteps were snuffed out, for my friend's spirit had ascended to the upper realm. The money from the watch I'd sold hadn't done him any good; his time had come too soon.

I attended the burial, my mind boiling over. Would anyone mourn for me when I died?

BACHIR

This is the second time I've been to prison since falling in love with Zakia.

About six years ago, I was gone from the barracks without permission for a whole day. I had rented a room in a two-floor brothel that was friendly to lovers and protected their secrets. You just had to present a medical certificate stating you were free of infectious diseases. I spent that time with her. She had given in to my promises of getting engaged and then marrying. She came dressed in a covering that hid her entire body, wearing a dress with a colored hem. Her neck gave off the scent of a perfume more delightful than any I'd smelled before. She didn't return to her family's house until sunset. In my arms, she forgot all about her brothers and her father, but she refused to let me deflower her: "We need to be patient until we consummate our marriage." We fell into touches and wet kisses. Whenever she uncovered her two apple-like breasts, I nibbled at them, neither of us concerned with the rising moans coming from the next room.

I didn't hear about the clashes that engulfed Nezrama following a football match between two teams from working-class neighborhoods when fans of the losing team attacked the winning team's fans. The police were unable to stop them. Blood was spilled, and one of the young men was kicked to death, which prompted the officer in charge to assemble all the soldiers in the barracks courtyard, advising them to prepare to intervene. He divided them into groups and noticed I wasn't there. When I returned, they shaved my head and threw me into a truck trailer without food or drink for five days. I slept and woke up in darkness. I could hear the chittering of rats and skittering of cockroaches that shared the space with me. I dealt with my isolation by conjuring up memories of my beloved. The situation calmed down once the town's wise men got involved. They reconciled the two opposing sides and paid the blood money, so the officer pardoned me after giving me a scolding in his office.

This is the second time now that I've been thrown in jail, although it's a crowded cell this time. They might transfer me to another one if they insist on the charge they're leveling against me.

WEDNESDAY

Rahhal and I have one enemy in common: Maimoun Belassal.

Eight years ago, he lit a fire in his own food warehouse without the police ever finding out who did it. "He claimed there was a food shortage and raised the price of fine flour even though the state was subsidizing its cost," Rahhal told me. Rahhal used to go to that warehouse to buy flour for his father's pastry shop. I wanted to tell him what I knew about Maimoun, but my eyes fell upon a small news item that appeared in the newspaper that always came late. It silenced me. YOUNG WOMAN'S BODY FOUND. The journalist insinuated that Zakia Zaghouani, or Z.Z. as he called her, had fallen victim to one of the faith-healers who live in the meadow. But she didn't frequent any faith-healers. No doubt his source was none other than Cheikha Edahabia; may God forgive her and him.

THURSDAY

Rahhal told me that he dropped out of the Agricultural Sciences program at the university and was in prison for driving a car without documents, meaning it was stolen. ("The important thing is that I bought it with honest money.") If I had a writer's imagination, I would write his life story, even though he practically deafened me with his ramblings about politics ("Wasn't it provocative of that communist, Fidel Castro, to visit our country the night before the *mawlid*? And then his comrade, General Giáp, came to visit the night before the holy Feast of the Sacrifice.") As he said this, he pointed his finger in my face as if I was the one who'd invited them. I responded by saying that the communists seek justice. I worked for a public company and had every right to defend communism. But he had no patience with me and proceeded to complain about how the women in government agencies are so cocky.

SATURDAY

It's five in the afternoon now. As had become our habit, I should be with Zakia now, smoking and drinking hot or cold drinks at Si Miloud's three-star Saâda Café, its walls decorated with pictures of European forests and rivers. The price of a coffee there is double what it is in regular cafés, and you have to pay in advance. It is frequented by men in neckties with thick mustaches whose features suggest they're in a hurry. But there was no other place we could sit without risking one of the hotel employees seeing us and telling Maimoun. He had given her the choice of leaving me or leaving her job. She would always come wearing a veil and sunglasses to ensure no one would recognize her. She'd hidden her hair and face ever since the time she'd ventured out and run into one of the nightclub customers on the way here. He loved to dance to the sound of her voice, and when he'd met her in the street, he'd hit on her. He grabbed her hand, and she turned around and slapped him, calling him a mangy dog. She waited for him to say something else, to slap him again, but he left her alone, her eyes glowing with anger.

In the Saâda, we lose ourselves in conversation about how we spend our days. I notice she's wearing the earrings I gave her, and I take her hand while the waiter, who never blinks, watches as if he wants to chase us off.

I used to forget everything around me when I heard Zakia's voice, with Umm Kulthum's song in my head always asking, "*Has love ever seen two people as love-drunk as us?*"

SUNDAY

Prison rules only allow visits from close relatives. That means I won't be seeing Kamal here. After Zakia, he was the person I had the most intimate memories of. He was orphaned young and raised by his older sister, Ouarida, who was like a mother to him. Even though she was just over forty, anyone who saw her would think she was much older. She spent her life caring for him and their sisters, along with her three sons, which is what prematurely aged her. Whenever I see Sidi Zerzour with his broad, rhinoceros-like face, I remember my friend, who told me about his knowledge and insight in curing sick people and those who have been touched by jinn. The prisoners avoid Zerzour out of fear of his spells. It is said that he can make even the most manly of men lose his abilities; he can put people to sleep with words or by writing a talisman that will make them lose their sight. Kamal used to be a customer of his. Had he found another faith-healer to satisfy his desires? I missed him and missed listening to his stories, so I wrote him a letter and posted it to the administration, hoping it would get to him.

WEDNESDAY

Whenever I went to bed, I imagined Zakia's image, but without the sexual fantasies that used to accompany it. I couldn't imagine myself fooling around with a woman who had died. I need to erase her memory from my mind. When her body died, my heart died along with it. Memories of my colleagues at the Rubber & Plastic Co. have begun to fade, whereas my beloved's image becomes more fixed.

FRIDAY

I turned thirty-two years old.

As my mother told it, I was delivered by a one-eyed midwife in my grandfather's old house, which was no more than two rooms constructed of gypsum, stone, and palm leaves. That was before he got his house in Gambetta, or First of November as the neighborhood was called after the French left. When I let out my first cry, at close to 9:30 in the morning, my mother felt that death was near. Then she was reassured by my weight of six and a half pounds and length of twenty inches, so she moistened her throat with water and honey. She rubbed me with olive oil and hung a charm around my neck, then argued with my father about what to name me. She wanted to call me by her father's name, but my father wouldn't have it, giving me his father's name instead. I am a Libra. I'm supposed to be a successful and balanced person, but I'm not. Yesterday, I saw myself in a dream, handing my mother a feverish baby and then rushing out of the house. I don't know how I'd become a father, but I do know that if I were free, I would buy a cake and light candles. I celebrated my thirty-first birthday with Zakia, and she blew the words *I love you* into my ear as I had never heard them before. I'll never forget that moment, just as I'll never forget three other moments that brought us closer together: When I went out with her for the first time, she told me, "I want you to be my protector and ally, not just my boyfriend." Then, when she came to live in this city, she said to me with half-closed eyes, "Having you close to me makes me feel that I'm worth something." And the third was after she and I made up after a fight, and she said, "I might forget my mother, but I'll never forget you." Now, I just wish I could forget her.

Her death has increased my appetite to live.

BOOK 3

THE END OF
THE SAHARA

NOURA

I secured a front seat in the shared car heading to Nezrama. Five passengers were sitting behind me. I sat next to the driver with my head tilted toward the window. He had thick eyebrows that came together as one and was wearing cologne that couldn't hide the smell of his tobacco breath. He stared at my thighs and hands. I wasn't wearing a wedding ring, and the conventional belief was that when a woman is past thirty and hasn't yet gotten married, she has "missed the train." My mother had castigated me for my insistence on pursuing my university studies, which, in her mind, made getting engaged unlikely: "A woman's capital investment is her husband, not her diploma." I often heard harassers whispering things about me that didn't make me happy at all: miserable, old maid, childless. "All a woman has is her husband or her grave," my aunt would say. However, I believe in sitting pretty instead of marrying and regretting it bitterly.

It occurred to me that I had not traveled anywhere since I'd gone with my mother to my aunt's house in the capital last winter, after my father had left. They'd both been unable to convince him to come back home, and my work was taking up all my time. Hassina advised me to relax some. "Otherwise, your ass will get old," she added. The important thing is that my heart doesn't get old, I always say.

I got bored of looking at the road, which cut through a flat wasteland scattered with wild plants and dwellings. The car shook as it moved along. I took a magazine from my briefcase and flipped through an article about how French women married to Algerian men refuse to comply with the government's decision to place their children in local schools rather than French mission schools. If they want their children to have a foreign upbringing, let them take the children somewhere else, I decided, convinced that these French women had no trust in our country, or its culture or religion. They just wanted to impose their laws on us.

I'd set off on my journey without knowing what would come of it. Would I find out anything new related to Bachir's case? I called the number Hamid had given me, and the victim's aunt answered, asking me to call back in an hour. When I did, Halima answered and was brief: "Our door is open to every guest."

The police inspector's words were still ringing in my ears: "He stole her innocence, then doubted her loyalty to him, so he killed her." Was it jealousy that had driven him to it?

I arrived a little after ten in the morning. The sky had started to blow its heat out like a hearth. I took a folded piece of paper out of my bag on which I had written the address Zakia's mother had given me: 6/145 Nineteenth of June Street. The road was also known as Light Street because, I later learned, it was the only street where public lighting had been installed. The surrounding roads were plunged into darkness at night. I asked a woman, who looked as glum as my mother and who was dragging three children close in age behind her by their arms, how to get to that address. She explained that I had to walk for nearly half an hour until I reached a mosque with four minarets, then turn down more than one side street. It seemed difficult, and searching for the address might be a waste of time. I thanked her as I turned my head and looked at an unfinished building with workers standing around it. It reminded me of my city, where cement was steadily advancing over everything. I convinced the driver of a gray Peugeot 404 – a "clandestine," or illegal, taxi whose owner was working outside of the law by not paying fees – to take me where I wanted to go, despite being unable to escape his leering looks at my thighs bulging underneath my jeans. I sighed at the fact that I gained weight no matter how much I tried to lose it. "Beautiful as a gazelle," he commented as I paid the fare.

"I've been expecting you." Zakia's aunt welcomed me with a broad smile, the scent of ambergris emanating from her bosom. She wore a loose green garment suitable for women who stayed at home. She offered me a seat in the living room, which was decorated with a picture of two horses. On the wall were two shelves lined with glass cups and earthenware basins, and at the side of the room was a locally made television. She brought me a cup of juice and asked about me, my family, and my job. To every question, I responded: "Everything's going well."

She expressed how angry she was about the scarcity of coffee and baby formula, as well as her fear that semolina flour and sugar would disappear in the coming days. "Our faucets haven't seen any water in a week," she added. She looked exasperated.

Because her husband worked at the postal and communications office, she owned the only telephone in the neighborhood. I assured her that we were as thirsty as she was. We had to rent water tanks, which had become increasingly expensive.

"We can't afford a tank. We use water from a nearby well and add bleach to it."

I cut off her complaining by asking about the victim's family's house, the reason for my visit.

"It's fifteen minutes from here on foot."

I remained silent until the woman I wanted to meet with arrived. I tried to imagine Zakia's life in her hometown. Had she been one of the naughty girls or one of the charming ones? Had she loved her hometown, or had she hated it as much as I hated mine?

Before Halima had even entered the living room, pale-faced and hair unbrushed, I rushed to kiss her cheeks: "May God grant you patience." But she answered me coldly as her eyes gazed up at the white ceiling. The mourning period had passed, and sympathetic words no longer concerned her.

She told me her tears dry up every night before she goes to bed. She never tires of hugging the picture of her daughter standing next to a swimming pool in a light blue summer shirt, white shorts, and sunglasses. And she never tires of kissing Zakia's gold necklace, which she puts under her pillow as if it were a charm warding off sickness and poverty.

I gazed at her face and noticed she was shorter and fatter than me. Her forehead had two deep creases in it. I tried to find a resemblance between her and her daughter, but besides the thin lips, Zakia must have inherited her father's features. It was quiet for a moment, then Halima began to speak after her sister slipped out of the room.

"They took my daughter from me."

I stared at her face, eagerly anticipating what she would say next. I was careful not to ask too many questions, to give her the chance to say what was on her mind.

Halima started with some stories about her lost daughter and the hostility with which her brothers had talked about her after learning that she sang in a nightclub.

"They called her a whore."

I, too, have been called a whore by people because I associate with men at work, I said to myself.

Halima had wanted to meet me at her sister's house rather than hers to avoid sparking her sons' curiosity. "If that son of a bitch hadn't killed her, her brothers would've," she added.

I delicately asked whether Zaza might have been the victim of a family settling of accounts, but she denied that. Then she called in her niece, Nassira, to corroborate that Bachir had dated Zakia while he was doing his military service and had urged her to leave her family home, and that he had then doubted her loyalty and killed her.

"My niece used to talk with her all the time."

Nassira recounted a phone call she'd had with Zakia during which her cousin had said: "I'm going to rule this hotel" and that she intended to marry someone else.

"She didn't find the right person in Bachir. He took so long to propose to her." I asked her to elaborate, but she wouldn't.

Nassira had been close friends with Zakia, or Zerboute, as they used to call her, because she was always in motion, like a spinning top. She was just two months younger than Nassira. They always sat together in the Kuttab school leaning against the back wall, memorizing short suras by rote without understanding what they meant, with other young boys rocking back and forth repeating God's words. At home, Zakia would practice *tajwid* so she could recite the words of the Qur'an, and would soften her voice by eating honey with cinnamon.

They'd sat at the same table in elementary school, exchanged clothes with one another, stolen chalk from the teacher's office, and were members of a musical group when the Minister of Education came to Nezrama. They'd appeared on television, and Halima had been pleased with her daughter, who, soon after, failed out of school, thus relieving the teachers from her restlessness and quarrelsome behavior. Nassira had done well, but her father had forbidden her from continuing to middle school. Her mother had allied herself with him, their justification being that she was nearing puberty. She'd given in to their decision without protest. The same thing had happened with her older sister, whom they had forbidden to go out into the street alone once she turned eleven, until she'd married and moved to her husband's house at sixteen. Nassira's relationships with her peers had been cut off, and her cousin had become her only friend. After working hard and persevering in convincing her husband, Halima had allowed Zakia to go to the Professional Training Center to learn how to make pastries.

Zakia had visited Nassira regularly, supplying her with news, rumors, and jokes from the few women at the training center. Her visits became a drug that stirred Nassira's imagination. In the summer, they would go to family weddings, where they would dance or help distribute food and clean up afterward. This continued until Zakia left Nezrama to become a singer at the Sahara.

Instead of standing face-to-face with one person, I faced two: the victim's mother, who kept repeating Hamid's words, and her niece, whom I didn't like despite the innocent look in her eyes. She was as thin as a locust, and her skin color tended toward brown. Her hair was black and pulled back with a red clip. Her two front teeth stuck out, and she had bulging cheeks.

I didn't say a word about how I was related to the suspect, thinking that would upset them. A feeling began to take root that my cousin had lied to me. He had not revealed the whole truth about his relationship with the deceased, and I became increasingly uneasy. *Lawyers ask questions that don't occur to others.* I'd learned that rule at university, but I was unable to apply it that day.

Halima sensed what I was feeling and said: "Lives are in God's hands, and the final reckoning will come on the Day of Resurrection." Then she rested her chin on the palm of her hand and swept the ground with her eyes. She recalled the day her daughter was born. "My pregnancy with her was easy." This had not been the case with Zakia's brothers. And breastfeeding her hadn't been difficult at all. "She lived gently, and she went on her way gently." I concluded that this meeting with Zaza's mother would not give me what I was after. She was unyielding. I gave her my office phone number in case she had anything else she wanted to tell me in the coming days. All I could do was leave, muttering "What a waste of time" under my breath.

She tried to insist I spend the night and travel back home the following day, but I declined. She asked that I pass along her greetings to Hamid, imagining we were friends, and tell him she would come another time to visit the deceased's grave.

Nassira walked with me to the street, where low-rise houses stood close together. We didn't say a word to one another, as if we were at a funeral. Before another illegal taxi arrived to take me back to the travelers' station, she addressed me:

"Bachir needs to tell you what happened."

I looked at her, confused.

"He knows something my Aunt Halima does not."

IBRAHIM

I read in the newspaper that the state takes care of martyrs' families, so I asked myself why I hadn't received any help looking for my father's grave. I persuaded myself to record a final take of "Salma ya Salama" and send it off to the radio station. After all, others who have their songs played on-air are no better than me. I've come to have decent control of my vocal range, relying on my throat and the nasal pronunciation of certain letters. If my cover version of this song worked out, I'd try covering others.

I counted out some bills that had accumulated in the cash register after an influx of customers. Some of them had come from the neighboring socialist village that was built so the farmers wouldn't leave their farms. They rent enough cassettes to last the week, and some leave me a tip so I'll get them more adult movies.

It dawned on me that I hadn't bought new clothes in a year or more. I hadn't purchased a pair of shoes in a long time either. I was thinking I might find some suitable imported or smuggled goods in the contraband market when Kamal came in, howling, "I'm the one who treated you like a brother, and you betrayed me!" He grabbed my neck and shook my head back and forth, yelling like a crazy person. "I'll bury you alive!" I felt like a chicken in his hands. There was nothing I could grab onto to get him away from me. He was taller and stronger than me. His face was red, and his eyes were spewing sparks of anger. I could hardly breathe. I was hoping for someone to intervene and save me when I managed to push him off by kneeing him in the testicles.

I stood up straight to defend myself. Kamal regained his balance, and I saw that he was breathing with some difficulty, with a look that resembled that of a reckless boxer. I was sorry I didn't have a knife on me so I could carve a cross on his face. When he spat "Son of a sellout!" at me, I wanted to unload all my hatred on him. I couldn't stand that insult. Quickly, I grabbed the broom with the thought of hitting him on the head with it. I was afraid he would lose consciousness in my shop, though, so I brought it down on his shoulder, which made him scream, "You break into my house and smash my car window, then you attack me, you fucker?!" "You're the fucker, son of a fucker!" I replied. We got all tangled up, and his punches landed on my face and upper chest like pickax strikes. I'm not sure how my hands moved on their own in response. I felt as if I had come to possess the strength of two men and punched him in the face and the stomach. We continued to rage and swear at one another. Then, a flailing swing of the broom hit the store window and shattered it. A man whose face I could not make out got between us. Kamal took a few steps back, his nose bleeding as he cursed at me.

Some of the other merchants gathered in front of the Desert Rose's door to satisfy their curiosity, and no sooner had my adversary disappeared than a wave of voices all speaking at once came: "Thank God for your safety…" "Avoid fools…" "Go back to work and forget all about him." I glanced at the glass that had fallen out and figured I would have to spend a considerable amount of money to get it fixed. I could forget about buying new clothes. A question bore down on me: How had Kamal known what I had done? I'd smashed his car window with a hammer after getting loaded on beer and snuck into his house to get back at him for not paying what he owed in videocassette rental fees. I resolved to bring a metal rod with me the following day to defend myself with if necessary, and to take another route home that evening, just in case he was waiting to ambush me, as highway robbers do in Westerns.

I turned to the man who had gotten between us and realized he was the same person who had put out the burning butane gas tank at the zalabieh shop. A string of prayer beads was hanging from his neck.

"Forgive me, but I don't know your name."

"Hadj Khider Arkoub."

My knees trembled when I heard this. It was Noura's family name. I didn't dare ask if he knew her, and my fears that Kamal would attack me again did not subside. I put off recording the final version of the song.

HAMID

The telephone woke me. I jumped over my clothes, which were strewn on the floor, to get it.

The commissioner informed me of a policeman's death. "Look into what happened," he added.

"I'll do it in the morning."

"The sooner the better."

There was some commotion in the background, as if he were sitting in a nightclub or at a wedding party. I looked over at Zinab as she lay on her left side, snoring lightly. I envied her for how she slept. The watch I had given her for her birthday, which had previously adorned Zakia's wrist, was in a drawer. She had only worn it once.

I went to the station and wrote up my report on the police-man who had committed suicide, including what had been in the crime scene officer's report. In one of the dead man's pockets he had found a list of debts: food and medications, along with other invoices. I wrote that the burial would take place that afternoon, hoping the chief would attend for me. He had promised to hire a second investigator to provide some relief but never had, claiming budgetary constraints. Ever since the government had settled on a policy of auster-ity because of the fall in oil prices, I have made do with the help of a single brigadier who occasionally steps in for me.

Returning home, I went back to bed and saw myself in a dream picking up the phone receiver. All I could hear was Zakia's muffled voice.

When I got back to the station in the morning, my boss told me of his intention to leave as he cleaned his ear with his index finger. He was headed to the dedication of a municipal stadium, then to the dead policeman's funeral with an honor guard detachment. He spared me that but ruined my day by tasking me with something else.

"Mrs. Ferrahi's body needs to be exhumed so we can establish what happened to her."

Last week, a fifty-year-old woman had died following a surgical procedure, and after her burial, her widower had requested a reinvestigation into the circumstances of her death, accusing the surgeon of making a fatal error.

The chief placed a pipe between his lips – a habit he had acquired after numerous visits to East Berlin for training courses – and his tone softened. He slicked back his oiled and well-coifed hair and asked me, "Where does the Zakia Zaghouani investigation currently stand?"

"The shepherd who found her body has requested a meeting with me."

"When?"

"I'll arrange a time with him."

"The sooner the better."

I nodded. The way the chief slowly exhaled the smoke reminded me of the police commissioner in the capital's suburbs, the one who had ordered my transfer to this city after he imagined I was competing with him for the heart of a girl who worked with us in the precinct office. "There's nothing between us," I had said, to which he had replied, "I'm not foolish enough to trust you." He had treated me like an enemy for days. He would pass by me without responding to my greetings and avoid eye contact. When he issued the transfer order, it was out of malice. I had so badly wanted to spit in his face that day but feared being sent to the Disciplinary Council. I had kept El Mejdoub's words in mind:

> *Whoever loves you, love him back, and in loving him, be pure.*
> *And whoever hates you should not be scorned. Leave him in good health and vigor.*

I got to the meadow just before noon and mumbled: "How can people stand living in houses made of tin and mud?" There's no shame in poverty, but it teaches laziness. Even though this place is technically part of the city, the police avoid interacting with its residents to avoid becoming targets of their anger, like that day when municipal employees had come to tell them of the government's intention to tear down their illegal residences. People had gathered and got up in the government officials' faces until they backed down.

As soon as I rolled down the window of the car that had picked me up with two other policemen, I was hit by the smell of burning plastic. One of them had undoubtedly started a fire to get rid of the garbage. The image of Zaza laid out in the morgue was stuck in my mind, and I hated Bachir, The Camel, twice as much. The investigation wasn't going to lead to another suspect, and he would pay the price by spending the rest of his life in prison.

After questioning all the criminals who had completed their sentences and been released in the past few days, I determined that they had alibis the night of her murder. Still,

223

the medical examiner's words rang in my ears: "Maybe she fell, hit the back of her head, and died." He thought the case might be no more than a fluke accident, as we never found the murder weapon. There had been no blood where the body was discovered. No doubt she had been dragged there from another location. But the three policemen tasked with combing the meadow in search of her other earring had come up empty-handed, even though they had used a search dog.

I was having trouble finding Achour's shack, so I motioned to a teenager with curly black hair who was peeing on a carob tree. I called over to him, and he turned around, confused, buttoning his trousers, which had gotten wet in the process. He walked with me down a dirt road lined with eucalyptus trees, and I found Achour standing in front of his shack. He was dusty and wearing the same crimson-red shirt he had met me in the last time, but he had added a third button. He was busy cutting wood. "Cutting down trees is forbidden," I said to him.

Beads of sweat shimmered on Achour's face, which seemed relaxed, in contrast to how terrified he had looked when I met him at the station before. He wiped away the sweat with the back of his left hand and stood up straight as a soldier, mumbling, "We've got no gas, Boss."

"The government wants to lay gas lines to Spain while people here still cook their food over woodfires," I muttered. There was a cut on his forehead; the result of a fall while he was chasing his flock, he said. He invited me in for a cup of tea, so we went through the whitewashed door over which there was a sheep's horn to ward off the evil eye. Next to the door was a waterskin and a *mahlab*, a goatskin used for churning milk. We each sat down on a brick while the two policemen who had come with me remained outside.

Six years ago, Achour and his wife and daughter had come to this shack on the meadow's eastern side. At the time, it was nothing more than an enclosure surrounded by cane stalks and bricks. In those first days, they had slept under the stars wrapped in blankets, relieving themselves in a hole. Then, with the help of two neighbors, they had built a room of clay. Whenever the wind blew, he had been seized by fear that the roof would fall in. After that, he had built another room, smaller than the first, which he had made into a kitchen. Then, within that, there was a corner set aside for bathing. And then his son had been born. He had insisted on putting a knife close to the baby's head during his first days to guard against "evil spirits" as he walked around the bed with incense. He had waited a week, as custom dictates, before giving him a name. He had slaughtered a sheep and promised to slaughter another to celebrate his circumcision, hoping to save enough money to move with his family to a house with many rooms. He had hoped to find a better job than trading in sheep or toiling on construction sites, but the years went on. Others had come and built similar houses, but his situation hadn't changed. Still, he lived by the proverb *We live on bread and water with our heads held high.*

"The cattle business going alright?"

"The rain is fighting us, and prices have dropped." There was a touch of gloom on his face and a fear in his words that illness would strike his animals after such a long drought. I could hear chickens clucking in a nearby house. How did they avoid the scorpions that roam around at night like sheep? I kept the question to myself, then jumped to another topic. Two flies buzzed around us persistently.

"Do you intend to spend the rest of your life here?"

"Until the Lord provides another house to live in."

He called to his daughter: "Bring the tea!" After just a few moments, a barefoot girl with unkempt hair came out of the room they had made into a kitchen carrying a tray with one sugar cube and two cups of tea topped with foam. I took her in with a pitying look, feeling a pang of tenderness toward her.

Achour grabbed a knife from a cord holding up his trousers and cut the cube into two pieces. He sunk one into each cup without asking if I wanted sugar. His daughter was about to leave when a toddler rushed out of the same room she had just come out of and nuzzled up to her. He had an *ayyacha* dangling from his earlobe; this thread was believed to prolong the male child's life. She picked him up in her arms and took him back inside.

"Anything new with the case?"

Achour adjusted himself in his seat and drank the tea down in one gulp. "The muezzin told me he saw a Peugeot 505 the night before I found the body."

"What color was it?"

"White."

Had it been Maimoun Belassal's car? Had he killed her while claiming he had traveled to Sétif?

"My daughter saw a blue Peugeot 103 moped before the time of the crime."

I hit my forehead with the palm of my hand. Farhat's moped? I asked Achour to call the girl back in, which he did. She hadn't known what kind of moped it was until she had seen one like it while walking around with her father. "Do you go to school?" I asked her.

"I stopped going this year."

"How come?"

She looked up sheepishly at her father, and he did not hesitate to jump in. "The school's far away, and my daughter is nearing puberty."

I did not want to get involved in their affairs. Simple people tend to keep their daughters from going out before their charms mature.

"Who was driving the moped?"

"A tall man. He stopped for a bit, then left."

"Did he come more than once?"

She nodded. I thanked her and turned back to her father.

"Where's the muezzin?"

"He's at home."

He traced the path to the muezzin's house in the dirt with his knife. Then I gulped down what was left in the teacup. I felt sorry for Achour and wanted to help. "I hope God brings you relief," I told him.

His eyes sparkled as he stood to whisk away a fly that had landed on my shoulder and then leaned over to kiss it, but I backed away, rejecting his fawning. I said goodbye and reminded him of El Mejdoub's words:

> *The one who does good, compliment him with joy and*
> *gratitude.*
> *The one who does evil, forget about him and let his deeds*
> *come back to haunt him.*

I headed off to the muezzin's house, where he told me the following: "When I saw that car while I was on my way to the mosque – I sleep in the closed-off space near the mihrab before calling out the dawn prayer – I thought one of the neighborhood loafers had come to smoke hash or have sex.

I prayed wholeheartedly that God guide him to the right path. I didn't think someone had died."

When I had finished speaking with the muezzin, I drove back to the station, delighted with the new statements I had gathered. However, when I got there, I found something disturbing. I read the post-exhumation report of Mrs. Ferrahi's body and saw that the medical examiner had found evidence of high levels of morphine in the samples. Another case I needed to look into.

I leaned back in my chair, hoping to take a nap, and felt a scorpion crawling on my arm. I remembered the dream where I'd seen myself talking to Zaza. Her heart had stopped, but her story kept beating. I thought of the people's bafflement at the sight of a police car in the meadow. I felt sorry for the children who were born and grew up there, as if they were Gavroche's brothers and sisters. I doubted that Farhat and Maimoun had worked with Bachir in perpetrating the crime and then concocted a hostility between themselves to make it impossible to think they were mutually involved. But why had the muezzin waited until now to report what he knew? Why hadn't he come down to the station before?

IBRAHIM

SEPTEMBER 28

I was near my shop, worrying that my father's grave had been washed away by floods that had inundated the city ten years ago, just as other graves on the riverbank in the Lalla Ammoura Cemetery had been, when I bumped into Tijani, whose left leg was in a brace. I felt sorry for him.

"Two masked men attacked me. They were carrying metal rods and looked like nutjobs who had escaped from the loony bin."

The police had refused to register his complaint because of a lack of witnesses. He believed the attackers were people who lived in the meadow who'd been reacting to a story the newspaper had published about the singer's murder, which had hinted that the perpetrator was from there.

"People from the meadow don't read," I said.

"But news about what's written still reaches them."

I didn't deny this and was sorry I had urged him to publish that news item. I did inform him that the police had put the accused in jail, then said goodbye and went back to my shop. I was looking at the movie jackets on display in the smashed window when Boulanouar sauntered in.

"I heard you got in a fight with one of them!"

"Son of a bitch rented movies without paying."

Boulanouar's assistant, John Travolta, explained to him in sign language that a mad beast had attacked me.

"Aren't you going to fix the smashed glass?"

"The handyman will come by in a little bit."

The pastry chef gazed at me and smiled. "I'll pay him for his troubles." His generosity made me feel awkward, and I wanted to politely refuse, but he insisted. Then he left, adding cantankerously: "You never brought me a movie about making pastries."

"I'll make a movie about you!" I responded, laughing out loud for the first time since Kamal had assaulted me.

I spread out a newspaper in front of me to do the crossword puzzle, but I stopped on the classifieds page. A man had his house with a satellite dish up for sale, another was selling his furniture, a woman was selling her jewelry. Everyone was advertising their most valuable possessions as if we were living through one of those lean years that come around every so often. I decided it would be a good time to record the final version of "Salma ya Salama" that evening when the street was free of daytime noise. I had a prepared lie for when the customers came: Two friends playing ball inside had broken the window.

As I sat there, Saâdi came in. His nickname was Iblis because he was devilishly clever at buying and selling. He had dropped out of high school and used to collect postage stamps with me, my hobby when I was younger. He would always sit at the last desk in class, making the teachers nervous with his fidgeting; they said he had wasps nesting in his ass. That was before he started to deal in imported clothes. He's the one who lent me the money to pay two years' rent in advance for the shop. I didn't know he had just gotten out of prison with the help of his father and that the tax collector he had beaten up had withdrawn his complaint.

"Saâdi, brother," I greeted him, and rushed to hug him. This was the second time he had come into the Desert Rose, the first time being when it opened. I usually visit him on holidays to stay on his good side. "Can I get you a cold drink?" I asked, and offered him my seat so I could go order two glasses of lemonade from a nearby café. His breath was so bad it almost made me sick. Despite how difficult he found it to pronounce, he insisted on speaking in an Algiers dialect to distinguish himself from the rest of the city's young men.

"Could you pay me back what you owe me in the next few days?"

That was the last thing I'd expected, since I'd committed to paying him back in installments. I had already paid him a small portion, and he'd promised to wait for me to pay off the rest, so why was he pressuring me now? "Are you in a hurry?" I asked.

He spat out a wad of chewing tobacco that he had tucked into his lower lip, and it stuck to the bottom of the door. "I got some new product I need to pay for."

Because he was slightly cross-eyed, I didn't know if he was looking at me or something next to me. I had signed a notarized pledge with him but didn't have any money to pay back the loan right then. While it was true that business was growing, I would have to work for another year without spending a single dinar to save up what I needed. He had dealt me a punch that hurt more than Kamal's.

MAIMOUN

The smell of rodent and cockroach poison filled my nostrils. The pharmacist, Djelloul, walked behind me to look at the medicines and bargain with me to settle on a price that would satisfy both parties. He went on about how clean and well organized the warehouse was. I acquired it about twenty years ago. It represents my spoils from a time when I couldn't lie in my bed without being seized by nightmares.

On the morning of June 19, 1965, our brother, President Ahmed Ben Bella, who had visited us here in this city and promised to lend a helping hand with whatever we needed, was removed from power. My friend Belkacem Belattar and I typed up posters urging people to revolt and not recognize his successor. However, the hotel cook betrayed us, and the police put us and a handful of other resisters onto a Citroën truck and drove us to a prison in the heart of the deep south. They tied us together in pairs and didn't let us relieve ourselves for the entirety of a trip that lasted a day and a half through hot, silent dunes. The trailer came to smell like a dead dog, and when I stepped out my legs were numb, which made me walk lopsided like a lame sheep as my feet sank into the sand. They gave us less than two pints of water per day, and we didn't know whether to drink it or use it to wash. Some of the prisoners suffered from skin ailments while others slid into madness, like Suleiman, a former sergeant in the Liberation Army, who got to where he could only walk backward, and as soon as darkness fell, he would start howling like an injured wolf. I spent my nights thinking about my wife and family, who didn't know what had happened to me. My beard grew long and was filled with lice, and I didn't have a change of clothes. We heard about the death of Belkacem's wife; he asked the guards to allow him to attend her funeral, but they refused, so he tried to run away and ended up getting shot. Sadness for my friend lasted for days as I faced storms and merciless cold nights and endured the fifty-degree heat during the day in a small tent where poisonous scorpions scampered about. I had lived as a free man under French occupation and as a prisoner following independence. I went on hunger strike, but it was futile. I became emaciated and suffered from severe stomach cramps. But I didn't die, even though death surrounded me, so I repented for what I had done. I begged for forgiveness and did what I was told. I returned to this city and participated in a mass gathering, addressing the people: "Whoever disobeys the new president is legitimizing a return to colonialism." I cried, and I made them cry. And I rescued my Sahara from the list of properties the state wanted to nationalize. I hung a picture of the new president in place of that of our brother, President Ben Bella, which had graced the reception hall before. I slaughtered a cow and gave its meat to the poor, praying to the Lord that He bless my livelihood. Then I learned that the cook who had betrayed Belkacem and me had opened a restaurant in the capital. It wasn't long afterward that he was killed in a fire that broke out there. The municipality gave me this warehouse for a nominal rent in exchange for my devotion to the party. The same was done with other fighters. This happened the same day people crowded in front of the Dunyazad Theater to watch *The Battle of Algiers.* I stocked up on heaps of durum wheat and soft flour, coffee, sugar, and dry beans. Along with my competitor, Si Miloud, my political and professional equal, we control the prices. I carry out my trade with a savvy I inherited from my father, who had engaged in buying and selling sheep; who had returned from World War II with a medal and three amputated fingers. My father taught me that money can determine a man's worth.

I opened the door to the fully stocked refrigerator, allowing the pharmacist to rummage through the contents: injections, pills, ointments, and cough and allergy syrups. He furrowed his brow, then smiled at me.

"That's just what I need."

"I can supply you with all the medications you need, even the hard-to-find ones."

Djelloul stroked his light mustache, then his long, spectacle-topped nose as he went through the stock. For weeks, he had been suffering from a lack of funds and feeling bad at having to tell patients that he couldn't fulfill even the most basic orders. "Where does all this goodness come from?" he asked.

"From a generous Lord."

I did not get into the details with him. He's nothing more than a customer. He looked like his father, who had been highly skilled at breaking into homes left behind by colonists. I'd got to know his half sister, Noura, whom I'd agreed not to meet until I'd had a chance to consult with an older lawyer she had worked with. And I couldn't bear her sticking her nose into the Merzaka Soualem case. But I didn't mention any of that to Djelloul, because all I cared about was him making the payment, me shipping the product, and him going on his way.

The pharmacist settled on buying the entire lot for thirty percent more than I'd paid the smuggler in Sétif. On a piece of paper, he wrote down the names of other medications he needed.

"I'll do my best to get them for you."

There was a glint of delight in Djelloul's eyes as he gave me a curious look while handing me the agreed-upon amount. "I heard a rumor about a merchants' strike."

"There are rumors every day."

The strike rumor had spread like a sirocco wind. Not a day goes by without people chewing on meaningless words. One time, someone said he saw a talking dog. Another person said they saw light seeping out from a grave. A third swore he saw a locust as long as his arm. And there are always those passionate listeners who add seasoning to that chatter and dish it out to those who will believe it.

"Not a thing was mentioned on the news," Djelloul continued as he rubbed his temple.

"You still watch television?"

Despite my involvement in the revolution, I've never been invited to appear on television, even though less worthy colleagues of mine who only joined the war in its final minutes have been so lucky. I'll continue to hate the television bosses until I get my full coverage.

I sat down in a chair at the entrance to the warehouse, the toxic smells invading my nose. I listened to my friend complain about the robbery his pharmacy had suffered about two weeks ago. The police had been unable to identify the perpetrator, so he'd found the thief with the help of his half brother, Faudel.

"The thief had been prosecuted before, for dealing in controlled medications."

"You should hire a detective to guard your shop when you're not there."

I finished counting the cash but stopped and stood up when I spotted a pearl earring on the floor among the sacks of sugar. I picked it up without the pharmacist noticing and hid it in my shirt pocket.

On my way back to the hotel, I couldn't stop looking at that earring, questions bearing down on me: Who did it belong to? Did I know her?

As soon as I got back to my office, I sat hunched over with my legs apart and reexamined my find. Was this Zakia Zaghouani's earring? The one Hamid was looking for? I had seen one just like it in her ear. Had she bought it herself, or had she received it as a gift?

My eyes focused on the stamp of Lazhari, the jeweler. Then, after checking over the accounts and taking my heart medication, I left. I waved to Kamal, who was chewing on something and engrossed in his work, and headed to the jeweler's shop, which faced the Foreigners' Villa. I found the long-faced Lazhari smiling as usual, his mustache looking groomed. "I'm at your service, Hadj. Do you need gold or silver?" he asked.

I don't always go to him, but when I do, I spend twice as much as his regular customers, purchasing gifts for important people's girlfriends and lovers. I've learned through experience that a gift is no less valuable than a cash advance. To win people over, I lavish them with gifts, just as I did with the police chief's wife, or Merzaka when I heard about her divorce. I draped her in gold and silver until she felt utterly indebted to me. As long as she dreamed of following her high political ambitions, she would be my right hand. But she disappointed me when death took her. Same with Zaza, to whom I had given a gold necklace. Despite my extravagance with other women, my family only gets money from me with great difficulty. In this, I follow what my father always said: "Problems start with your family."

"Actually, I came about something else."

I showed him the earring through the metal bars that protect his shop against thieves and make it look like a prison. I asked him if he remembered who he had sold it to. His face darkened, and I only learned later that the police had asked him about a similar earring. He tried to keep me from noticing his discomfort. He chose to deal with me the same way he'd dealt with the policeman who had come before.

"I've stopped selling pearls."

I cast him a silent, frustrated look.

"It must be an old order."

He took out a register with yellowed pages, where orders and their corresponding names were recorded. Most were newlyweds or members of the nouveau riche. Everyone else bought fake jewelry from sidewalk vendors or shops offering copies. He spent more than a minute flipping through the book, wetting the tip of his index finger with his tongue every time he turned a page, trying to make it look like he didn't know who the earring belonged to. I played with the inside of my ear, thinking I wasn't going to get what I was looking for. Then he raised his head, checked the weight of the earring theatrically, and answered.

"This is an order from someone named Bachir Labtam."

"Bachir?!" I rubbed the back of my neck. I felt as if my head would explode, I was so angry. I had banished him from the hotel when I'd learned of his relationship with Zakia, and I'd reprimanded Kamal for allowing him to sneak into her room at night. I'd watched him for days, threatening to cut off his balls if he went up to the third floor again. He'd felt the same shame Adam did when he was banished from paradise. I thought he had broken up with her.

I waved to Lazhari as I left, ignoring his persistent question: "Why are you asking whose earring that is?"

IBRAHIM

SEPTEMBER 29

I heard that visiting graves is one of the things forbidden by religion, so I felt the futility of searching for my father's. I went over the names of people I knew but could not think of anyone well-off enough to ask for help. Noura had disassociated herself from me. Tijani struggled daily for a pittance. Life and its hardships had dashed my neighbors' dreams. I've not been lucky enough to win the lottery, and I don't own a valuable mine I could sell for a lot of money. Then I thought of my uncle, so I headed to his house in the morning to ask to speak with him alone.

My uncle lives in a slum near the Emir Abdelkader Mosque, known as the Kabul Mosque ever since a young man who returned a year ago from Afghanistan with a wooden leg had started to lead prayers there. People living in that area have no doctor, so they treat their sick with herbs and supplications. And rather than go to court, they settle their disputes through retribution. My uncle shares his house, which is no more than three narrow rooms, with his wife and six male sons. He washes his legs every night before going to sleep, in the belief that whoever does so won't be taken unawares by Azrael in bed. His wish is to be blessed with a daughter, even though he grumbles about running into girls in the street; he just needs to see one of them dressed in skimpy clothes for him to toss an audible insult her way, as he did when he saw some young women on their way to school as we approached the café.

"What can I do for you?"

I felt awkward, as it was the first time I'd asked him for something. "I'd like to borrow a bit of money."

He took a sip of coffee and shooed a buzzing fly away before letting out a burst of laughter. "You're old enough to get married."

I responded with a smile, explaining that I needed the money to pay a debt to keep the shop. He repeated the same old song about how I should take another look at my situation and stop engaging in what he called "commerce of the forbidden." He invited me again to work with him at the Rubber & Plastic Co., but I had had enough. I thanked him and excused myself after paying for two cups of coffee, begging him not to tell my mother about what we had just discussed. He boiled over with anger and made sure to wait for the waiter to pass by with a broom before stomping his cigarette out on the floor. Customers have stolen the coffee shop's ashtrays, so the owner no longer puts them out on the tables.

"You're as hardheaded as your father," my uncle told me.

I was plunged into a maelstrom of rising anxiety. I thought about the pastry chef but then thought better of it. He had already been too generous with me. Then I remembered Khider Arkoub, who had saved me from Kamal's attack.

At Boulanouar's shop I bought a cake and, lucky for me, I only found his assistant there. Then, I headed to Arkoub's house with its mustard-colored walls. Its modern furniture gave the impression that its owner lived well. I reclined with my host on a brown leather couch in the living room, facing purple floral curtains, and imagined how much they would please my mother. I proceeded to present my case.

Khider smiled reassuringly. "What weighs heavy on you is light for me." He asked me how long I'd been running the shop and what the average monthly earnings were, and I told him. "I'll tell you what. I'll pay your debt, and we'll transfer your business over to me," he suggested.

I didn't see any other way out and had to accept in order to continue working at the Desert Rose, now as an employee rather than as its owner.

BACHIR

The guard called me, and I got up as if I had just heard a piece of great news. "Follow me," he said.

I thought my mom had come back to visit, so I prepared to ask her to tell Noura I wanted to meet with her. However, when the guard turned right, my eyes lit up. As soon as I saw my cousin, I felt as if I had just been delivered from impending danger. I wanted to embrace her, but she stepped back and made do with a limp handshake. That's what she usually does to make others understand that she isn't a woman with endless free time on her hands.

"I've been waiting for you to come," I said. I couldn't hide how scared I was. "But my trust in the Creator has not faltered," I continued.

We sat at the table, and she looked straight at me. "You deflowered her. You thought she had betrayed you, so you killed her."

I stared at Noura as I rubbed my earlobe. No girl had ever betrayed me, and I didn't recall plucking any roses. My teenage girlfriends had never allowed anything more than apprehensive kisses, just as Zakia had resisted and preserved her virginity by firmly refusing my entreaties. I held my hands together without taking my eyes off hers, and responded in a lowered voice like someone afraid the walls might hear. "Wrong."

She wasn't convinced, so I told her to ask a relative of Zakia's named Nassira, who she had confided in about what was going on between us. "That one?" I thought I heard her sneer.

She had come intent on pressuring me to spew out everything I knew.

"I've already spoken with her!"

My forehead was sweaty, and I said, "I take refuge in God."

Noura stood where she was, surprised at my words. She had never personally witnessed any piety or proximity to religion on my part. I had no idea which direction to face when praying toward Mecca.

My face darkened, and it occurred to me that she had noticed I'd lost weight and that my hands trembled. I lowered my head, then looked up again. Shyly, I proceeded to recount how my relationship with Zakia had started – when I'd promised that we'd get engaged and then married, my rendezvous with her, her being satisfied with just hugging and kissing, and her insistence that she had never felt such love and warmth before meeting me.

"She was involved with another man before you?"

"That's why I wanted to meet with you."

Noura covered her mouth with the palm of her hand, and I held back tears as I brought my hands together.

"Her previous fiancé's name was Bensalem. He became so obsessed with her he couldn't stand them being apart." I thought it likely he was behind her murder and felt increasingly doubtful that Maimoun had been involved. I figured it wouldn't be in his best interests to have a murder sully his hotel's reputation.

She jotted down what I said, and I sensed that she felt bad for doubting my initial account. "When did you last write to her?"

I looked up at the ceiling. "More than three months ago," I told her. I'd written to her the day I'd seen Miriam Makeba sing on television; her brown face had inspired me with words of love.

Noura looked at me in silence, not believing what she was hearing. "My mother wasn't wrong when she called me the Godmother of Divorced Women. I'm no good at anything other than family cases," she mumbled. She had believed what was contained in the interrogation report, where I had acknowledged writing a letter that had been falsely attributed to me.

"I was forced to sign it."

I told Noura what I had gone through at the station, and she said she felt for me. I recited bits of letters I had written to my beloved, who was now buried in the ground, and not one of them contained a single insult, rebuke, or threat. It was all just sweet talk quoted from ghazals. My cousin decided to request that the court conduct an analysis to compare my handwriting to that in the aforementioned letter.

"Zakia was going to tell me something before she drew her last breaths."

Noura remained silent as she waited for me to continue.

"She called me at home while I was out."

"This is a point in your favor," she said, citing what the police inspector had reported ("The victim telephoned Bachir's family home hours before her death.").

That I hadn't answered her call right then might take the heat off me, even if just slightly. She had gotten into the habit of calling me from the phone booth next door because the telephone lines at the hotel were under surveillance.

"Was she planning on going back to her old fiancé?"

"I don't think so."

"Did she love another man after you?"

"No, she didn't."

"Do you have any proof of that?"

"I gave her a pair of silver pearl earrings. I wanted to make her happy after a spat we'd had. They served as an agreement between us. If she had returned them to me, that would have meant our love had run dry. But she didn't."

People don't consider earrings mere adornments. They're a statement of a lover's loyalty to his beloved, something which was not lost on Noura. She asked how Zakia had come to possess my ID card, which she'd used to rent the VCR.

"I gave it to her to rent the machine to watch a recorded concert of hers."

"Why didn't she use her own card?"

I explained how she'd been on the missing persons list at her local police station since she'd run away from her family home. To keep it from falling into the hands of an informant or someone who might report her, she'd only showed her ID card to people she trusted. Noura's face flashed a look of surprise, but she quickly hid it.

"Did she sing anywhere else besides the hotel nightclub?"

"Only at the Sahara."

Noura obviously thought she had put her finger on a sore spot when she asked: "How do you explain the bloodied shirt of yours I found at your home?" She told me she had burned it so no one could get ahold of it, as it would have implicated me. I spoke frankly about the fight between Kamal's neighbor and me. She thought I should go see a doctor.

"It's nothing to worry about."

That day, my friend had taken me to the hospital in his car, and a nurse had bandaged me up as he finished his cigarette. The nurse made me wait for the doctor to examine me.

The clamor of sick people filled the corridor. "It was chaos...
ass-backward," I told Noura. But the police had arrived
before the doctor showed up; the hospital administration
had reported me, as they always do when someone arrives
with an injury from an accident or a fight. I was taken to the
station, where I waited even longer before the brigadier took
my statement. He wouldn't record my complaint towards
the aggressor unless Kamal agreed to appear as a witness!
I returned home that night, walking down sidewalks lined
with homeless families. The following day, I found myself
accused of murder.

Noura told me about Merzaka Soualem, whom I used to
hate because she'd been so egotistical. "Had she and Zakia
had a falling out?"

"Merzaka argued with everyone. She considered herself
better than everyone else."

"Zakia never complained about her?"

"The only thing she used to complain about was gaining
weight from eating too many pastries."

Before glumly bidding Noura farewell, I told her: "This
Bensalem fellow never got tired of looking for Zakia, and
he was always leaning on her relative, Nassira, to tell him
where she was."

I could tell my cousin wanted me to elaborate, but the
guard came between us at that point.

IBRAHIM

OCTOBER 1

My mother was furious when my uncle told her what I had asked him for. She called me every name in the book – filthy, cheap, nasty, mangy – while I made do with insulting my uncle.

"Relatives are like scorpions."

"You're the biggest scorpion there is!"

She tried to convince me to leave the video shop and find other work, so I shut my bedroom door, not telling her that I had settled my debt and was now no more than an employee. I looked through the things I had brought back from the Desert Rose: a blanket, pillow, eating utensils, guitar, cassettes, a tape recorder, and a handful of books. I said goodbye to my previous life; I'd now have to comport myself at work in a dignified manner out of respect for the shop's new owner.

I left my room with the idea of grabbing a half loaf of bread from the kitchen to gnaw on as I made my way to work. The shouts of a traveling kitchen utensil salesman reached my ears through the open window, then there was a knock at the door. I opened it.

"Ibrahim Derras?"

I responded with a nod to the policeman brandishing a summons in his hand.

"You need to come to the station."

Thinking the inspector wanted to question me again about Zakia Zaghouani, I went back inside to tell my mother that the police wanted me for something. "I hope they take you to prison!" she snapped at me. *Prison makes men stronger*, I wanted to respond, but I kept this to myself.

I brushed my hair, put on some of the perfume Nabil had given me, and headed out with *The Sheik* under my arm to give to Tijani for his amusement. I passed by the Christian cemetery and pictured a skeleton with a set of gold teeth, an image I had come to associate with the place. When I got to the station, I spat into my hands and, in an elegant move, fixed my hair before going in. I presented my ID card to the policeman at the front desk, and after making a call that lasted no more than thirty seconds, he indicated I should go up to the first floor. I entered the inspector's office but was met by another person with a thick face and brown eyes who held the rank of brigadier. He ordered me to sit down without even looking in my direction. He stared at the papers in his hands, then looked up at me.

"Why did you attack Kamal Belattar's property?"

"Who told you that?"

He informed me that the complainant had a witness – Faudel Arkoub – and that things would become difficult if I didn't confess. It felt as if he was threatening me. I looked at the policeman sitting next to him, typing my words on a typewriter like the one I used in front of the post office. He was just doing his job, listening but not speaking, his fingers gliding over the black keys. I felt heat rising to my cheeks, then they went cold as the blood drained from my face.

"He's the one who wronged me."

"I don't understand."

"He didn't pay me what he owed."

"So instead of submitting a complaint, you attack his property?!" The brigadier blew his nose into a cloth handkerchief like someone stricken suddenly with a cold. He then folded the handkerchief in two and, without giving me a moment to defend myself, added sharply: "You're under arrest."

I didn't understand what was happening. It seemed that some sort of mistake had been made, although I hadn't denied what I had done.

When the cell door closed, I felt like an orphan in a dormitory, as Dalida had sung in French. I waited for the police inspector to intervene and let me go to work, to watch him overrule that brigadier who had ordered that I be put in prison. I hoped he would come and save me, and I vowed to implicate Six for what I suspected was his involvement in the hotel singer's death. But the only one who approached me was a young policeman, who handed me a container of water to quench my thirst and asked, "Why'd you trespass on someone else's property?"

"To defend my dignity."

"Your dignity got you thrown in prison."

I ignored his provocation, hoping Khider Arkoub wouldn't hear about what had happened and kick me out of the shop. I prayed to God that He would get me out of this. I flipped through *The Sheik* with trembling fingers. I was dazed and unable to concentrate on the words, although I knew the story by heart: Diana, an Englishwoman, is born looking more like a boy than a girl. Thin, with deep blue eyes and small breasts, masculine with short hair. She rides horses and is good at archery, which she is taught by her older brother, who, following the death of their parents, takes care of her as if she were a brother rather than a sister. She comes as a tourist to Biskra, that city lying beyond the dunes and among the oases like an old fennec. She attracts attention with her smooth face and tweed knit skirt. She mixes with Arabs, whom she describes as impatient. She insists on taking a tour of the vast Saharan desert tracks, after which she plans to head to Oran by land, board a ship to Marseille, then continue to northern France. From there, she will sail again to rejoin her brother. She tasks a camel driver to lead her caravan, without knowing he is in cahoots with a sheik named Ahmed ben Hassan, who kidnaps and imprisons her in his tent, just as I was imprisoned. However, the difference between Diana and me is that Ahmed provides her with a servant and a horse to ride around on, which she eventually uses to escape. But the sheik catches up with her, and their relationship turns from arm-twisting into love. The whole time, her brother is baffled by her disappearance. Then she discovers that ben Hassan is not an Arab after all. He is from the same blood as her. His adoptive father raised him and made him look like the rest of the Arabs. Although I had enjoyed the novel, I wasn't comfortable with its ending: Why do romantic novels always insist on happy endings? Isn't the most beautiful love also the most painful one? I pursed my lips, having decided that imprisonment doesn't make men stronger. It just makes them really have to pee.

HAMID

I considered reaching over to grab the newspaper lying on the edge of the commissioner's desk, but I held back. I glimpsed a story on the front page about a national symposium to protect minors from violence. There was another one next to it about the Olympic Games in South Korea. I wondered what was in the local news pages, since the paper's regional reporter, Tijani K., had been absent for the last couple of days. He had been punished by two ex-convicts after publishing a story about Zaza's death that hinted that the perpetrator was a faith-healer who lived in the meadow, an action that was likely to influence the investigation. He has only himself to blame, I thought. I refused to register his complaint against the assailants because his only witness was his wife.

"Will you drink something, Inspector, sir?"

The commissioner usually called me by my name, not my professional title, or he would point at me with his finger or chin. I wondered where this newfound respect was coming from.

"No thanks, I just had a coffee."

The commissioner leaned back next to me on the couch, rubbing his left arm with the palm of his right hand, his eyebrows furrowed as if laying an ambush for an opponent. He asked me how Zinab was doing. I had gone with her to the doctor the previous day when her back pain had worsened.

"Better," I answered.

"Eight years we've had the pleasure of your company."

I'll never forget the day I arrived in this city. It was just after the cancellation of a lecture by Mouloud Mammeri on ancient Amazigh poetry, when strikes broke out in Tizi Ouzou as a result. My meeting with the commissioner that day had lasted no longer than fifteen minutes, during which we had exchanged greetings and pleasantries. Prior to my arrival, a detailed report on me had come from the station in the capital's suburbs where I had worked before.

Why are you being so friendly all of a sudden, I wanted to respond, but he didn't give me a chance.

"A decision has come down to send you back to your previous post."

I stared at him in disbelief. The room was silent except for the sound of the electric fan. I caressed the soft couch with my fingertips. I hadn't requested to go back and hadn't done anything wrong that would necessitate my transfer. I said what I was thinking, and he seemed measured as he spoke.

"The police chief you quarreled with has retired."

He had retired five months ago, and I knew for a fact that he'd never got what he wanted from the girl we had argued over. I asked why I was being transferred right then.

"The Security Directorate there needs you."

Then he yawned without covering his mouth as he instructed the brigadier to take over my duties temporarily.

His tone became firm. He stood up and headed toward the door, cleaning his ear with his index finger. "You'll receive a copy of the transfer decision tomorrow."

I understood that the meeting was over and that my relationship with this city was done. I learned that I had a week to empty out my office. It occurred to me that what was happening was connected with Zaza's case. When lions grow old, the wolves swoop down on them, I thought. I was a lion whose fangs had fallen out, and I had become a delicious morsel for whoever wanted it.

In my office, I looked around as if bidding a broken-hearted farewell to a beloved. As I left the building, the policeman at the front desk asked me what he should do with the people sitting in the waiting room who were complying with summonses they had received. "Lick their asses!" I screamed at him.

El Mejdoub's words came to mind:

> *Friend, be patient and forbearing about what has happened*
> *to you.*
> *Lie down naked on thorns 'til your day dawns anew.*

I called Noura's office that afternoon and asked her to meet me at the Nakhil.

"Why?"

"It concerns something that might interest you."

This lawyer seemed nicer than her father, whose real estate scams I had heard about. On the way to the restaurant, I cursed everyone I worked with as I spat out of the car window – the whole lot of them bastards, degenerates, wretches, despicables, and lechers. I recalled incidents that had stuck in my mind, like that psychopath who had chopped off his mother's head, stuffed it into a paper bag, and gone out for a walk downtown. Or that old woman who had cut off her grandson's hand so she could use it in some sort of witches' brew. Or the woman in her forties who had hidden a bag of cocaine in her vagina the day we'd raided her house to conduct a search.

When I reached my destination, I realized it was the first time since Zakia's death that I had gone out without a security escort. I was no longer "Boss." Just Hamid. A man stripped of all standing and history. My head swirled with thoughts about what my life would look like in the capital, with its alleyways and streets, its port that smells of sardines. I thought about taking my sons to visit the Martyrs' Memorial. They would no doubt be impressed by the monument's three stylized palm fronds rising high into the air in eternal memory of the War of Independence. And also by the shopping center next to it, where we could buy European products.

I got a table in the far corner of the restaurant, its walls decorated with ceramics. At the entrance goldfish swam in an aquarium whose sides were adorned with hanging bunches of plastic flowers. Younger customers sat at the other tables.

Noura came right away. She was wearing jeans and a long red shirt that covered her buttocks. I stood up, wanting to kiss her cheeks and smell her perfume, but she took a step back and contented herself with shaking my hand, after which she quickly withdrew hers.

I glanced at her face, and she looked more beautiful than when we had met at the station, when I had lured her in by arresting her aunt's husband instead of just sending him a summons. After learning that she had gone to the hotel more than once, I wanted to hear what she knew about Zakia's case. A pang of guilt hit me as I thought about how badly I'd treated her aunt's husband, Makhlouf Labtam, a skinny man with an egg-shaped head who had looked as scared as a chicken with a knife to its neck when I'd arrested him.

"What can I get you?" I asked her.

"Just tea."

I ordered her tea, and a bowl of soup and a bottle of soda for me. She was surprised at how the waiter smiled at and ingratiated himself toward me, unlike the rest of the city's sullen servers. She didn't know she was sitting with me in the same restaurant I'd brought Hassina to when we first started dating. I haven't stopped coming since. Uncomfortable, I tugged at the chest hairs that sprang out from the top of my shirt. A pair of speakers at the nearby Art Stars shop was blaring out a song popular with the youth. It was by a young, unknown male singer named Hasni and a strong-voiced female singer named Zahouania. In the song, they talked about themselves as they performed their romantic rituals in a ramshackle hut, just as I had with Bahija in Bab El Oued when I was seventeen. That had been my initiation into the world of women.

I looked into the lawyer's eyes and said in a crushed tone: "You won't be seeing me in my office anymore."

She thought I was joking.

"I'm going back to the capital."

The waiter handed her a cup of tea, but her desire to take a sip seemed to leave her, as if my words were stuck in her throat like a pebble. He brought me some soup, which I proceeded to slurp calmly. Then he handed me a soda.

"You've had enough of us!" the lawyer quipped in an apparent effort to get me to level with her.

I told her about the decision to return me to my previous station and about my suspicion that it had something to do with Zaza's case. I didn't hold back about what had happened to me since the murder, from the smashing of my car's windows to my haunting fears that I would be targeted next. I told her how I tossed and turned in my sleep and had lost a few pounds, I was so anxious. Sympathetically, she covered her mouth with her hand.

"I didn't want to meet up with you to complain about my situation, though."

"…"

"Rather, I want to be of help with the murdered woman's case."

"You won't be of any help to me as long as Bachir's in prison." She reproached me for forcing him to sign the interrogation report.

"You want me to end up a laughingstock!" I retorted. Every case that ends in finding the perpetrator results in a bonus at the end of the month. That was why, since taking this job, I had strived never to have to write off a case as "accused unknown."

"Why were you so rough with him the day you arrested him?"

"It was a fit of anger that I regret."

The difference between Columbo from the old TV detective series and me is that I have a short temper. She revealed that, before Bachir, Zaza had been engaged to a man named Bensalem.

"I suspected her heart belonged to someone else too," I told her. I felt like an idiot for believing Zaza all that time. I informed Noura that Zakia had run away from her family home and that her town's police had "posted her picture in the travelers' station, restaurants, and mosques, but to no avail."

"I know."

I made her understand that all of that wouldn't change a thing.

"My cousin was injured that night. He wouldn't have been strong enough to be able to commit murder!"

"I don't think he was the only one involved. Someone was working with him, and someone covered it up."

I informed Noura that the blood analysis results had arrived from the lab but hadn't pointed to anything significant. Zaza hadn't been drunk, and she hadn't taken any drugs before her death. And all the prints we lifted from her room had been hers. I suggested to Noura that she go back to the hotel. I outlined in detail what I had heard from Achour, his daughter, and the muezzin, along with Farhat's statement, making clear that what had happened had not been planned by one person alone. I mentioned what Halima had said about how her daughter had not felt safe around the people she had worked with.

Noura's lower jaw was trembling, and she muttered what Zaza had said to her cousin, Nassira ("I'm going to rule this hotel"). I fixed my gaze on her face, and through tightened lips I said, "There's no way anyone will rule that place without getting rid of Maimoun." Had the hotel owner taken revenge on Zaza for conspiring against him? I thought.

I finished my bowl of soup and sipped what was left in the soda bottle, moistening the corners of my lips. Noura had not swallowed a drop of tea. The whole time we sat there, she moved the small spoon around and around in her cup. Out of nervousness, she took out a cigarette and asked for a match.

"I didn't know you smoked!"

"I didn't know you were so much nicer than people say."

I couldn't keep from laughing.

She turned to me and asked, "Why did you want to help me?"

"So you can help me ensure that Zakia's blood wasn't spilled for nothing."

It was clear she didn't believe me, but she appeared to appreciate my friendliness toward her. "I need you to do two things for me."

I expected her to ask for something connected to her cousin, and I prepared to beg off.

"Investigate her former fiancé."

"And?"

"Punish Ibrahim Derras."

I pretended not to know him. I hadn't been comfortable with his statement. I was sure he was hiding something.

"The movie rental shop owner you questioned," she continued.

"What did he do?"

"He bothers me."

You're a lawyer and you don't know how to defend yourself? I thought. "What's the charge?"

"Disseminating pornography."

I had overlooked Ibrahim's complaint against Noura's brother for lack of witnesses, and I didn't tell her that he would be punished for leaking news of Zaghouani's murder to the reporter, as Tijani had admitted to the two men who had disciplined him. He had stuck his nose into a hornets' nest. I assured her that I would call the police station in Nezrama to have them forward the statement of the person known as Bensalem. I wrote down her request in my notebook, even though the legal procedure required a formal letter. Then, I began to pick my teeth with the nail of my index finger.

"Who's this Farhat you mentioned?" Noura asked me.

"He was the dead woman's accompanist."

She asked me about Merzaka Soualem, so I gave her the facts about her suicide and how her family had rushed her burial without having an autopsy done so as not to prolong the sadness of her two sons. I also told her how we had found a medical report in her room stating that she was pregnant.

"She was pregnant?!" Noura drew on her cigarette and continued: "As far as I know, she was divorced."

"Doesn't a divorced woman have the right to love another man?"

The lawyer remained silent for a bit, then told me that she suspected Safia Bechiche, even though she seemed gentle and gave the impression of only being interested in using her makeup-caked face to turn men's heads.

I told her I didn't consider Cheikha Edahabia a suspect, and that was the last time I saw Noura Arkoub.

That evening, my baby girl was born, and I remembered a snippet of Abderrahman El Mejdoub's poetry:

> *Don't be deceived by the oleander flower that gives shade on*
> *the river's banks*
> *And don't be deceived by a child's beauty until you've seen*
> *what she does.*

Over the objections of Zinab, who had tried to convince me to name the baby Lamia, I insisted on calling her Zakia, hoping she would not meet the same fate as the singer at the Sahara. It wasn't long before my wife gave in. She knew she would move with me to the capital and throw herself into the embrace of her blind mother-in-law with the tattooed forehead, who was thrilled by the news of my return.

I was watching something on a French channel when Hassina Eidache called to congratulate me on the birth of my daughter and to comfort me after hearing that I was leaving. During the conversation, she asked me sadly: "Do you think Bachir will ever get out of prison?"

"I don't know, but what I do know is that Noura won't come out of all this unscathed."

NOURA

I got to the hotel and found Kamal stretched out on a sofa in the lobby, wearing leather moccasins that had never been touched by dust. He was watching the calm movement of the employees around him as he listened to Umm Kulthum on his tape player. As soon as he saw me, he stood up. He looked delighted to see me.

He walked over and shook my hand, accepting my apology for coming without an appointment. I'm sure he noticed my pale face and thought it likely I was suffering from stomach cramps or my period. He offered me a cup of juice, which I did not refuse.

The flood of foreigners had stopped, he told me, and he no longer had to listen to their complaints about snot-nosed children who annoyed them downtown as they begged for money or sweets. The only person who still came was a young expat studying archaeology. He was surprised at how dour she always looked: "She hasn't shown her teeth since she got here." According to him, a woman's beauty lies in her teeth. "Once, I pretended to laugh in front of her to try to get her to smile, but she refused," he said. He figured the place was not to her liking, which he took umbrage at: "Let her go to the roach-infested Nour, home to transients, fraudsters, and vagrants." The Sahara is where the locals go; couples who spend their honeymoons there, or bachelors who have suddenly come into some money and who book rooms to satisfy their pleasures and spend time in the garden among the palm trees, fox geraniums, morning glories, Indian jasmine bushes, and lavender. Or they might avail themselves of the swimming pool during the day and, at concerts in the evening, move their bodies like dervishes animated by Cheikha Edahabia.

He stopped the tape and asked me about Bachir, seeming heartbroken, while I drank my juice. I looked at him as he calmly smoked and answered him curtly: "Truly with hardship comes ease." I sat up straight; my red shirt had stuck to my belly, I was sweating so much.

"Do you remember where you were the night of Zakia Zaghouani's murder?"

Kamal had obviously thought he was done with all this when he gave his statement at the station, but he went along with me. "At work." He had proof that he had been welcoming foreign tourists who had arrived from the capital in the wee hours of that morning. He offered me the records so I could look into the date and time of their arrival.

"It's OK, I trust you."

Nothing in how he moved made him look guilty, and I had learned that people's movements give them away before they say anything. He probably figured it was nothing more than a routine question I needed to ask as my cousin's defense lawyer.

I tucked a lock of hair behind my ear and fixed my gaze on his nose, which went well with the rest of his face. It was as if I was seeing him for the first time. I was convinced his lips were made for kissing. Kamal was one of those men who would remain handsome even after turning fifty. I imagined his taut stomach underneath his white shirt, unlike Ibrahim's flabby baklava-dough-like stomach.

"It seems that your relationship with the deceased wasn't good!"

Kamal understood that I had come armed with secrets only those closest to him knew, and he kept his cool as he answered. "She couldn't stand how strict I was," he said, saying she had disliked him because she was easily offended. I didn't comment, since I had not known the victim personally. I sought clarification as to whether he used to go to the meadow, hoping to get him to divulge the names of hotel employees who used to go there.

"May God forgive me." He told me about how he used to go there with someone named Farhat, who had a moped, "to smoke joints." According to him, Farhat enjoyed smoking hash out in the open rather than sitting cooped up inside. "That guy puts his all into inhaling his joints until his face looks like a potato, and all he can do is laugh as if someone's tickling him."

"I've given up smoking things that are haram."

I held off asking him about this Farhat who never stopped going to the meadow to get high as a kite on hashish. He sounded like a shadowy character to me. Then I asked him about that neighbor who had assaulted Bachir.

"He'll get his."

He answered me confidently, but I didn't fully believe him. Why had he only attacked my cousin? Who was to say that Kamal hadn't been the one who had provoked Bachir? The smell of his perfume made me swoon, and I wondered if I was being overly suspicious. I thanked him for the juice, then asked if I could see Maimoun Belassal.

Lazily, Kamal picked up the receiver and called the manager from the reception desk, then told me with a friendly smile: "You know the way."

Belassal regarded my face, which must have been shimmering with beads of sweat, making me shine like a photograph. "I don't know when this brain-frying heat will break," he said.

A greater heat in the fires of hell awaits you, I said to myself, surprised Belassal had agreed without hesitation to meet with me. He didn't stop chitchatting about the weather that made it easier for the locusts to feverishly multiply by day, he said. Breezes did nothing to cool the night air, and electric fans were useless.

I smiled to put him at ease. He passed his hand over his bald spot and the wrinkles on his forehead. He offered me a cold drink, but I declined. "As you wish," he said.

I had a strong urge to scratch my armpit. I asked him when he had last gone to the meadow.

"Being so busy keeps me from getting around much." Then he looked up at the ceiling and added: "I haven't set foot there in years."

I guessed that he had prepared himself to dodge a question like that. He was a war veteran after all. No doubt he was accustomed to deftly getting out of difficult situations. However, I put his past aside and faced him head-on.

"Someone saw your car in the meadow around the same time that Zakia was murdered."

I had repeated this sentence to myself many, many times before getting to where I could say it without emotion. I wanted to be sure he felt the seriousness of what I was saying.

Belassal adjusted himself in his chair, ignoring the telephone that had started to ring. He glared at me in a way that reminded me of my father when he'd get mad when I was young and slap me or rub my lips with a hot pepper.

"Perhaps it was just one that looked like it."

"No, there's proof it was yours." Without blinking, I told him clearly that the muezzin had seen his car and license plate number close to the scene of the crime.

Belassal's face froze and he sat as still as a piece of furniture. I also remained still, waiting for a response. His lips lost their color, and he began to sweat. If not for the movement of his eyelashes, I would have thought that he had fainted.

IBRAHIM

OCTOBER 2

Instead of finding my father's grave, I started to dig my own.
I threw my ass down onto the cement floor, surrounded by
prisoners, some weeping, others laughing. I was irritated
by the sound of the guards' footsteps in the hallway, upset
about the small window at the top of the wall through which
a sirocco wind blew, and annoyed at the strong fluorescent
lights that constantly lit the place without any of the power
cuts people experienced in their homes. After spending half
an hour in silence, baffled by my situation, I saw Djeghloul,
a former customer of mine, looking emaciated. He had
just four teeth remaining in his mouth. "What brought you
here?" he asked me.

"Trespassing."

Djeghloul had worked for years in a shop where they
made knives the tourists went crazy for. Their scabbards were
goatskin, their handles carved ivory. After that, he'd headed
up a gang dedicated to stealing cars, in a country that didn't
have enough cars to go around! According to a statistic I once
read, there are six vehicles for every hundred people here.

He asked about the identity of the owner of the house I
had broken into and whose car window I had smashed.

"A bastard who didn't pay what he owed." I didn't mention his name.

"You're always getting yourself into shit."

You're right, I answered him silently. I'd thought I understood life from how much I read and that the hours I'd spent flipping through books – more hours than I slept – would be of some help to me. But I'd come to understand that I was no more than a half-wit. Although the Eagles sung about people who sometimes lose and sometimes win, I never win a thing. I'm up to my neck in losses.

At dawn the next day, a young man as fat as a pregnant sheep came to wake me from a slumber that hadn't lasted more than a few minutes. I'd dreamed that I had gray hair. Isn't gray hair one of the signs of wisdom? "Prayer," he said. His stern gaze and blackened teeth frightened me.

I tried getting away from him. "I haven't performed my ablutions."

"Use the dirt to perform them," the man said, nodding toward the ground. Other young men were doing just that, and all I could do was copy them. I barely remembered the short suras; it had been a long time since I had knelt down and bent over to pray. Ever since childhood, I'd mimicked my teacher and classmates. The last prayer I'd attended was the Prayer of the Dead, for Nabil, and there had been no kneeling or bending over.

Sluggishly, I stood with the worshippers. Then, a young man who performed the call to prayer before had us line up: "Shoulder to shoulder. Foot to foot. Make sure the row is even!"

When the prayer was done, I felt a pain in my calf as if I had just been forced to perform a strenuous task. The guy who called himself Sidi Zerzour prayed a little away from us.

It was rumored that he hid his money in his ass, wrapping banknotes in sticky tape and licking the tape before inserting it into his anus.

Chaos returned after prayer. No one lay down comfortably where they were. Instead, each prisoner sought to gain control over every extra inch they could, like drunken locusts. I listened as a young man with a severed nasal septum raised his hands to pray for water to return to the tap after a two-day absence.

"They want us to die of thirst."

"Aren't we already dead?"

I withdrew to my corner, unable to close my eyes, and played around with the novel in my hands. No use in reading or writing or a diploma now, I thought. I remembered something Malek Haddad once said: "Exile is a bad habit we need to get used to." Prison was also a bad habit I needed to get used to. What I craved the most was the flavor of nicotine. I hadn't had a cigarette since my arrest. I came to crave the fava beans I'd hated so much before, the news on the radio about AIDS, coups, floods, earthquakes around the globe, and young people being arrested for hiding on ships headed for Europe. I longed to hold my guitar close and smell the outside air; it didn't matter that it was polluted with fumes from municipal insecticide trucks. The air inside was unbearable. It smelled of sweat, armpit odor, and stinky feet. What was my mother doing in my absence? Did Khamisi know what had happened to me?

Prisoners were reciting prayers, which masked the groans of two young men hiding what they were doing with one another under a blanket. I cursed them both under my breath and thought of Noura, the only lawyer I had ever met. I regretted that my relationship with her had deteriorated, since I didn't have any money to hire another lawyer, and no lawyer would defend me for free. I recalled my years at school and my work at the Desert Rose. All is lost, I thought. As I hugged my knees to my body, the prison muezzin walked toward me. His fluffy beard looked like a newly hatched chick, and he had a *miswak* between his lips.

"Where are you from?"

"Achacha."

"I know it."

Who doesn't know that ghetto where I was born and grew up, where people live in coops and not houses? The children there grow up fast, fighting each other all summer long like bulls, the winner rising to the role of leader. He who commands is obeyed. They tell dirty jokes. They bum cigarette butts from one another. They come to blows over an egg or a sugar cube. They defecate against walls, unbothered by the smell. They grill birds and trap scorpions and locusts, and whenever they see lovers walking together, they pelt them with the nastiest words. They pull up every seedling, and the neighbors – who compete with one another in reproducing – find nothing but walls remaining if they leave their house for more than a day. All they watch are Westerns and action movies, and whoever insists on something romantic is called the worst names. Not a year will go by without a baby of unknown parentage being found. The police have grown so tired of trying to keep up that they just leave these babies next to the dead in the Christian cemetery to scrape at the graves and pray for God to prolong their lives.

That muezzin seemed to feel sorry for me and sensed from how I looked that I had been mistreated.

"Do you have any family?"

"My mother's downtrodden, and my younger brother can barely make ends meet."

"Consider me a brother." He asked me what I had in my hand.

"A novel."

"What's it called?"

"*The Sheik.*" I cut short his stream of questions by asking his name.

"Bachir Labtam."

HALIMA

I stood in front of the policeman at the front desk, who was busy flipping through a sports magazine. Without looking up, he asked me in a robotic voice: "Do you have a summons?" I asked him if he thought I was one of those women suspected of dealing in counterfeit or stolen jewelry. Or buying and selling umbilical cords, which sterile women cook and eat to get pregnant? He looked up and replied, "No."

He scrutinized my face. I'd imagined they would treat me with some decency, considering I had just lost my daughter. I was hit again by the smell of camphor that had made my nose run in the morgue when I'd taken a last look at her body. The only thing I could come up with to say to him was: "Is Hamid here?"

As he tried to figure out who I was, he looked me straight in the eyes for so long it made me uneasy. "No," he eventually answered.

I waited for the policeman to tell me when Hamid was coming or where I might wait for him. I was beating myself up because I hadn't told the inspector when I was coming. I'd called his office phone numerous times the previous day, but he hadn't answered. I'd just thought he was busy, so I'd rushed over to seek his help. My oldest son, Tali, who works as a chicken butcher in the daily market, had been hauled off to prison after a run-in with someone named Bensalem, who the police had summonsed to give a statement. He thought he'd be implicated in Zakia's case, got mad at my son, and they'd come to blows. He'd called my daughter the worst names, loud enough for all to hear, boasting that he'd done "nasty things to her" before getting stabbed in the right shoulder and landing in the hospital. Tali is quick to anger. He's my son, and I know him well. None of my other pregnancies were as difficult as his. I nursed him two months longer than his other siblings, but he still grew into a short young man with a long tongue, like his father. His blood is always boiling.

I remembered when I had come back from burying my daughter on that day so hot it felt like a fire had kissed Nezrama's lips. He approached me rudely and hissed, "Your daughter brought shame whether alive or dead." I told him she'd been a victim of foul play, but he didn't show any pity. He yelled in my face without giving a thought to my grief. As for Yahya, who's two years younger, he was spitting mad and insisted I tell him who did it. "He's in prison," I told him. "I swear I'll rip his guts out with my own two hands," he threatened as he waved a knife in front of me. My eyes filled with tears, and I almost fainted. I found myself a prisoner to the rage of my four sons. The youngest two didn't hesitate to insult their sister's soul.

"When's he coming back?"

"He went to work in the capital," the policeman answered.

The capital is over five hours away by car. I thought he was kidding at first, but he was insistent.

It's one ulcer after another, I thought. I was upset I had come alone. My niece, Nassira, was being kept inside by her parents, who had forbidden her from going out alone or with her female relatives. This is what people do when a family intends to marry off a daughter. They keep her inside. It's common practice among the neighbors. She isn't allowed out until a groom comes for her.

I only had enough money to get back to Nezrama, with a few dinars to spare. Not enough to pay for a room. I'd been counting on the police inspector to find me a place to stay like he had before. When my daughter died, my source of income was cut off. If not for her, I wouldn't have been able to afford the gold tooth in my mouth. I'd given my children all my savings to stop them from saying I'd brought her up badly.

I took a step back without the policeman noticing. I realized his face was elongated like a fava bean. I hate fava beans, and I don't like people who look like fava beans. I left with a sneaking suspicion that Hamid had betrayed me by hiding his intention to be transferred to somewhere far away. Our last conversation had taken place after that lawyer had visited me at my sister's house. I'd told him what we had talked about.

The only thing I could think of was to call Noura to complain to her about my situation and then make the most of coming here by going to visit my daughter's grave. I called her in a hushed voice, and for a moment she thought I was one of her clients.

"This is Halima, the dead woman's mother."

Her voice rose like someone who had been stung by a bee. I told her I was calling from a telephone booth in front of the post office.

"I'm coming."

When I caught sight of Noura, it was like seeing the morning light after a long period of darkness. I felt bad for being so rude to her when she'd come to take my statement, and I hugged her as I would hug a loved one after not seeing them for a long time. "I'm in your hands."

We got into an illegal taxi that charged more than a regular cab and headed to where the lawyer lived.

Noura's mother thought her daughter had brought one of her clients home, and she offered me tea in the living room. It tasted as bitter as my days, but I didn't dare ask for sugar. I'm just a guest, and guests don't complain. A cat roamed between our legs, swishing its tail as if it wanted me to pet it.

The lawyer sat on the couch between us, and her mother asked her if she had called her aunt. The mother talked about how sorry she felt for her sister and how Bachir's uncle's wife, as she put it, had come asking about him. Her daughter cut her off.

"Halima… the mother of the woman who was killed…"

Noura's mother's eyes widened when she heard that. Then she stared at my graying hair once I pulled my veil off. I need to darken it with henna to complete the mourning process for my daughter, I said to myself. With her hands clasped under her belly, she told me in a kind voice: "My nephew's been put in prison by mistake."

I didn't understand what she meant, but a heat crept up to my ears as Noura grabbed my hand and explained what left me practically breathless – that the man suspected of killing Zakia was none other than Noura's cousin. I thought I had fallen into a trap. O Lord, watch over me, I thought. I covered my mouth with my hand and silently cursed Hamid, thinking he had left his post just to put me into this predicament.

Noura seemed to notice how perturbed I was as I touched the back of my head. "You're at home and among family," she reassured me. Her mother, for her part, swallowed her tongue. She didn't know this was a chance visit. The lawyer surprised me by saying the suspect hadn't forced the deceased to do anything she hadn't wanted to. This called to mind the inspector's denial of my suspicion that the murderer had deflowered and then killed her. She asked whether my daughter had been previously engaged to another man. She kept her hands clasped with her thumbs up, forming two sides of a triangle. I understood what she was getting at, so I told her what had happened to my son, who was now in jail, and I couldn't avoid telling her what Nassira had confided in me after the police had arrested Tali. My eyes filled with tears as I talked about what had happened to Zakia the day she disappeared six years ago.

When my daughter was almost eighteen, she met a young man named Bensalem, who did business in spare car parts. She liked how soft his hair was and how shiny his black eyes were. He wanted to get engaged. However, their relationship only lasted a month, and she split up with him when she learned he was from a tribe that was hostile to ours; they accused our family of cooperating with the colonial system. He couldn't accept that she'd left him and flew into a rage, feeling he had been made into a laughingstock. During the early days of their relationship, he'd lavished her with gifts of jewelry and foreign perfumes, all of which practically emptied his pockets. Then something terrible happened. She disappeared, and we thought she had run away from home after quarreling with her older brother, who chastised her for going out so much. She came back the next day and endured Tali's abuse and her father's insults. She claimed she had been at a wedding all evening, when in fact she had spent the night in the cemetery, pissing the whole time due to the fear raging in her heart.

Zakia had waited two months before she told her cousin what she was hiding.

"Bensalem and a friend of his kidnapped her and..."

She couldn't go back home that same day out of fear that a slip of the tongue would give her away. Even if forced to do something against her will, every girl bears the sin alone. Ever since that day, she'd kept her nails long to jam them into the skin of anyone who forced her to do something she didn't want to do.

It wasn't enough for this Bensalem that my daughter had left Nezrama, first to work at a resort in the north and then to go wherever Bachir went. Out of a desire to ruin her life, he persisted in asking Nassira about her. What baffles me is that Zakia told Nassira on the phone that she intended to marry a man from the hotel where she worked. I was almost convinced my sons were right when they'd openly declared that I hadn't provided her with the best upbringing. My sons were right, and I was wrong.

I went on to tell her about how shocked I'd been by what I'd discovered about my daughter's life and what Nassira had hidden for so long. Noura listened as she sat next to her mother. I barely moved my lips as I spoke.

As soon as I finished, the three of us sat there in a daze. Right then, we heard a knock on the door. With the cat clinging to her leg, Noura grumbled as she stood up and muttered that it was probably one of the neighbors coming to borrow something from the kitchen. People had become stingy and dependent on one another. However, when she opened the door, there stood a middle-aged woman with gray eyes and dry skin as yellow as safflower, wearing a black djellaba that went down to her ankles. She introduced herself as Daouia. Then, she rambled on about why she had come. The lawyer screamed that she wanted to kill her father, and I regretted ever calling her that day.

MAIMOUN

I wolfed down two spoonfuls of vegetable soup and closed my mouth as I looked toward Mehdi, who had spent the last three nights at my brother's house in Biskra. I thought about how I'd met the smuggler in Sétif and sent my son with my car to deliver the first shipment of medicines. The next day, when we'd gone together loaded up with the second shipment, Zaza had already been dead. Had he taken vengeance on her out of deference to his mother, Yacout? The one who had returned home after having spent a few troubled days thinking her only fate was to end up a divorced woman, and who was now smacking her lips and staring at a show on TV about the conquest of space? As soon as we finished our lunch, I stood up, claiming I had some work waiting for me. I asked Mehdi to come with me to deliver some orders to my Sahara.

Before getting to the long road that leads to the hotel, I turned right into the Martyrs' Cemetery, where five acquaintances of mine are buried along with the rest of the soldiers from neighboring villages and cities. I parked in front of its empty entrance; no one, not even officials, visits except on national holidays. I fixed my gaze on my son and asked him point-blank when he'd last gone to the meadow. Surprised by my question, he looked at me.

"I haven't set foot in that place in years."

I reached over to his left shoulder and tried to get him to talk by agreeing to help him open a shop that sells music tapes, if only he admitted the truth.

"I swear, I haven't been there in a long time."

Mehdi's life is limited to the house and the Peace of Mind Café, where he sometimes meets friends. Other times, he goes to his cousin's to play dominoes and hang out in the street. Young people's lives today are incredibly dull.

There was an innocence in his eyes and I felt he was telling the truth. So how had my car got to the meadow, then?

"What did you do when you came back from Sétif?"

"I rested up in room 302, went out to a café, then ate dinner in the restaurant and went to bed early."

"Where did you park the car?"

"In the hotel parking lot."

The following day, he'd taken off for Sétif again, and then we'd returned together.

I couldn't help feeling the lawyer was accusing me of committing a crime. I'd wanted to find out why she was digging into Merzaka Soualem's case and had been happy last time to meet her without a prior appointment. But before I'd had a chance to ask, I was surprised to learn that a witness had seen my car near the crime scene. I felt like the lawyer wanted to implicate me to save her cousin.

"Kamal took the keys from me so he could transport the shipment. I don't know where to, and I didn't drive it again until the following morning," Mehdi said.

"When did he get back from delivering the medicines?"

"I don't know."

I couldn't figure out a link that might implicate my son, so I hurried him along. "Can I take you someplace?"

"You said you needed my help!"

"I changed my mind," I responded in a more jittery tone than the usual composed way of speaking he was used to.

Dropping Mehdi close to the contraband market, I returned to the hotel. I found the receptionist, Kamal, stretched out on a sofa in the lobby, listening to Umm Kulthum on a tape player. I asked him gruffly to accompany me to my office. He got up and came with me, understanding that I wasn't in a good mood, thinking it had something to do with an error in the accounts, since most of the time I'm angry it's because I've come across an accounting error. The end of the world might come, but it won't bother me as much as discovering something wrong in the cash box.

"How's work?" I asked him, as if we didn't know one another.

"No pressure these days."

I remained calm as I questioned him to get him to reveal something I didn't already know. "Did you get your car fixed?"

"Yes."

"Did you have a lot of work to do the day Mehdi delivered the medicine shipment?"

"I was up all night waiting for some tourists to arrive in the wee hours of the morning." He slicked his hair back as he answered.

I asked him if he went to the meadow a lot, and he laughed.

"I've come to my senses."

"What do you mean?"

He told me how he used to go there with Farhat to smoke joints. I was furious. I didn't want any of my employees falling into addiction.

"When's the last time you went there?"

"I don't remember."

I could hear Umm Kulthum singing the "Rubaiyat of al-Khayyam" through the office door, which was ajar.

> *The heart is exhausted by love of beauty*
> *By what is not said, made angry.*
> *Does this thirst satisfy you, O Lord?*
> *As fresh water flows before me?*

As we moved over to the sofa, I reassured him that I wanted to listen to what he had to say, no more.

"Do you not trust me?"

"I'm trying to protect you."

I assured him that I would defend and protect him, just as I had when he'd taken the life of Merzaka Soualem, who'd had a predilection for younger men. More than two years ago, he'd got involved with her. She'd wooed him with her short, colorful skirts, sweet, shiny-white smile, and the self-confident way she walked. He sat with her in her room and they would drink together, each craving the other. I'd warned him not to go too far with her, telling him, "She's older than you." "My mother was older than my father," he'd responded.

Merzaka had divorced and been given a room at the hotel after her election to the Municipal Council and her retirement from education; she had grown frustrated by the overcrowded classes, the administration's and parents' indifference to the students' poor performance, and the meager salary she received. Kamal kept getting closer to her – with a touch, then a kiss – until she forgot herself and was swept away in the sea of love even though they were unable to find condoms in the pharmacies. She told him about the feelings that had taken root in her heart, but he made fun of her. Then she became pregnant by him, thinking a new son would renew her life. She pressured him to acknowledge what was in her womb and marry her, but he begged her to get rid of the fetus. She refused, and their relationship turned into arguments and harsh words until she yelled in his face: "You're a son of a bitch, and you want a son of a bitch like yourself!" He knelt on top of her so she couldn't move, smothered her with a pillow, and then threw her from the third-floor balcony. He was drunk. The night sky had been thick with clouds, but there was no rain and a north wind was blowing in from Biskra. Radio stations had been racing to report the news of what had happened in Chernobyl. He'd rushed into my office, where I was bogged down dealing with some things that had kept me there late. His hands trembled, and his face dripped with sweat, which he was trying to wipe away with his light purple shirt. I told him not to leave the office while I dealt with the police, who put it down as a suicide, Hamid being satisfied with my testimony. "What was the reason behind her suicide?" he'd asked. I'd lied that her ex-husband was keeping her from seeing her two sons and was pressuring her to go back to him, adding, "Perhaps he never buried his love for her." Kamal had taken a three-week vacation at Sidi Zerzour's house, which smelled of incense, herbs, old clothes, and animal bones. He ate dates, drank camel milk, and gave himself over to spells and washing his body in water suffused with charms, thinking a jinni had possessed him. Merzaka besieged him in his dreams. She asked him why he had killed her until he felt she would rise from her resting place to take revenge on him. He repented to his Lord and prayed for days, then gave it all up.

I had put Merzaka up in the hotel, smitten by the long chestnut hair she always flaunted like a peacock's tail. I'd showered her with gifts and jewelry, determined to convince her to run for parliament. She was supposed to be my winning card. I praised her eloquence and benevolence toward the underprivileged, but her ambitions didn't extend beyond her room's ceiling. Even though I kept advising her to take an interest in her political path, she was overly arrogant and sought only to satisfy her whims and collect enemies by exposing gaps in the municipal budget and defaming those she suspected of embezzlement. She would also pick fights with Zaza after the singer refused to hand over a portion of her earnings from a downtown nightclub as they had agreed until I intervened. I'd paid her out of my own pocket and reconciled things between them. I'd wanted to get rid of her anyway, so her death didn't sadden me. I concealed the perpetrator's identity to protect the hotel's reputation, sealing her room even though I was tempted to reopen it for the money.

Now I pressed Kamal to tell me what he'd done with the car after Mehdi left him the key.

"I took the medicines to the warehouse."

"Then what?"

"I went back to work."

"You spent the night here?"

"I had to wait for some tourists who were due to arrive late."

Kamal didn't usually sleep at the hotel, especially when the bus driver called in advance and told him they would be arriving late. But nothing in what he said betrayed any agitation on his part, even if it didn't help me. I was a suspect because someone had seen my car in the meadow that night. Had Bachir Labtam killed her alone? I wondered. Despite that, I tried one last time with him. Perhaps he knew things I didn't.

"Farhat told me that Zakia complained about you."

Without revealing that what I was saying came from what I had read in the police reports made available to me by the commissioner who had taken over the case, I addressed Kamal. "The police took his statement."

I concealed the fact that Hamid had left his post after complaints had piled up against him. Si Miloud had disapproved of his negligence in investigating the torching of his car and Hamid's interference in his projects, some of which had been thwarted altogether. Residential neighborhood committees had also denounced his random surveillance patrols. Then came my report, in which I'd condemned his raids on the hotel under the pretext of investigating Zakia's case, something which frightened the tourists, and the fact that he'd leaked news of her murder to a reporter. The commissioner hadn't wanted the police station's reputation to suffer, so he'd called on the Security Directorate to have him sent back to where he came from.

> *Don't fill your soul with fear of the unknown,*
> *Snatch from today the security of what is certain.*
> *For the soil will cover whomever dies tomorrow,*
> *Just as it covered those who died thousands of years ago.*

The receptionist knew that no secret could be kept from me in my Sahara, and that the waiter, Khalil, and the chef, Khayati, also kept me abreast of what goes on when I'm not there. He knew I moved mighty men like a set of Russian dolls. His face turned red.

"You're the only one who has a copy of the warehouse key," I said, and I showed him Zakia's earring, which I had found.

Kamal's lips quivered. Beads of sweat glistened on his neck and fell from his forehead onto his cheeks. I waited for him to implicate Bachir, but he just mumbled something before saying clearly, "You don't want to believe she was robbed, then."

That was the theory he had convinced himself of.

"I've never heard of a thief who would kill without stealing anything."

He understood that I had made up my mind not to take him at his word. His knees shook. "I... I... I didn't do anything."

In his agitation, his hands shook, as if an electrical current had touched them. I reminded him that he was like the son I'd always wanted.

"I'm not denying how kind you've always been toward me."

I looked calmly into his eyes, like a teacher who pities his student. I remembered the medical examiner's report stating that there were traces of isopropyl alcohol on the victim's cheek. Kamal is the only one in the hotel who insists on cleaning his hands with this type of alcohol because of how much he shakes hands with customers and other people going in and out all the time.

"I didn't mean to do her any harm."

"..."

"She's... She's... the one... the one who was conspiring against *me*."

"Who?"

"Zaza."

Kamal launched into an explanation about how the dead woman had harassed him and threatened to tell the police about the seed he had planted inside Merzaka. He hid his face in his hands, his words mixing with broken sobs.

"How did she find out?"

"Merzaka... told her. She told her... everything."

Zakia had kept the secret for a long time so as not to harm the reputation of my Sahara and not to involve me, the one who had transformed her life from ruins to tranquility. That is, until this past month, when she began putting pressure on him. She blackmailed him, revealing her conviction that he was behind Merzaka's death. She demanded money from him so she could run off with Bachir, and I realized she had been laughing at me this whole time. She hadn't wanted to marry me. All she'd wanted was for me to give her gifts and presents.

"Why didn't you tell me?"

He got up in my face without drying his tears and reminded me that I'd always stood with her. Full of self-hatred, I didn't deny it: "I was a fool." I stuffed my hands between my thighs, a chill creeping through my limbs.

> *You know the secrets we keep in our hearts,*
> *You are the one who comforts our pain,*
> *You are the one who accepts our excuses.*
> *We have returned to Your shadow,*
> *So accept the repentance of those who repent.*

Right then, we heard screams from the lobby mixed with Umm Kulthum's voice, which never gets old. I rushed through, terrified.

A young man was slapping and punching Fouzi, the carriage driver, leaving his face smeared in blood.

KAMAL

My shortness of breath returned as I left the hammam that provides mattresses to bathers during the day and at night to people passing through. I'd tossed and turned like a hungry infant without sleeping a wink. I've been going to that hammam since I was five, when my mother used to take me. She would wash my entire body and massage me as I looked at the naked and half-naked women around me, water streaming down between their breasts. My mother died of tuberculosis after becoming emaciated and turning into a handful of bones. I was nine when my father joined her, and my confidence in anyone but myself died too. Before last night, I had not been back since that time. I preferred sleeping there to sleeping in my own bed. I was terrified Maimoun would report me, and I'd even left my car in front of my house. I hope Bachir can forgive me, I thought. I grew even sadder for him when I read his letter.

In the name of God, the Compassionate, the Merciful

My dear brother, Kamal,

I am writing to you from a prison that, despite how small and constraining it is, has enough room for new acquaintances and for my patience to bear what has happened to me. I have met some

good people and am keeping my spirits up as much as possible. My
cousin, Noura, has taken it upon herself to defend me, and I am
still waiting for my trial date to be set. Please send my greetings
to all our mutual loved ones. I met a young man named Rahhal,
and I hope he and I will be released and that you will also get to
meet him. My memories of you never leave me and I pray for you
always. Know that I have been wrongly imprisoned and that the
pleas of the wronged will be accepted.

    Take care of yourself,

Bachir

I didn't shave or get the chance to brush my teeth. I couldn't get the image of Fouzi's blood-smeared face out of my head. After I'd brought the carriage driver's attacker down with a kick to his right knee, the very tall young man had confessed that Six had assigned him the task of watching over Cheikha Edahabia. And because of how much time she spent with the carriage driver, the attacker had thought they were involved in an intimate relationship.

Tearing an undershirt, I wrapped it around my head like someone with a migraine. My gray tweed jacket and blue jeans, and the sunglasses hiding my eyes, made me look much older than my actual age. I left the hammam and headed to the post office at 7:30 to withdraw all my savings and take the bus to Biskra. I figured I would travel after that to any remote location and wouldn't return until I was certain Maimoun Belassal wouldn't turn me in.

I arrived fifteen minutes before the post office opened and joined a line of gloomy-faced men and women, like newlyweds whose wedding night had been canceled. I waited until nine before it was my turn. I stood in front of a metal window opening above which a sign read WORK AND RIGOR

TO SECURE THE FUTURE. I faced an employee who looked as somber as the math teachers in school. He addressed me with an edge to his voice: "What do you want?" I was taken aback by his question, sorry the wife of Hamid, The Scorpion, wasn't there, as she generally treated people nicely. "What else do people standing in front of this window want besides to withdraw money?" I asked him. "I mean, how much do you want?" "Everything," I responded firmly, shedding the nice boy act I had performed ever since graduating from the Hotel Institute. My nose detected a rank odor, like how my mother had smelled when she was dying. I received a wad of bills, which made me the envy of the other customers, who hungrily watched my hands as I verified the amount, like they would a piece of meat on the grill. I could almost hear their whispers and feel their desire to divvy up what I had. It was the sweat of years of work, lying, and cheating. I proceeded to count down my final minutes in that city suspended in Satan's innards. That city where I was born, where I dreamed and loved. Where I met defeat, fear, and joy. Where I felt my first shivers while making love. The languages I had learned were no longer of any use to me. The only thing useful to me now was running away.

Outside, I felt sorry I would not be able to follow up on my complaint against Ibrahim Derras, just as I wouldn't go to the doctor after finally being able to book an appointment. "Health is in God's hands," I said to myself.

Voices and shouts began to rise. At first, I couldn't figure out where they were coming from, then the noise got closer. On the side of the street, people young and old were waving a banner that said MERCHANTS' UNION. They were marching in an orderly fashion like Boy Scouts and shouting, "Here... we... come... For our rights, we won't keep mum!" They approached the Foreigners' Villa just yards in front of me, and the shouting grew louder. The day of the promised merchants' strike was upon us, and they had organized themselves into a demonstration. Food was scarce at the grocers and farmers' market, the water was always being cut off, and the hospitals didn't have enough medicine or doctors. Things did not bode well.

Not more than a few moments passed before the crowd grew from dozens to hundreds. Heads of black hair were moving like spots of oil and calling out rage-filled slogans. I had never seen anything like it. I stood and watched, stock-still, as if my feet were nailed to the ground. Young people came out of the post office and joined the demonstrators.

I expected the thread of anger to be short, as I had never heard of this city's people rising up before. They never emerged from their apathy. During the War of Independence, only very few individuals had joined the fight. They were comfortable in their laziness, and I guessed they wouldn't shout for too long. They would voice their concerns, then go peacefully on their way. The merchants from the contraband market in front of me locked their doors, while others folded their metal tables, stuffed their goods into duffel bags, then rushed to join the protesters. It hadn't occurred to me that that day, which had started with partly sunny skies, the temperature lower than it had been in days, would turn into something like hell.

Angry people gathered in front of the Foreigners' Villa, and their echoing slogans grew louder as I parked myself on a corner in front of the post office, dividing my cash between my jacket and trouser pockets. As I recited God's name, which I only did during Ramadan, policemen began leaving their posts at the traffic barrier and running toward the protesters brandishing weapons.

The demonstrators turned and ran, kicking up dust; although the road was paved, it had become covered with sand over time. I didn't know what to do. I was unable to move forward toward the travelers' station for fear that I would be taken for one of the demonstrators and get arrested. A shiver ran down my legs.

Two policemen advanced toward the post office to prevent the protesters from getting to it, so I stepped to the side and put my sunglasses in my jacket pocket. The guard rushed to lock the door. A third policeman joined his two colleagues and fired a shot into the air to disperse the crowd. People ran in the opposite direction, and I trembled at the sound of the shots. My legs moved on their own, and I joined the protesters running away from the policeman who kept firing warning shots. The crowd didn't get more than a few hundred yards before running into a security barrier preventing them from continuing to City Hall. They fell like trapped prey, like flies trapped in an empty juice bottle, and I was there with them. Right then, the policemen became rattled by the chaotic scene, and clouds of tear gas rose up.

Things started to look more like a battle than a demonstration. I felt like I was sleepwalking. I ran without knowing where I was going. I blotted out the bodies around me. All I could see was a dark corridor in front of me. I ran like never before, as if I were racing Carl Lewis. I started to gasp, having forgotten the difficulty in breathing I suffered from. The city faded from my memory, and I became an animal running toward who knows where. All that was important was getting away from the clouds of tear gas. I was oblivious to the fact that I was carrying years of savings in my pockets. I ran, taking side streets and avoiding the city's main arteries, without feeling tired or getting a cramp. I feared my heart would let me down, as I was a regular smoker and had not exercised since I was a teenager.

My legs brought me to the meadow, that forbidden zone, like the Kaaba that pilgrims circumambulate in Mecca without entering. I had run four miles, but it felt like thirty. I knelt under a carob tree to catch my breath. I asked for God's forgiveness and pronounced that there is no power nor strength save but in Him while the sound of bullets still reverberated in my ears.

Since the beginning of the year, I'd felt that 1988 would be a bad one. My neighbor, Saliha, had passed away, leaving behind a child, something that reminded me of my own orphaned state. My sister Ouarida's heart had failed as she was going into surgery. And Sidi Zerzour had been put in prison and was awaiting what might be a life sentence. Same with Bachir. O Lord, ensure things end up well, I thought. An inner voice urged me to step forward and inspect the spot where I had laid Zakia's body to rest.

A man with a prominent bald spot was tranquilly herding some sheep. He seemed calm despite what was happening, or else he didn't know anything about it. I licked my dry lips and thought about asking him for a sip of water, but then I backed off. I knew well that there was nothing charming in these displaced people who are nothing more than locusts feeding off the bread of others. I dragged my feet to the edge of the road, where I found a Renault 5 stopped on the sidewalk, a sign installed behind it advertising anti-bug spray. The fat driver, who hadn't been able to get downtown, helped me out with half a bottle of water. I asked if he could take me to Biskra, which is in the opposite direction, not more than an hour to the north.

"Demonstrations have broken out there too," the driver said. *The only thing people have ever agreed on is destruction*, I almost responded. I bribed him with money and asked him to head south, to take National Route 3, without realizing I was taking the very same road my father had taken to his imprisonment and death. It was as if this country's history just repeats itself rather than moving forward in a linear fashion.

I threw my sweaty body onto the car seat and stuffed my hands between my thighs. I lowered my eyes and recalled the scenes I had witnessed that morning, my head ringing with the sounds of the protesters' voices. I touched the ID card that I had picked up in my office at the hotel before leaving and put in my pocket. A previous customer had forgotten it. My name became Samir Laâroum, same age and appearance as me. I'd got rid of my own ID card in case we came across any security barriers, and my boss had reported me.

I'd done it. I'd run away. My eyes darted around in every direction. I was leaving all the people who had passed through my life: my mother, my father, my sisters, Bachir and my other friends, my neighbors and acquaintances, girls I had fallen in love with and others with whom I had only spent a day or two. I thought of Zakia, Cheikha Edahabia, and Merzaka. I thought of Hassina Eidache, my Hassouna. When I first met her at the hotel, she stopped my heart despite our apparent incompatibility – her blood type was A positive and mine was B positive. Nonetheless, I smelled something in her that returned tranquility to my heart. There was something about her tired eyes and soft skin that I found attractive. When we started seeing one another, I was annoyed she was friends with Hamid, The Scorpion. "My job requires me to socialize with him," she told me at the time. I'd wished at first that she would leave the legal profession, but then I just ignored it. I loved the way she held me in her arms as her fingers ran between my tight buttocks, and I would whisper a sentence I'd heard in the movie *La dolce vita* ("There are three things I like most: love, love, and love"). I didn't object to rough sex, her pinching my flesh or biting my neck. It made me want her more. We wouldn't get out of bed until sweat dripped from our foreheads. It occurred to me at first that she was one of those who would quickly move on. I never imagined our relationship would last so long. I quit smoking hash to make her happy, so had I truly loved her? I wanted to convince myself of that.

I've lived during the colonial period and into independence. I have known three of the country's presidents. I remembered what I heard from news announcers about the agricultural, industrial, and cultural revolutions. I remembered how our national team had played twice in the World Cup, and how they lost the Africa Cup.

On the other side of the city, it was total chaos. I later learned that young men had stormed institutions where the national flag was flying. They had also attacked the farmers' market. They'd run off carrying sacks of semolina, sugar, and coffee that were piled up in the warehouse while women stood on balconies and rooftops, trilling joyfully at what they saw.

To the Head of the Judicial Police Squad
SUBJECT: Body found
REFERENCE: Your request of October 5, 1988 at 8 p.m.
VICTIM: The late Derraji Aouina
LOCATION: Soummam

On October 5, 1988, at around 8 p.m., we went immediately after being summoned to the location and discovered the body of the late Derraji Aouina, born February 20, 1956, the son of Ammar and Fatna Majdal.

LOCATION DESCRIPTION

The body was found in the hallway that leads to a staircase to the roof, in a house rented by Kamal Belattar.

FORENSIC INSPECTION

According to instructions, upon our arrival we donned special clothing (protective suit, head protection, a mask, shoe protectors, and gloves), then:
- We found a male corpse lying on its stomach, wearing a light purple shirt and black trousers.
- We saw a bullet hole corresponding to the victim's liver.
- We saw blood on the ground.
- We saw that the lock on the door was broken.
- We lifted fingerprints.
- The body was identified after listening to the neighbors' testimony.
- We drew a diagram of the house where the body was found. It consists of two rooms, a hallway, a kitchen, a bathroom, and a roof terrace.

The medical examiner confirmed that the victim sustained a wound to the liver, which caused him to hemorrhage heavily.

IBRAHIM

OCTOBER 6

It was almost noon. As I stepped out through the prison door, which looked like that of a high school, I imagined how displeased my father, in his final resting place, would have been with me. I tucked my red shirt into my jeans and looked down at my worn-out leather shoes. I hated myself because I couldn't leave the country. "This is a country of monsters," I said to myself as I walked along a rain-dampened sidewalk in front of the Foreigners' Villa. The shops surrounding it were either locked or had been vandalized. I was terrified to see that the post office had had its windows smashed, and that next to the entrance were traces of a fire. Only the metal skeletons and dangling wires remained of the phone booths. There was nothing left of Lazhari's jewelry shop besides metal bars standing upright with shards of glass piled up inside. People passed by with their heads lowered in fear; angry graffiti about government officials was scrawled across building walls. Fortunately, my father hadn't lived to witness such ugliness. I saw charred rubber tires, and there was a smell in the air that resembled that of burnt milk. I hurried toward home like a stray cat or a miserable escapee from an old French movie or novel, trying to remember the face of the lawyer who had defended me. She'd had a black handbag under her arm, like the one with which Assia Djebar is often pictured. She only said a few quick words to me: "Your case doesn't warrant imprisonment." Then she said goodbye and left to take care of her obligations at the courthouse, one of the few institutions spared Molotov cocktails thanks to the security personnel that had encircled it. Ever since the police inspector had returned the VCR and tape of the dead singer to me, I'd been expecting something bad to happen. But where had this lawyer come from? Why had she helped me?

I found my mother squatting in the kitchen, her hands busy cutting tomatoes for drying to use in the winter. She was humming a song: "*Tell my mother not to cry… Your son, O Lord, isn't done yet!*" She called "Briha!" to me with a tenderness I had been longing for. She got up gleefully and hugged me before taking two steps back. "Your friend's sister, Noura, is a whore!" she said and told me what had happened that day I was gone so long. She thought I had holed myself up in the shop as I had done before. That was before the policeman who worked at the station front desk knocked on the door and told her what had happened to me. "He's in jail." He knew my address from my ID card. The word "jail" terrified her, and she imagined I would never come back. He advised her to go to the courthouse and request a visit. My mother stayed in the courthouse waiting room for an hour before the court clerk met her. She recounted how he had fixed his spectacles on his forehead and the words had flowed between his saliva-dampened lips. He asked her to come back the following week because there were so many requests for visits right then. She pressed him to tell her what I was being accused of, but he just said: "When you see him, ask him yourself."

On her way home, disappointed, she had felt a folded piece of paper in her djellaba pocket. Noura had written down her number when she had visited. My mother hadn't thought a day would come when she would need that number. She shoved a coin into the payphone slot next to the post office, dialed the lawyer's number, and asked about her and her family as if she were a relative. Noura was surprised by how my mother spoke, thinking she wanted to give her something that would help in her defense of her cousin, Bachir. Then my mother explained what had happened to me. "For the sake of the angels, help me," she pleaded. Noura replied, "Let's let justice do its work, then."

My mother realized she had been wrong to call Noura, and hung up as she muttered insults. She likened the lawyer to Fatiha, the other cleaning lady in the hotel, whom she avoided out of fear that she would accuse her of stealing things from tourists' rooms, which made it necessary for her to ignore her suspicions that Fatiha's daughter, Cheikha Edahabia, had been involved in Zakia's murder.

I explained to my mother that Noura's disdain for her stemmed from the fact that she hadn't provided any assistance in the hotel singer's case.

"What does her murder have to do with me?" my mother said.

I avoided revealing anything that had transpired between Noura and me regarding blackmail.

"How come they threw you in jail?"

"A fight with a burglar in the shop."

She shot me an angry look. "I've talked myself hoarse trying to make you understand. Get away from that shop!"

If not for that job, she would not have been able to get her tooth pulled, nor would she have been able to pay for the drugs that soothed her stomach pain. I ignored her. I just wanted to take a shower, but there was no water. No difference between prison and home.

"There's water in the mosque's well," my mother said.

The taps had been cut off for six days. She only had a tiny bit for drinking and cooking. I had no choice but to go to the ablution fountain to wash myself, but before leaving, I asked about Khamisi.

"He went and joined the army," she sighed. She had hung his picture in her room. "He left me all alone." Is that what he'd meant when he said "I know how to become a professional boxer"? He'd been intending to join the military boxing team! I slammed the door as I left, struggling to figure out how I could comfort her from now on and how I could lessen her longing for my younger brother.

After washing up, I felt ashamed under the gaze of my neighbors, who were all lined up for the noon prayer. I slunk away as they muttered under their breaths: "They head to God's house to take care of their sanitary needs, but not for religious purposes." *Do you speak on heaven's behalf?* I wanted to say to shut them up.

On my way to check on the Desert Rose, hoping it had not been burned or destroyed like other shops, I found the door to the pastry shop ajar, so I knocked and went in. Boulanouar met me with a hug and a kiss on each cheek. "When did they let you out, comrade?" he asked.

How did he know I had been thrown in jail? I wondered. "Today," I replied.

He'd feared I would be in for a long time, having experienced prison himself twenty years ago. He'd been involved in a secret opposition party before abandoning politics altogether, availing himself of some property along with his former comrades. Nowadays he limited his patriotic struggle to annual participation in the anti-imperialist festival at the neighborhood cultural center. He lavished words of gratitude on Hassina, the lawyer, describing her as a "tough woman."

"Do you know her?"

Hassina had lost her father when she was thirteen years old, leaving her mother to take care of her and her younger brother. Her Uncle Boulanouar provided them with enough money to get by, so she never hesitated to do whatever he asked of her. She was quick to respond when she asked why I'd been arrested and was able to convince the investigating judge that Six's testimony against me had come out of nothing more than malice. The release order had been issued two days ago but hadn't reached the prison administration until that morning.

"Ever since I saw you getting into that police car, I've been ill at ease," the pastry chef said.

I wanted to tell Boulanouar about his son, Rahhal, whom I had left behind bars, basking in the prisoners' admiration for him, but I held my tongue, knowing how much he missed him.

Then I asked how the Desert Rose was doing, and Boulanouar reached out his hand to rub my shoulder. "Don't go back there ever again." He noticed that I was taken aback by what he said, so he added: "The new owner handed the shop's daily operations over to his son Faudel, and he changed the locks on the door."

He confided in me how much he hated Khider Arkoub, who had assaulted the family of the Jewish man who had taught Boulanouar how to make pastries, forcing him to emigrate so Arkoub could take possession of his house. I was astonished and saddened. Noura, you defend the oppressed, yet you disregard your oppressive father? I thought.

NOURA

I gave up any semblance of composure; all I could do was spew insults. I sat cross-legged on my bed and lit a cigarette. My mother sat in a chair facing me with her head pressed against her hands, her eyes fixed on my room's linoleum floor. She remained indifferent to the smoke that came out of my nose and from between my lips, avoiding her usual reprimands. She sat in silence as I poured out my hatred toward my father. I hadn't forgotten what she told me about how unhappy he'd been that I was born a girl, then about his desire to marry me off at seventeen to his friend who was a leader in the party, something he would have done had I not gone on hunger strike. And I couldn't stop thinking about the day he'd tried to prevent me from pursuing my university studies, only for my aunt in Algiers to intervene. When I'd been younger, he didn't take me to the photographer on the two big holidays to take pictures as other fathers did, ashamed I was related to him. And he'd only helped me open a law office so I could meet a man to marry, which would allow my father to get rid of me. "Gentle Noura" is nothing more than a trembling deer. Because of my intense hatred for him, I hate almost all men. Only Kamal remains stuck in my heart. Whenever I close my eyes, his image flashes in my mind. I hug my pillow before going to sleep, imagining I'm hugging him. I promised myself that if I married anyone other than him, I wouldn't have children, so my child wouldn't have to suffer a father like mine. *Do you realize how much luckier I am than you that no man ever mocked me so much?!* I wanted to say to my mother. Rouna walked around in circles, her tail sticking straight up and moving back and forth like the needle of a compass.

When my father had arrived at the house after the city erupted in anger, he assumed my mother would agree to rekindle their relationship, but she asked him to take a seat in the living room.

He slowed his walk when he saw Daouia's thick face and rounded nose. He went pale and understood that it would be difficult to get out of this scandal. No doubt he cursed the day he had seen her for the first time coming out of Zerzour's house after receiving an amulet to dispel her hallucinations. She was accompanied by her only daughter, Naima, who was tall and shared her pale skin and short black hair. The girl filled him with desire, so he asked for the faith-healer's help. Zerzour gave him their address in a village a few dozen miles away, where people tend to their mules and poultry more than they care for their children. My father sent a messenger to Daouia to act as a go-between in asking for her daughter's hand, but she refused on the grounds that she was a minor, an orphan who had no legal male guardian. He took advantage of their poverty and lavished money on the mother until she married her daughter to him the same day Maradona scored a goal with his hand. There were no witnesses or signed documents; it was a common-law marriage, on the condition that he have the marriage officially certified as soon as Naima came of age. He didn't object and bought them a decent house in the village. They left their hut, and he visited them frequently, withdrawing to be alone with his wife, who was unaware of what was happening. She was compelled to do what he commanded her to, and she complied with the wishes of her mother, who had recovered from her visions of ghosts chasing after her under the cover of darkness. My father continued in this way until Naima became pregnant, at which point he disappeared. Daouia gave him time to come to his senses, but he was stubborn. She was patient and had her only daughter show patience as well so as not to cause him any problems, but he remained blind to the situation. That's when she'd come knocking on our door.

"The baby will soon turn one, and we don't have anyone to provide for us."

He couldn't believe such a capricious act had resulted in a baby boy. I decided not to forgive him for what he had done.

"We can't register him with the municipality."

Her daughter had no piece of paper proving her child's lineage, and she had become aggressive toward her mother when she understood she had been deceived.

Naima's mother kept talking while Khider remained silent. He promised he would visit and pay them the support he owed. I listened in on them and looked through the door's peephole.

"And to certify your marriage to her," Daouia said.

He stammered and began to rub his temples.

When Six had hurried to inform him that my mother was looking for him, Khider could not find a taxi, so he hopped up behind his son on the moped. He wore a turban and hid his eyes behind sunglasses, careful not to be recognized by any of the demonstrators as he had been dismissed from the Municipal Council for embezzling from the municipality. He also hid on the way back, assuring his mother-in-law he would take care of all their monetary needs and keep them from going into debt.

My face froze in astonishment; a baby brother, right there in front of me. I remembered what my mother had said about the day my father married her after his first wife died bleeding out because they couldn't find a doctor to help her following Djelloul's birth. "His face gave me the impression he was a pure man," she said.

After finding out about the son he had concealed, my mother began to suspect that he had also had other relationships. Because of his money and real estate holdings, he could indulge in polygamy, and she did not believe that his last wife, who he'd also had intercourse with in an unofficial marriage while she was in her early twenties, was barren. She thought he'd only wanted her for pleasure, nothing more.

"I'd rather live with a dog than live with him," she said through gritted teeth. Isn't the cat that lives with us enough for you? I said to myself. I'm certain she uttered her words without really believing them, for nothing frightens her more than the prospect of my father dissolving their marriage and her being labeled a divorced woman, which is synonymous with a prostitute in people's minds.

Taking a drag from my cigarette, I thought about going to the hammam, whose owner has a good-sized well, more than sixty feet deep. The bath is reserved for women in the morning and men in the afternoon. I wanted to pour hot water over my body to wash away my anxiety; to lean back naked on the marble platform, close my eyes, and feel the steam seep into my bones; to rub my skin until it became as fresh and radiant as the heroine in the movie *The Sheik*.

I felt like my body was getting heavier and heavier. I had promised Halima I would help get her daughter's body transferred to Nezrama. I apologized for not defending her son, who had been accused of attempted murder, and advised her to seek help from Hassina. All I could do was return to the monotony of my life; to rely solely on misdemeanors, divorces, and inheritance cases; to truly become the Godmother of Divorced Women; to dive into the daily problems of my clients and not venture into another criminal case. But not until I secured Bachir's release by having the case dismissed without needing to analyze the handwriting in his supposed letter. The court knew who had done it, but I didn't, and I was waiting for Bachir to answer two questions. First, was there a connection between the deaths of Zakia Zaghouani and Merzaka Soualem? And second, who had the singer been intending to marry?

Khider had been convinced never to return to the house, to avoid any potential flare-ups resulting from fights with my mother or me. Six had transformed from a mere son into my father's servant after being entrusted with the Desert Rose so he could turn it into a shop that sold ready-made clothes. And Ibrahim Derras had come to be without a job. He'd learned that what comes around goes around, and that dog eats dog. Of course, now I didn't have anyone to loan me videotapes for free, and since there were no movies to go see that might make me forget my worries, I turned on the radio.

Talents on Radio Algiers was just starting; on it, amateur singers compete by singing famous songs to win a cash prize. The announcer introduced the first contestant: Zaza.

MAIMOUN

Some teens ran off after pelting my car windshield and the room windows with rocks, cursing the women heading into the hotel and calling them whores. *They're tourists!* I wanted to yell after them. These angry people have mentalities like locusts; they are easily injected with chaos hormones. They blow in with the wind. They imagine anyone wearing a short skirt and high heels is a prostitute.

I laid back on the lobby sofa, rubbing my bald spot and thanking the Lord they hadn't thrown Molotov cocktails as they had elsewhere, tears streaming from my eyes. Had I become a criminal? I howled like an idiot, my hands shaking. My Lord, what had I done to deserve such punishment?! I hadn't stopped praying for Derraji Aouina, whom Kamal had introduced me to when I'd visited him at the house he rented in Soummam. When I'd seen his car parked outside the house, I'd broken in to put an end to the receptionist, to spare him a prison sentence that might last until his final days, and to spare my hotel, my Sahara, his scandal. But I made a mistake. I broke the lock on the wooden door with a pair of bolt cutters and only saw Derraji from the back. He was wearing Kamal's light purple shirt. I raised my pistol, gripped by fear because I had never fired it. A 9 mm bullet hit the victim's liver.

What had Aouina been doing there? I figured he'd been waiting for the right moment to take revenge on Kamal, who had lodged a complaint against him. He had eluded the police that day, October 5, and guessed his adversary was staying at the hotel and would not risk returning home. I imagined Derraji had climbed the low wall of the house and then come down the stairs to Kamal's living room. Perhaps he'd intended to steal his things, but all he had taken was his purple shirt, and when I'd walked in, he'd run back to the stairs. I hadn't seen his face, and my face had been covered. I had a gun I'd held onto since the war years, just in case. I pulled the trigger, reconsidering for a split second, but it was too late.

"I've lived as a coward," I whispered, fingering the earring I'd found in the warehouse. Ever since Zaza's been gone, rumors have been running rampant. Some say her brothers took revenge on her, or that a swindler became overly envious of her, or that she stole a man's heart and his wife took it upon herself to get rid of her. No other voice has managed to move me quite like hers. Her death killed off half my heart. I listened to her songs in my Sahara, in this hotel now empty of customers and which reminds me of the ghosts of those who have left or died. That night I was away from her brought about her death. And Kamal has disappeared, too. Earlier, his sister, Ouarida, rushed into the lobby leaning on a cane and asked about him, surprised by his sudden disappearance. I was afraid to tell her anything that might make her even sicker, but she insisted that she had the right to know. She was like a mother to him. "If you report him, I'll turn you in for killing my father," she warned me.

She told me about the former sergeant in the Liberation Army named Suleiman who had gone crazy in prison in

1965. He had confided in her that I had encouraged her father, Belkacem Belattar, to try to escape, after which I had betrayed him to the guards. Ouarida had kept that story to herself in exchange for covering up her brother's involvement in Merzaka Soualem's murder, holding onto it like a silver bullet with which she would guarantee my support for him when needed.

"You believe the words of a crazy person?" I asked.

"He was saner than you and me both."

It was true. That night so long ago, I had urged my comrade to run away, knowing full well where his fate would lead. Other detainees had been unable to dissuade him, and he'd ended up getting shot. "You're delirious," I said to her.

"I'll protect you if you protect Kamal," she countered.

My head started to spin. I placed my index finger across my lower lip. I hated myself for the fact that I was behind the killing of my dearest friend, their father, Belkacem, just so he wouldn't dispute my ownership of the hotel. We had bought it from a colonist who gave it to us for a reasonable sum so he could escape with his skin after assassinations of foreigners had become widespread following independence. I realized I could deny Ouarida's accusation, but it might harm my relationship with Papillon, the secretary of the Veterans' Club, who had taken Belkacem Belattar as his right-hand man to do his dirty work, such as when he'd entrusted him to eliminate Ben Kaddour Derras. Derras had been one of the first to join the War of Independence but had resisted Papillon's rise to sole leadership in the fight. They had secretly buried him in the Christian cemetery under a stone on which was written Ben Kaddour's alias, Oultem. Then they spread a rumor that he had betrayed the revolution by revealing secrets to the colonists.

Ben Kaddour and his wife had converted to Christianity, as so many others did in St Philip's Church, out of admiration for the virtues of the nuns and the Pères Blancs who had helped him in his wool business, just as they had taught his wife how to sew and weave. They appealed to Jesus for help and made the sign of the cross on their chests. However, after the French left, orders were issued for all Christian converts to return to Islam. The birth of an independent Algeria discouraged Christianity. Wannasa had stood in a mosque and pronounced the Shahada, the Muslim profession of faith, and the women rejoiced, forgetting all about her the next day. She went back to being poor and gave up sewing and weaving out of grief for her husband. She never got over her love for him, and only learned a little from Islam as she gradually changed her mind about raising her two sons according to the love of Christ. Unable to forgive her past, her family and relatives avoided her. They were unwilling to visit her and claimed they didn't feel safe going to the poor neighborhood where she lived. That is, except for her children's uncle, who failed to convince her to marry him according to the custom of a man marrying his brother's widow (at least this is what she told me). Her relationship with him settled merely into what the duties of kinship imposed.

My knowledge of Ben Kaddour Derras's past made it impossible for me to hire his son, Ibrahim, as that could have resulted in him digging into the past and discovering what had happened to his father. I wasn't worried about his mother, Wannasa, though, who was still beautiful after all these years. I was sure she wouldn't kick up a fuss, so I hired her as a maid at the urging of Merzaka, who had met her at City Hall. Should I tell her where her deceased husband's grave is? Wouldn't it be fair for her to get a martyr's widow card that would allow her to live a better life? Her two sons have the right to know where their father is buried, too. And I must find an excuse to justify my actions to Papillon.

To avoid anyone accusing me after the muezzin saw my car in the meadow on the night of Zakia's death, I told the police commissioner about the receptionist confessing to her murder. Out of fear of being accused of covering it up, I didn't report what he had done to Merzaka. The courts released Bachir Labtam and issued an arrest warrant for Kamal. I thought I had done well with that preemptive strike, which would make Ouarida's charge against me seem like a baseless conspiracy of revenge. Anxiety drove me to liquidate my trade in foodstuffs, curb my activities in the drug trade, and sell this hotel where I had spent my life but which had now become unrecognizable to me. And I resolved to share the proceeds with Belkacem Belattar's daughters to absolve myself of their father's blood. I have spent my life climbing a staircase of sins, like a drunkard climbing a ladder who lurches backward with each rung he takes. It's time to retire. I'll take care of my garden and my son Mehdi, for whom I've decided to open a music tape shop in the contraband market.

I decided to shave and visit the doctor again to check on my heart condition. Right then, as I stood in the hotel doorway, I caught sight of a young man as tall as half an electrical pole waving an iron rod and chasing after a girl crying out for her mother, her hair flying every which way. I did not dare intervene, nor did anyone else passing by. We watched in silence as the girl fell to the ground.

IBRAHIM

OCTOBER 8

My mother informed me that the hotel owner knew the location of my father's grave and that he would show her where it was. A cold shiver ran through my body and I went back to the bookshop tucked away in an alley adjacent to the Electricity & Gas Co. I found it just as I had left it the last time I was there, a year ago. No one was reading there. It smelled of a mixture of incense and cleaning fluids, and there were so-called schoolbooks and other books on sciences, religion, and literature on shelves hung on the walls. The store received little sunlight. I showed the fifty-something-year-old owner the books I had decided to sell to secure the household expenses for the coming days.

The bookseller, who had a mint leaf stuffed in his nostril, wore a dark-colored Mao suit with four pockets and five buttons. He flipped through and examined the books. He checked to make sure the pages weren't torn and that there was nothing wrong with them. His hands stopped at *The Sheik*. He fixed his gaze on the municipal library stamp on the first page and on what Nabil had written before he died: *I have no money nor friend to help me other than you.*

"Where did you get this?"

"I bought it."

He handed me a tidy sum and wrote down my name and address so he could return the books to me if he didn't sell them, in which case I would return the money.

At noon, I arrived at the Rubber & Plastic Co. It had escaped the demonstrators' fury, having been defended by its workers. I became temporarily responsible for distribution, replacing a former employee who was lying in the hospital after having his leg amputated because of diabetes. I'd been recommended by Tijani, who is friends with the manager; he always publishes praise pieces about him in the newspaper. I was convinced to take the position for a while, reassured that I had the right to obtain the card exempting me from military service as the firstborn son of my mother and because my brother had joined the army. This would make things easier for her and allow me to get a teaching position in the coming school year. I regretted all the useless bribes I had paid to get the card.

I sat at a wooden table in a cramped office with a broken window. It kept me from seeing my uncle, who worked in the production unit. I'm disappointed I didn't stick to what I said ("I would rather starve to death than go work there"). I remembered what I'd heard Bachir Labtam say in jail about how his boss preferred the silent worker over the efficient one. I glanced at my worn-out shoes and then started to look over the orders that had arrived that day, smoking the whole time. I summoned a porter to get the pipes from the warehouse and prepare them for shipment. He had a curved mustache and a shiny bald head, and his face suggested he had had a rough life. No sooner had I issued the order than he politely asked me for a cigarette. I asked him his name. "Achour Hadeeri," he replied.

The porter told me he had run away from his village and settled in the meadow with his wife and daughter after a dispute with relatives over a piece of land. His cousin had tried to strangle him with an electrical cord, so Achour had plunged a knife into his shoulder, but the cousin had survived. Achour and his family did not return to the village, out of fear that his relatives would plot against him; there is no justice or law there, only blood revenge and retaliation. He had been blessed with a baby boy. He did business in small livestock and worked on construction sites. He had entrusted his sheep to his neighbor. He had a bandage on his forehead after the family of a veterinarian had assaulted him. "The vet's name was Nabil," he said. The family members had blamed Achour for not properly installing some wooden boards on some scaffolding that my friend had climbed so he could check on the construction's progress, which had led to his fatal fall.

Achour had spent years in this city but still felt like a villager. He told me that his daughter, Louisa, had returned to school and joined the music choir there, toying with the dream of becoming a singer one day. "Singing is haram. I don't want her going down that road," he told me. The police inspector had helped him get work with the company. That inspector hadn't helped me with anything at all.

"I helped him in the case of the woman who was killed."

I understood that he was talking about the singer. "Zakia?"

"I don't know what her name was," he answered.

Although I would have loved to listen to him, the noise of the workers around us made it impossible. We agreed to meet the following day at the Khayma so he could tell me the rest of this story, which is as murky as this country and its people.

I didn't finish my shift. I left early at 4 p.m. and shut myself in my room, twirling strands of my long hair between my fingers. I avoided my mother in the kitchen. She had been seized with fear that she would lose her job after someone in the hotel had disclosed that its owner had decided to sell it. "What's important is that he'll show us where Father's grave is," I said.

My friend Mellah knocked on the door. He showed me a VCR. "Name any price, and it's yours," he said. He'd got it from the Foreigners' Villa after protesters looted it on October 5. On the ground floor, they'd discovered a restaurant, in the middle of which was a pine table with more than thirty chairs around it overlooking a swimming pool. On the first floor, small tables and leather-covered chairs were scattered about a nightclub equipped with the latest sound system.

I told him that I had left my job at the shop and sold my machine, too, along with a bunch of personal items and books. All I'd kept was my guitar and the cassette recorder. As for the tape of Zakia's concert, I'd buried it just as her body had been buried. I told him that I hoped he'd find a buyer.

To calm my nerves and let off some steam, I decided to take a walk. I was thinking about what I had been told about how the salaries at the end of the month might be delayed due to the accumulation of company debts when a police car stopped in front of me as I was passing by the Christian cemetery. "Get in and ride with us," said a voice from inside the car.

In the office that I'd been in before being taken to prison, I came across neither the inspector who looked like Groucho Marx nor the brigadier who blew his nose into a cloth handkerchief. Instead it was someone else, also an inspector. He was clean-shaven, and I thought he looked like Humphrey Bogart in *Casablanca*, which I had seen three times.

"Where did you get this book?" He pointed to a copy of *The Sheik*.

I realized that the bookseller had brought this novel to the station, hoping for a reward promised by the police. They had offered cash to anyone who could identify people who had participated in the storming of state institutions over the last few days. After the trade union demonstration had been dispersed, people had returned even more angry, with fires breaking out all over the city center.

"I bought it from a sidewalk vendor."

"What was his name?"

"I don't know."

"Where does he live?"

"I don't know."

He got up from his chair and sat to the side of the table, tilting his head in my direction. He accused me of joining the young people who had raided the municipal library and stolen from it.

"I was in jail when the protests took place."

He flipped through his files to confirm what I was saying, then turned back to me. "But you bought it from one of the vandals who stormed the library, and then hid it."

Through the wide-open window, I watched a damp darkness spread softly over the face of the city and murmured: "Don't you know that government materials are being sold in the markets? Do I need to wake Nabil from the dead to testify on my behalf?"

"You're under arrest."

A refreshing breeze blew across my face, bringing me back to the night I'd passed the baccalaureate exam. I remembered what my neighbors had said at the time. One of them predicted I would become a scientist. Another one said I would be a professor, and a third foretold that he would see me on television. I'm nothing but a locust with its wings pulled off, I'd thought at the time. It bothered me that my mother would no longer have anyone she could shower with nasty words as she was accustomed to doing. She wouldn't find another Briha. She wouldn't have anyone with whom she could recite the Fatiha prayer over the grave of my father, who only visited me in my dreams with a blurred face. A sentence from *The Sheik* came to mind: "When an Arab sees a woman that he wants, he takes her." As for me, everything I once loved had been lost. I recalled the words to the song: "*Salma ya salama... we came and went safely...*" I wondered when I would get to record my final version of it and send it to the radio station.

I want a lawyer, I almost yelled. That's how we always see people accused of committing crimes asking for a lawyer in movies. Do things here happen the way they do in the movies? There was the sound of cars in the street, followed by men walking by and laughing. I didn't know them, and they didn't know me. I'm just Ibrahim Derras. No name. A complete unknown in a city where people never agree on what my name was in the first place, sometimes Ibrahim, other times Brihoum or Briha. Where children still entertain themselves by smashing streetlights with rocks.

Was this inspector as interested in eavesdropping on passersby through his window as I had been in the Desert Rose? Did he know what the investigation into the hotel singer had led to? He spoke very little, unlike his double, Humphrey Bogart. I couldn't meet Achour Hadeeri at the Khayma now, and I would never know what I'd missed. A sharp buzzing filled my ears, followed by a wave of nausea, as if I had eaten eggs, which disgust me! I opened my mouth painfully, without any sound coming out, and felt heat consuming my body as if I had been submerged in boiling water. This left my arms and legs numb and filled me with a desire to lie down and close my eyes, never to open them again.

KAMAL

It's been a month since I last caressed Hassina's cheeks, since I touched her soft hands that used to run through my hair, since I embraced her in room 302, which was filled with the perfume of lovers I used to rent it to.

As soon as she left, Zakia came up to me at the reception desk and repeated her demand that I give her a large sum of money so she could run off with Bachir to some city on the coast. She wasn't satisfied spending her life as a singer in a nightclub, and I couldn't pay what she asked for. She hated me because of how imperious and cruel I was toward her, although I was the same with all the other employees. Then she threatened to reveal what I had planted in Merzaka's womb; she'd heard our fight that night. Zaza knew I had killed her, but kept quiet for a long time so I wouldn't reveal to others that the security forces in her town were looking for her. But once she sensed Inspector Hamid would stand by her, she pressured me. She knew the inspector enjoyed her singing and would come to her aid if things got difficult. I was powerless before her and didn't get any help from her lover, who I invited to my house to help me drive her away after Farhat failed to do so. But my friend quickly got drunk and got into a fight with my neighbor, who stabbed him in the shoulder, so I drove him to the hospital. Then I went to see Ibrahim Derras in his shop. I returned some movies to him and complained about what was weighing on my mind, without disclosing the name of my blackmailer. I was naive. I listened to what he thought. I used to see him as strong, clever, knowledgeable, and enlightened. He recited sober words to me: "Close the door to the wind that's bothering you, and put your mind at ease." He convinced me to show no mercy to my enemies: "Whoever lacks dignity isn't a man." I returned to the hotel when my Hassouna called me to tell me that the seamstress had finished a new dress for her and she wanted to know what I thought of it. I didn't hide how annoyed I was with Zaza, but didn't go into detail.

"A man-stealer."

That's how Hassouna described Zakia Zaghouani.

"Do you know her?"

She didn't answer. She wanted to meet Zaza "to teach her some manners." She liked my idea of luring the singer to Maimoun's food warehouse, where she used to meet Bachir after Maimoun banned him from her room in the hotel. I would give her the key so she could be alone with him for an hour or more whenever one longed for the other. She would thank me profusely for that.

Zakia imagined I would give her some money the following morning and that her boyfriend wanted to see her after her show. Perhaps she thought he wanted to apologize for what had been in the letter the police found in her room. (Who wrote it? I don't know!) She knew it was impossible that Bachir was thinking of leaving her, so she went out, hoping to meet up with him after midnight. My lawyer girlfriend met up with her first, then I arrived and found them exchanging insults. The warehouse door was ajar, and Hassina was raising her index finger in Zaza's face, threatening to expose her relationship with Hamid. I was baffled. The Scorpion, smitten by her? A feeling of sadness crept into my blood, left over from the drinks I'd had that afternoon, to which I had added another glass just before leaving the hotel. I had the feeling everyone was against me and that Ibrahim had been right in urging me to crush my blackmailer.

She denied the accusation. "I'm not involved with him."

"You're lying."

"I don't even know who you are."

"And I know something you don't."

Zaza had no patience for accusations, so she grabbed Hassina by the neck with her long-nailed fingers, her eyes open wide and filled with a cruelty no one familiar with her calm demeanor would believe. She tossed Hassina between some bags of sugar in a way that sent a taste for revenge into my heart. I couldn't stand to see someone attacking the person I loved. I rushed toward the singer, who trembled when she saw me. I punched her as hard as I could out of anger and hatred, without noticing her earring fall to the floor. Then Hassina got up. Zakia ran out, her bag in her right hand. Hassina's scream practically burst my eardrums: "She's going to go to the police!" My joints trembled at the sound of the word *police*. I imagined Zaza would tell the police what had happened between Merzaka and me. People would know that I threw her from her balcony, and I'd go to prison for the rest of my life. I didn't know what to do. Then my eyes fell on the metal bar used to barricade the door from the inside. I saw Zaza running from me. I saw her hair flying every which way and heard her cry out for her mother. I also cried out for my mother, and just as I caught up to Zaza, she sped up. I was afraid she would get away from me and reach the road that crossed the meadow. A voice inside my head said it again: *Close the door to the wind that's bothering you, and put your mind at ease.* I hit her with the metal bar like a baseball player hitting a ball. I intended to hit her in the back to slow her down, but she bent over and the blow fell on the back of her head. Zaza let out a scream and fell. She started foaming at the mouth and writhing around like my mother had in her sickbed. Then she let out a rattle I will never forget. Whenever I think of her, that rattle comes to mind.

It was one in the morning. The curved crescent moon was in its usual position in the clear, cloudless sky. I was done once and for all with her blackmailing. I had extinguished all the memories and hopes that had swirled around in her head.

"She... she's... dead," the lawyer exclaimed through trembling lips. She called me the worst names, and her screams mixed with whimpers. My hands relaxed and the bar fell to the ground. I stood next to the body as I opened and closed my mouth without saying a word. Once again, I had confirmed that killing was easy. I wanted to flee, to run away. Terror seized me. The only light was a dim neon glow coming from the warehouse door, which was ajar.

We wiped up the blood and moved Zaza's body to the adjacent meadow as we dripped sweat and tears. All we could hear was the shuffling of our feet, which we had wrapped in plastic wrap from the warehouse. We laid her out on a slope, concealed among the wormwood, and turned her head toward Mecca. We used the flashlight from Maimoun's car, which I had come in. I cleaned the car with bleach just as I cleaned the iron rod, following Hassina's orders. She was well-versed in crimes, and she told me what murderers do. We covered our hands with our socks. I removed the dead woman's ID card from her handbag and was alarmed at the large sum of money I found there. Then my girlfriend returned to her family's house, and I went to the hotel after arranging the medicines that Maimoun had sent with his son in the warehouse refrigerator. I changed my clothes in the men's room on the ground floor, hoping someone would come up to me, slap me, and tell me that what had happened had been nothing more than a dream. In the bathroom, I threw up everything I had swallowed that day. I regained my equilibrium. I tore up Zaza's ID card and got rid of it. I imagined stray dogs drawn by the smell of her body tearing it to pieces, but the angels protected it. I waited up for the tourists whose bus was late rather than going back home to sleep for an hour or two. I wanted to make sure I was seen in my place of work the night she was killed.

In the following days, I made a real effort to act as if I knew nothing of what had happened. I ate too much, smoked too much, and drank too much. I was exhausted from lack of sleep and talking to myself like a lunatic. I had a feeling there was someone out there wanting to hurt me. I felt as if Zaza's ghost was watching me from every corner, and my Hassouna pressed me to ask her mother for her hand. "I want to carry your name," she said. She encouraged Noura to focus on Zakia's brothers as suspects, but we didn't know why Noura was looking into what had happened to Merzaka Soualem. If I got into trouble, Hassina was determined to pin it on Cheikha Edahabia under the pretext of Zakia's jealousy toward her.

What helped me remain strong was that Hassina was not under suspicion, since I'd confessed to Maimoun that I had committed the crime alone. I would not have confessed had it not been for how vulnerable she was, and my fear that she would reveal the truth after I'd told her on the phone that I needed time to think about the engagement because my sister was about to undergo surgery. She would think I intended to give her up. I took all the blame and regretted that I hadn't listened to Hassina's suggestion of burying the body. I was scared that digging a hole and then filling it back in would take too long and that someone would catch us in the act. Zakia had died with a heart that had beat out of love for Bachir, while now I remained with a heart that longed for my sister, Ouarida, who had raised me after I'd tumbled into this world by mistake. My parents hadn't planned to have another child. I'd been conceived out of carelessness. I came into this world on a whim and am leaving on another. Maimoun had no choice but to thank us for removing the corpse from the warehouse, which spared him from being among the suspects. I don't know what I'll do without him. He has always been my protective shield. Without him I am alone, a stranger, naked, a castoff.

What did I do to live a life other than the one I wanted to live? My existence was nothing more than a drawing in the sand obliterated by the wind. I have not been blessed with one of Sidi Zerzour's amulets that would protect me from the burden of what I have done, and I don't know how many more pages I need to fill about what happened after Zaza left our world. But I have grown tired of writing. I lay my head on a table in a hotel room which is nowhere near as clean and well-appointed as the rooms in the Sahara. I'm in this flat city in the far south, where no rain falls, six hours from Hassina. I hear footsteps approaching the door and men whispering while the radio softly plays a Moscow Philharmonic concert.

I was not alone in silencing Zakia's voice. My girlfriend took part in that deed; her brothers, who disowned her, took part with us; Bachir, who broke his promise of marrying her;

Cheikha Edahabia, who plotted against her; Maimoun, who fed her arrogance; Ibrahim, who planted a desire in my heart to take revenge against her; and Hamid, who made her think he was protecting her. The footsteps stop, and I hear a knock on the door. Two knocks. Then a third. Then a fourth. They get faster. Nobody knows me here. Who could it be?

Now I can't bear to look at my own face. I have been punished and sentenced to separation from the one I love. Will Hassina forgive me my sin? Doesn't love mean accepting the mistakes of those we love? I won't wait for her to answer, since lawyers only ask questions; they don't answer them. She didn't answer me when I asked her what she knew about the dead woman's relationship with the police inspector, even though I'd told her everything about my life. I never got to see her new dress, but the image of her laughing radiates in my mind.

When I was young, I was the best penalty kicker on my team. They called me Garrincha. People predicted a prosperous future for me. That I would play for Entente Sétif or Mouloudia Algiers. Little did they know that my future was to deliver death blows. The knocking on the door is getting rougher, and someone is calling my name. Did he call out the name Samir Laâroum or Kamal Belattar? I can only remember the words of Ibrahim Derras, who made me curse myself: "Whoever lacks dignity isn't a man." How I wish I had cut his throat that day in his shop. He is the reason I stomped on my dignity, humiliated myself, and ceased being a man.

"Open the door!" The voice at the door grows louder. A dampness spreads between my legs. The Moscow Philharmonic has not finished its piece, and all I can hear in my head are the words of Umm Kulthum: "*How much have we built out of our imagination / and walked on a moonlit path?*" The person knocking at the door must know I'm inside. He won't just wait there patiently; he'll break the lock.

The phone starts ringing. Who's calling? What do they want to tell me? My only hope is that someone will tell me that I've been asleep and that what happened was nothing but an illusion. Or that they'll reassure me that I'm dead. That I died a merciful death.

BACHIR

SATURDAY

I nodded off for a few minutes, during which time I dreamed of Ahmed ben Hassan, the hero of *The Sheik*, the novel Ibrahim Derras told me about. Towering over me, he walked past with his beloved Diana, but they didn't turn my way. I like their story. He abducts her and sacrifices himself to keep her from the shadow of any danger that threatens her. As for me, I stole Zakia's heart. I kept her away from her family yet didn't sacrifice anything for her. She double-crossed other men to remain faithful to me, and I wasn't there for her when she needed me most. I'm a coward, like a spider that builds its house but doesn't know how to protect it.

I got up to call the communal prayer.

SUNDAY

I have a desire to embrace Rahhal. To throw myself at his chest and tell him about my misfortune in love. I have always believed that the most beautiful love is incomplete. The most beautiful part of love is our desire, and if we end up finding our beloved, desire dies. But Rahhal has never tasted love, and he will never understand how much I miss my beloved.

MONDAY

People who write in diaries imagine themselves important, but my life is of interest to no one but myself. My life is a garden of losses. I'm lying whenever someone asks me how I'm doing and I answer "I'm fine." The word *fine* means I'm trying to conceal my sorrows.

WEDNESDAY

Zakia once said: "If you love me, then write about me."

I told her that I'm no good at writing about anything but myself and what goes on inside me. I don't take on other people's lives. I didn't fulfill her wish, and she didn't insist on me doing so, for she died and her story became known to all. Another person might write about her and document her life, as short as it was, but I am accused of killing her, and angry at myself for having known and loved her.

From the moment I emerged into the world, my life proceeded with relatively little pain. That is, until the dawn of the year 1988, which made me feel as though I had lived like a fool. I did not die, and I have no desire to die. I spend my nights and days trying to erase her from my memory. Whenever I close my eyes, her image is there, and I imagine her making fun of me from above.

After lunch, which was nothing more than half-cooked pasta with stale bread rolled up like plastic, I withdrew to my corner. I looked around in a daze; Ibrahim Derras squatted next to me, his head lowered, resisting the urge to cry. He had hugged his knees to his chest because there wasn't much space. Rumors began circulating: "There's been a coup," one of the prisoners shouted, claiming he overheard it from two guards. Another replied: "Actually, the president has resigned." A third prisoner exclaimed harshly: "There were clashes with rebels." I was lost in the crowd of gossip. I heard rough footsteps and then screams rising up outside. The prison door opened.

Five young men in their mid-twenties joined us. The prisoners organized themselves and made five new places for them. One of the newcomers laid down on his side, unable to sit on his backside because of how much it hurt. A surgeon, accused of unintentionally killing a patient, came forward to examine him. I insisted on hearing what happened, so one of them, smelling of shit, said that people had formed a demonstration after the merchants launched a strike. Another one continued that he joined some city youths in an attack on the farmers' market, where they took what food they wanted from the warehouse before the police dispersed them and made some arrests.

Things got louder when a third guy recounted that the demonstrators had set fire to government institutions, and the fourth one added: "We've turned things upside down, ass-backward." Why didn't they burn this prison down too? I doubt I have any other way of escaping unless a miracle were to occur, such as the prison burning down, for example, so that I could benefit from the chaos.

SUNDAY

I feel like another person.

I took a warm shower and shaved my pubic hair, which had grown like moss. I left the old Bachir in the prison I walked out of and emerged in a second Bachir's skin. The old Bachir Labtam lived as a coward. Anxious. Lazy. Mean.

A liar. Withdrawn. A failure. My wish is for the new Bachir Labtam not to slip up.

WEDNESDAY

It was the first time leaving the house since I'd been let out, and I noticed that the date was October 19 – forty days since Zakia's passing. I attended the funeral of the former head of distribution at the Rubber & Plastic Co., watching the mourners as they lowered his body into the grave. I held back my tears. The deceased had persevered in indoctrinating me with conviction, but I'd been a lousy student. I decided not to return to my job. No one would believe in my innocence. I hoped the Lord would bless me with something else to sustain me. I walked among the tombstones surrounded by wormwood until I reached the edge of the cemetery where my beloved's grave was hidden. I caught sight of Fouzi, his nose bandaged, reciting the Fatiha prayer over her soul. I didn't want to talk to him because he hated me on account of me once making fun of the breasts he had. Zakia had taught him how to remove the hair from his legs and armpits painlessly by rubbing them with castor oil to soften it. My tongue overtook me: "I wronged her… I wronged her." I had promised to travel with her to the coast, but that had never happened. I wished I had lived without ever knowing her. I said a prayer for her and wiped my face with my palm. I closed my eyes, but all I could see was an image of a smiling Kamal. Why hadn't he ever come to visit me?

FRIDAY

I saw myself in a dream. I returned to jail, and Rahhal told me all about his job while he stood next to his father, the pastry chef. Then I woke up and noticed that the wound on my left shoulder had healed, leaving a dark, rectangular scar. It had healed just as my longing for Zakia had healed, leaving her ghost floating before my eyes.

I talk to Zakia's ghost in my room, where I've gotten rid of my books and pictures of singers and athletes. My father tells me they're turning the Sahara into a hospital. Patients will look in on my memories of my girlfriend. "The central hospital can no longer handle the influx of people," he says. And I can no longer handle my life. I remain condemned in my relatives' eyes. I was an accountant for a national company but forgot to hold myself accountable. I'm like that Frenchman, Dreyfus, whose story I read; I am presumed as guilty as he was, despite my innocence.

My parents decided to sell the house, thinking it was inhabited by misfortune, and move to another. They didn't believe what I told them, that what happened was nothing but fate. I offered them the money I had saved for the engagement that had never taken place, and they did not refuse it. No one believes in me in this city where the buildings are getting taller, where the clouds of tear gas have cleared from the skies since the president appeared on television promising a better tomorrow and giving people hope.

As for me, my only hope is to forget prison and the clamor of the prisoners. But the biggest prison I need to rid myself of is writing. I'm no good at blackening paper with words. This notebook is destined to turn into ashes, scattered by the wind, just as the years have scattered the love story of Diana Mayo and Ahmed ben Hassan.

MAIN CHARACTERS

NARRATORS (IN ORDER OF APPEARANCE)

Ibrahim Derras – also known as Brihoum or Briha; runs the Desert Rose video rental store.

Achour Hadeeri – a shepherd who lives in an area known as the meadow.

Inspector Hamid – also known as The Boss and The Scorpion; married to Zinab.

Maimoun Belassal – also known as Hadj; the Sahara Hotel's owner; married to Yacout.

Bachir Labtam – Zakia Zaghouani's boyfriend.

Noura Arkoub – defense lawyer; Bachir's cousin and Faudel's older sister.

Kamal Belattar – the Sahara's receptionist; son of Belkacem Belattar, a member of the FLN (Front de libération nationale) during the War of Independence.

Cheikha Edahabia – stage name of Safia Bechiche; sings at the Sahara; Fatiha's daughter and Lotfi's older sister.

Faudel Arkoub – also known as Six; a local petty criminal; Ibrahim's friend, Noura's younger brother, and Bachir's cousin.

Halima – Zakia Zaghouani's mother.

MAIN SUPPORTING CHARACTERS
(IN ALPHABETICAL ORDER)

Ben Kaddour Derras – Ibrahim and Khamisi's father; killed during the War of Independence.

Boulanouar – pastry shop owner; Hassina's uncle and Rahhal's father.

Derraji Aouina – one of Kamal's neighbors.

Farhat – Zakia's backing musician at the Sahara.

Fatiha Bechiche – a cleaner at the Sahara; mother of Cheikha Edahabia.

Fouzi – owns a horse-drawn carriage; works the tourist trade in and around the Sahara.

Hassina Eidache – a lawyer; Noura's friend; niece of Boulanouar, the baker.

Khamisi – Ibrahim's younger brother; aspires to become a professional boxer.

Mehdi – son of Maimoun and Yacout.

Khider Arkoub – Faudel and Noura's absent father.

Lotfi Bechiche – also known as The Pharmacien; Cheikha Edahabia's younger brother and Fatiha's son.

Merzaka Soualem – a former teacher; local politician and resident of the Sahara; died under mysterious circumstances before the start of the story.

Nabil – Ibrahim's friend; returns to Algeria after years studying and working in France.

Wannasa – Ibrahim's mother; works as a cleaner at the Sahara.

Yacout – Maimoun's wife.

Zakia Zaghouani – also known as Zaza; a nightclub entertainer at the Sahara; Halima's daughter.

Zinab – Police Inspector Hamid's wife.